PRICELESS BETRAYAL

A DOTTY SAYERS ANTIQUE MYSTERY

VICTORIA TAIT

KANGA
PRESS

PROLOGUE

I t was a bright but chilly morning when Dotty Sayers arrived at Cotswold Airport in a black chauffeur-driven Mercedes. Situated to the south-east of the historic town of Cirencester, the airport catered for private charters only.

"As-salamu alaikum," greeted Tariq Kazem as he walked across and held his hand out to Dotty's companion David Rook.

Tariq and his father were business associates of David's and it was their plane Dotty had been invited to travel on to visit a large international antique fair in Istanbul.

"Are you excited about your trip?" Tariq asked, turning to Dotty.

She nodded and blew on her hands to warm them up. She was excited, who wouldn't be when offered an opportunity to fly on a private jet and not have to pay for food or accommodation in a top four-star hotel, and Dotty had never visited Istanbul.

David Rook was very knowledgeable about antiques. He'd explained the history of the Ottomans and their treasures, and she was eager to see what was on display at the international antique fair.

But Dotty was also nervous. She was only a young, trainee antique expert. Her main role at Akemans, an auction house and antique centre in the Cotswolds where she worked, was admin, office work, and cataloguing items for the monthly auctions.

David was a respected expert in the antique world and, while she didn't know Tariq's level of expertise, he and his family clearly had money to invest.

Tariq broke into her reverie. "My father and his friends will arrive shortly, so if you'd like to identify your bags, they can be loaded onto the plane."

Tariq pointed to a white jet parked close by. As they watched, a hatch door opened behind the long cone-shaped nose of the plane and a blue-clad steward appeared as a set of steps automatically extended towards the ground.

"If you'll come with me," instructed Tariq with a smile.

"That's mine." Dotty pointed to a black case, standing on wheels, the handle already extended. She sighed with relief, it didn't look too out of place with the other luggage and she was travelling light, unlike one of her companions who had five matching designer suitcases.

David pointed to a brown leather holdall.

"Thank you. Now we can board," Tariq declared.

Dotty lifted a small green holdall which contained her handbag, and other items for the flight. She could hear the wheels of her suitcase trundling along the tarmac and she turned to watch a blue overalled man lift it up and slide it into a cargo area towards the rear of the plane. She took hold of the handrail and was about to step onto the bottom step when bright spotlights lit up the scene and a voice, amplified by a megaphone, shouted, "Stop there and put your hands on your heads."

Dotty froze. Her heart pumping madly in her chest and her hand still on the handrail.

"I repeat. Put your hands on your heads."

Dotty felt David move beside her, so she pulled her leg back and lifted both her hands above her head. This was not the exciting and luxurious plane trip she'd been anticipating.

CHAPTER ONE

Twenty-nine-year-old Dotty Sayers rested her head on her folded arms on top of a grey Formica table. Her limbs felt heavy, and she had no idea how long she'd been sitting, alone, in the police interview room. It was hopeless.

Her friends in the police force had turned against her. Some said they still believed she was innocent, but she saw the doubt in their eyes. And Sergeant Unwin. Attractive Sergeant Unwin. He had no such reservations. He openly displayed his disappointment in her, whether or not she was guilty.

She heard the door open, and the chatter and general hum of the Cirencester police station invaded the interview room.

"Sit up," ordered Sergeant Unwin, sharply.

Dotty opened her eyes and stared at a grey trouser leg. The slight shine gave away the polyester mix in the material.

"There's no need to take that tone, Sergeant," admonished the voice of Chief Inspector Ringrose.

That was interesting. Sergeant Unwin didn't work for Chief Inspector Ringrose. The chief inspector, who headed up the Rural, Heritage and Wildlife Unit, had already interviewed her, several times, about a missing Middle Eastern chapan robe. The valuable antique had been found inside her suitcase, in the hold of the private jet she'd been invited to travel on to attend an international antique fair in Istanbul.

She heard chairs scrape across the vinyl floor and two figures sat down opposite her.

"I'm afraid we have to ask you some more questions," said the chief inspector.

Dotty lifted her head, looking up at him. There it was. The doubt. Even though she knew her landlady and friend, Aunt Beanie, who worked as a consultant for the chief inspector, would have protested Dotty's innocence.

He crossed his arms. He wore a discreet cherry red and blue double-check shirt with a bold cherry red and blue striped tie embroidered with a red rose and 'England Rugby' beneath it.

Dotty sat back, rubbing her eyes. Her interrogators weren't going away, and she didn't want to spend the rest of the day in this interview room. It was beginning to feel like a prison cell.

Chief Inspector Ringrose stated, matter-of-factly, "We're still trying to piece together how the chapan robe was stolen from Timeless Treasure's stall at the antique fair near Malvern and transferred to your suitcase where it was discovered at Cotswold airport."

Dotty didn't know how to respond.

"You had the opportunity to steal it at the fair," Sergeant Unwin observed, "and you were carrying a bag which you could have stuffed it into."

Dotty bristled, and replied defiantly, "You saw the size of my bag. I had to remove my phone to put Billy Edwards' coke can in it. The one you wanted me to carry so you could check his fingerprints, as he was one of your murder suspects."

Sergeant Unwin leaned back, looking uncomfortable, but countered, "You could still have hidden it away. Maybe you put it in the old lady's bag before driving her home."

Dotty leaned forward, her eyes narrowing. "I drove Edith home on your instructions. In your car. Is that the problem? Are you worried your Mercedes might have been used to transport stolen goods?" Dotty snorted in disgust.

Sergeant Unwin shuffled uncomfortably in his seat.

Chief Inspector Ringrose's voice was measured as he stated, rather than questioned, "But you could have stolen the chapan."

Dotty turned to him, feeling her fingers tighten into fists on the table, and replied, "For the short time I was at the stall, there were always other customers and the stallholder there. One of them would have seen me if I'd tried to remove the robe from the partition wall."

Sergeant Unwin rallied and retorted, "Not if you'd waited until their attention was elsewhere. A skilled thief could easily have lifted the robe without anyone noticing."

The rest of Dotty's body tensed and in exasperation she cried, "But I'm not a skilled thief. I'm not a thief at all." She swallowed to calm herself before continuing. "You, me and Keya, Sergeant Varma, were fully occupied looking for suspects in the Roger Dewhirst case, and then after I found poor Ethel's body, we were looking for her killer."

Sergeant Unwin crossed his arms and, his confidence returning, stared unkindly at her, his lips drawn into a thin line.

"Don't tell me you think I killed Ethel," Dotty exclaimed.

Sergeant Unwin continued to smirk as he remarked, "We don't have any other suspects."

"But why would I want to kill her?" Dotty knew her voice sounded shrill. Desperate.

"You tell me." Sergeant Unwin sounded calm, but Dotty felt like a mouse her cat Earl Grey had spotted, and she had nowhere to run. "Maybe she saw you steal the chapan robe, or the copper jug at the Cotswold Antique Fair."

"What?" exclaimed Dotty, feeling hot as she fought to control her breathing. "Are you going to accuse me of every unsolved crime committed this year?"

"Please calm down, Mrs Sayers," interjected the calm but authoritative voice of Chief Inspector Ringrose.

Mrs Sayers now. No Dotty or even Dorothy.

The chief inspector continued, "But you have to admit that when you lay the various incidents out - the stolen jug, the stolen robe, and Ethel Lee's death - it's quite feasible they could all be connected."

"Definitely," Dotty retorted, "But I didn't have anything to do with them."

Dotty's petulant words hung in the air as the chief inspector studied the ceiling. Calmly, he suggested, "Shall we return to the stolen chapan robe? How do you think it ended up in your suitcase?"

Dotty shrugged. "I don't know. Maybe that missing ground crew member, Bernard someone, hid it there." Her eyes narrowed as she looked from the chief inspector to Sergeant Unwin and back again. "By the way, has he been found?"

The two police officers exchanged nervous glances.

Dotty continued, "I read that someone had offered a reward for information about his whereabouts. I wonder who that was?"

"I don't think that's relevant," Sergeant Unwin responded curtly.

Dotty stared at him and argued, "Why? Because it might reveal who's actually responsible for trying to smuggle the chapan robe out of the country?"

It was Chief Inspector Ringrose who answered. Dotty shifted her attention to him as he stated,

"No. Because he was found dead in Cotswold Water Park. His body washed ashore."

"Oh, no," cried Dotty, her hand shooting up to cover her mouth.

Sergeant Unwin rubbed his chin, looking confused as he asked, "Did you know Bernard Ingram?"

"No. But another death." Dotty looked down at her hands and mumbled, "And I bet you're going to pin it on me as well."

Dotty felt Sergeant Unwin lean towards her as he asserted, "It makes sense if you're trying to cover up your other crimes."

Dotty slumped back in her chair, exhausted and deflated. Her earlier defiance against the two police officers accusing her of crimes she hadn't committed gave way to anxiety, and she picked at her nails as she realised just what a precarious position she was in.

Sergeant Unwin broke into her introspection.

"Thinking of giving us a full confession?" he suggested, a hint of satisfaction in his voice.

Dotty whispered back, "Am I under arrest?"

Chief Inspector Ringrose replied, "No, you're not."

"Then I'm free to leave," Dotty said weakly.

"You are," agreed the chief inspector. "But as we're not satisfied with your answers, or explanation of events, we will continue this interview in the very near future."

Dotty stood up, but grasped the edge of the Formica table as her legs trembled and threatened to buckle underneath her.

Sergeant Unwin jeered, "I suggest you find yourself a good lawyer. You're going to need one."

Unsteadily, Dotty left the interview room, but once outside, she slumped against the stained off-white wall in the corridor.

"Dotty, are you OK?" asked the kindly voice of Ryan, PC Jenkins.

"No. No, I'm not. I've just been questioned … about everything, by Sergeant Unwin and Chief Inspector Ringrose. I know they're going to pin something on me. But I didn't do anything."

Dotty felt her legs give way, but as she started to slide down the wall a strong pair of hands lifted her up and she felt her arm being draped across a muscular set of shoulders.

"You're in shock," advised Ryan. "What you need is a sweet cup of tea. But not here. If I help you, can you walk out of the station and round the corner to a local cafe?"

Dotty nodded. "I'll try."

With Ryan's help, Dotty placed one foot in front of the other.

As they passed through the reception area, she heard Ryan ask the duty sergeant, "Can you call Sergeant Varma and tell her to meet me in the Copper Kettle? Tell her it's about spotty, and it's urgent."

CHAPTER TWO

O nce outside, the crisp March spring air revived Dotty, and she removed her arm from Ryan's shoulders. He straightened up but placed a hand on her back as he guided her across the road and down a narrow alleyway. They ducked beneath a stone arch and into a secluded courtyard.

Even though the temperature was in single figures, several couples and a lone man sat outside at metal tables. Blue pots of yellow daffodils were scattered around the courtyard, and two tall, chrome, gas patio heaters warmed the hardy customers.

Ryan guided Dotty to a table in the corner and as she sat down on a chrome slatted chair, she immediately felt the warmth of one of the patio heaters.

"Wait here," Ryan instructed.

Dotty leaned back, closing her eyes.

Several minutes later, Ryan returned. "Here you are," he said. "A cup of Assam tea, with sugar, and a piece of chocolate cake."

Keya dashed into the courtyard but stopped abruptly when she saw Ryan and Dotty. Next to her, a chair clattered to the floor. As she picked it up, her eyes remained on Dotty and Ryan and she blurted, "So that's what you meant by 'spotty'. I was really confused."

Keya pulled out a spare chair and sat down between them. "I know you were being interviewed by Sergeant Unwin and my chief inspector," she said. "What happened?"

Dotty recounted the interview as best she could.

At one point, Keya interrupted and exclaimed, "I know Nick is upset and feels you've let him down, but I'd no idea he'd become so vindictive." Nick was Sergeant Unwin, one of Keya's colleagues and Dotty had worked closely with him and other members of Inspector Evan's team investigating crimes during the past year.

When she finished, Dotty sipped her tea. Its sweet but malty flavour was welcoming. She looked up, catching Keya and Ryan exchange glances.

Keya cleared her throat before conceding, "Nick is right about one thing. You do need a good lawyer. They're not going to let this drop. Not when you're the only suspect."

"But I don't know any lawyers," Dotty protested.

Ryan responded by pushing the chocolate cake towards her. "Eat this."

"What about the lawyer who saw you and David when you were brought back from Cotswold Airport? The one from London?" asked Keya.

Dotty sighed, "I think he only visited me to make sure I didn't implicate his client, Ahmad Kazem. Once he was satisfied, he left."

Keya's shoulders slumped, but she said, "I'll speak to Aunt Beanie. She's bound to know some top-class solicitors."

"But how can I afford one?" implored Dotty.

"I'll ask around some of my mates," offered Ryan. "A couple of them are lawyers and while they might not be experienced, they are passionate, hardworking … and relatively inexpensive."

"Thank you." Dotty laid a hand on Ryan's arm, before reaching for a small dessert fork and slicing into the cake.

"Mmm, that looks delicious," said Keya, eyeing the cake.

"Finish it," responded Dotty, pushing the chocolate cake towards Keya. She looked apologetically at Ryan. "It's too rich at the moment. But the tea is perfect. Thank you." She looked from Ryan to Keya and added, "And thank you both for your support. I think you must be the only police officers who don't think me guilty of at least one of the crimes Sergeant Unwin accused me of this morning."

Keya and Ryan exchanged an uneasy look.

Turning back to Dotty, Keya asked, in a falsely bright voice, "What are you going to do now? Go back to work or go home?"

Dotty lifted her teacup and replied, "Back to work. But first, David Rook has asked me to visit Barnton Manor and collect a painting for him." She sipped her tea. "But I think I'll sit here for a little longer."

David Rook and his wife Marion helped out at Akemans, the antiques centre and auction house where Dotty worked. David was a knowledgeable and highly respected member of the antique's world, and Marion was extremely efficient at organising and running auctions.

"I have to get back to work too," apologised Ryan.

Dotty nodded her understanding.

"I'll stay with you," offered Keya.

Ryan rose and left.

Dotty smiled weakly at Keya. "I really am grateful to you and Ryan. Everyone else, including Chief Inspector Ringrose, seems determined to pin one crime on me, if not more."

Keya looked serious as she replied, "Aunt Beanie won't let that happen." She cut a portion of cake with the edge of her fork.

Dotty sighed. "She might be overruled. As you said, I'm the only suspect for the theft of the robe, and I don't know how much progress has been made with either Ethel's or Bernard Ingram's deaths."

"Bernard Ingram?" spluttered Keya through a mouthful of cake. "The body that washed up in Cotswold Water Park. What could that possibly have to do with you?"

"The chief inspector thinks it might be linked to the smuggling of the chapan robe, and I agree with him. I think Bernard put the robe in my suitcase, but as I didn't ask him to, who did?"

Both Keya's eyes opened wide as she whispered with a note of awe in her voice, "Do you think there's a criminal mastermind operating in the Cotswolds?"

Dotty sat back. A year ago, she would have laughed at such a question. The Cotswolds were considered quaint and even sleepy. People visited in the summer to walk beside the rivers and streams, through the woods or across the gently rolling hills before exploring the honey-coloured stone villages and having a drink or a meal in one of the numerous pubs.

She'd never imagined an underworld of crime linking murder, theft, and other antique-related crimes.

Keya's eyes were still wide, and she held her breath, waiting for Dotty's reply.

"Yes, I do. One person, or more likely a gang. There's something out there that we're missing. Think of all the cases we've been involved with over the past year. Counterfeit furniture, stolen and copied paintings, missing antiques smuggled out of the country. And the dead bodies are stacking up," she added flatly.

"But we solved most of those cases," counted Keya.

Dotty picked up her cup of tea, but it was empty. Placing it back on the table, she explained, "I know, but take the counterfeit furniture. You found and arrested the craftsman, but not the person who ordered or paid for the furniture."

Keya's face fell. "And he's still refusing to give me any names."

Dotty looked round before continuing. The couples had left, and only the lone man was still at his table, reading a newspaper.

Returning her attention to Keya, she lowered her voice and said, "I know you have your suspicions. Aunt Beanie certainly does. And there's Operation Bumblebee."

Keya blanched. "I've told you. I know nothing about that. In fact, it's all meetings behind closed doors between Sergeant Unwin and Chief Inspector Ringrose. Aunt Beanie and I have both been pushed out."

Keya looked down and examined her hands. "If I'm honest, I'm getting rather fed up with it all. I like being involved in the local communities, but I'm sick of being sent to sort out every petty argument and misunderstanding. It's as if I'm no longer welcome at the station."

Dotty felt her chest tighten. Her friend was a hard-working police officer and popular amongst the inhabitants of the Cotswolds. She'd been so proud the previous year to be promoted to sergeant, after many years as a constable, and to be part of Chief Inspector Ringrose's new unit. It wasn't fair if she was now being excluded from police activities. Was it because of their friendship?

Dotty had felt a change in the atmosphere at Cirencester police station, but thought it was only directed towards her. But what if she was wrong, and it affected others, like Keya and Aunt Beanie?

Trying to lighten the mood, Dotty asked, "And what about your troublesome villagers in Lemington?"

Dotty thought back to the previous month when she'd driven Keya to a meeting in Lemington village hall, which had turned into a food fight.

The inhabitants of Lemington were notorious for squabbling amongst themselves over sabotaged vegetables in the allotments, overhanging branches, and cars parked in the wrong places, but when the Kazem family bought the neglected Lemington Hall, the villagers turned en masse against the incomers.

Keya tapped the table. "The trouble is this time the villagers might have a point. There's a wood between the village and the hall which they've been using for years.

It's a great place for the kids to play. There are paths for dog walkers and horse riders. Even the teenage kids have even started riding their motorbikes through it, although that might be taking it too far."

She paused before continuing, "But the Kazems' estate manager has built a difficult to climb stile, blocking access for all but the most agile inhabitants of Lemington. He set his dog after a group of children, so they're too scared to use it anymore."

"I can understand he doesn't want people wandering about the grounds, and motorbikes might cause damage," defended Dotty.

"I know, but the footpath between Lemington and the neighbouring village of Eaton Common is popular for dog walkers and mountain bikers. And one of them broke the stile, so the groundsman is now threatening to block the path all together."

"But surely he can't do that?"

Keya shook her head. "He can't, but the council is fed up with the inhabitants of Lemington always complaining about something and is currently ignoring their protests. Of course, I've been sent to intervene and all the council has told me is that it suggested the path be diverted around the woods, which just makes the villagers even more angry."

Dotty brightened and suggested, "But why not speak to Tariq Kazem? Or I could do that for you."

Keya wrinkled her nose. "I would, but he left on that trip to Istanbul you missed and I'm not sure when he's due back. Neither the groundsman nor the housekeeper at the hall will tell me. And talking of getting back, someone might be missing me at the station, if only to ask me to go and speak to speeding drivers after one of the local village's speed awareness campaigns."

She stood and smiled weakly before asking, "Are you OK to drive?"

Dotty pushed back her chair and replied as she rose to her feet, "I'm fine now." And she was. Her legs no longer trembled, and she walked purposefully out of the courtyard cafe with Keya. "I only need to collect that painting for David before returning to work at Akemans."

CHAPTER THREE

Dotty drove her compact green Skoda Fabia north-east from Cirencester to the typically picturesque Cotswold village of Barnton. She passed an old Cotswold stone building with small windows and a sign hanging outside stating simply 'The Village Pub'.

Turning left between crumbing stone columns, she drove fifty metres up a gravel drive, dotted with tufts of grass, before parking in front of the main house.

Dotty was surprised that it was constructed from red and grey brick rather than honey-coloured Cotswold stone. It was two storeys high and looked old, Elizabethan probably, judging by the very tall, narrow chimney. A two-storey brick tower made up the right section of the house.

Dotty opened a squeaking metal gate and walked towards the front door, feeling an air of neglect hanging over the property. The front door was ajar, but she knocked on it and called, "Hello."

There was no reply, although she thought she heard a scuffling noise.

"Hello," she repeated, pushing the front door wider.

This time, her call was met by silence.

David had warned her that the owner, Sir Reginald Spencer, might be out and that she'd find the painting of Judas betraying Jesus for thirty pieces of silver, wrapped up in the hall or library, ready for her to collect. Had Sir Reginald intentionally left the door open for her?

Nervously, she stepped inside the stone-flagged hall and stopped. The house was still.

Looking around, she couldn't see a painting-shaped parcel. It must be in the library, but which room was that? To her left, a corridor led to a brighter room, and she spotted an Aga range cooker.

Not that way. She pushed the heavy wooden panelled door in front of her. No, the chintz sofa and chairs gave that room away as a living room.

Dotty turned to her right towards what she presumed was a room in the ground floor of the tower. She pushed the door open, stepped inside, and froze.

Tariq Kazem lay on the floor, bright red blood around his mouth and smears of it across his shirt. A partially wrapped painting was propped against the bookcase behind him.

Dotty screamed, but quickly covered her mouth. Unlike many people, she had seen a dead body before but, today, after all she'd gone through, the horror of the scene hit her in the stomach.

Bent double, she backed out of the room, turned, and stumbled out of the front door, only stopping when she reached her car and leaned against it.

Where was the house's owner? And what was Tariq doing inside? In the library? It was like a twisted version of the board game, Cluedo.

Her phone. She needed to call the police.

She retrieved it from her bag in the car and called Keya, but only succeeded in reaching her voice mail.

Nick, Sergeant Unwin? No. She wasn't calling him. Not after the way he'd treated her this morning.

Her call to Ryan was answered promptly by the young constable, who asked in a concerned voice, "Dotty, are you OK?"

"No. There's a dead body. In the library. And blood."

Calm, but with a note of surprise in his voice, Ryan asked, "Which library? Where are you?"

"Barnton Manor," Dotty managed to gasp. "And the body. It's Tariq Kazem."

Dotty slumped onto the front seat of her car, leaving the door open and the chill air kept her senses alive as she waited.

Sometime later, a tall gentleman with a military bearing stepped out of the house. He spotted Dotty and strode over to her calling, in a strong voice, "Are you David's girl? Here for the painting?"

The shock had subsided, and Dotty climbed slowly out of her car. She looked up at the man she presumed was Sir Reginald, wondering if she could trust him. Had he killed Tariq?

"I am," she replied hesitantly.

"Well, come with me. I wrapped it up as David requested and left it in the library. I thought we agreed that you'd collect it from there if I was out."

"We did," agreed Dotty.

She was saved from explaining why she hadn't followed the instructions by the arrival of a car.

She groaned. It was Sergeant Unwin's metallic grey Mercedes.

Ryan pulled his tall frame out of the car before it had stopped and bounded towards Dotty, repeating his earlier question, and asking again, "Are you OK?"

"Of course she is," replied Sir Reginald. "Why would you think there's anything wrong with her? And why are the police at my house?"

"Sergeant Unwin and PC Jenkins from Cirencester Police Station," explained Sergeant Unwin, joining the group and holding up his warrant card. "This woman called about a dead body she found in the library."

"Don't be preposterous," blustered Sir Reginald. "Is this some sort of joke?"

"I do hope not." Sergeant Unwin stared at Dotty. "I don't appreciate my time being wasted." He looked at Sir Reginald and asked, "Is this your house, Mr?"

"Sir Reginald Spencer, and yes, this is my house. And I can assure you there are no bodies in my library, or anywhere else, for that matter. I don't know why this silly woman would think there are."

Ryan appeared to be taking the situation more seriously than the other two men. "If I could just check, sir? Where is the library?"

"In the bottom of the tower." Sir Reginald turned towards the house. "I'll show you."

"If you don't mind, I'll go alone. So inside the hall and turn right?" asked Ryan.

"Yes," replied the disgruntled homeowner as he drew his lips together.

Dotty waited outside, feeling Sir Reginald's displeasure and Sergeant Unwin's disappointment, although she tried to ignore both of them.

Maybe the body would change Sergeant Unwin's mind? Or would it be just another crime he'd think she'd committed?

She shuffled her feet on the gravel drive.

Ryan reappeared, a pained expression on his face. As they all looked up at him expectantly, he shook his head and called, "There's no body."

"Just as I said," reported Sir Reginald.

Sergeant Unwin considered Dotty grimly before declaring, "I've a good mind to charge you for wasting police time. But that's trivial compared to the other crimes you're under suspicion for."

Sir Reginald took a step back. "Other crimes? What other crimes?"

"Theft, and smuggling antiques to start with," sneered Sergeant Unwin.

That wasn't fair. She hadn't been charged with anything. And she had seen Tariq lying on the floor of the library.

She looked up, fixing a defiant gaze on the sergeant.

"I haven't stolen anything, and I did see a body," she hissed.

Sir Reginald's face flushed, and he exclaimed, "Theft. The painting," before rushing inside and pushing past Ryan.

Sergeant Unwin gave her an insolent look before following Sir Reginald.

Ryan joined Dotty, and she pleaded, "But I did see a body!"

Ryan raised his hands. "I believe you. There are small spots of red ink on the floor and a faint smear which looks recent."

"You mean if Tariq was pretending to be dead, he might have used ink as fake blood?"

"Exactly. There's an old-fashioned desk with bottles of blue and black ink, but no red. It was definitely Tariq Kazem you saw?"

"I'm certain, although earlier Keya said she thought he was still abroad."

"I'll check if he's returned."

"You better not let Sergeant Unwin know that. He's convinced I've made the whole thing up. But why would I?"

"Dorothy Sayers," announced Sergeant Unwin as he strode out of the front door. "I'm taking you in for questioning about the theft of the painting of the Betrayal of Jesus."

CHAPTER FOUR

Dotty stared at the bare grey walls of the police interview room. The same room she'd spent the morning in.

The door opened and Chief Inspector Ringrose entered, followed by Sergeant Unwin.

The chief inspector's mouth was pinched, and his eyes narrowed as he regarded Dotty. As he sat down at the grey Formica table, he remarked, "That was a short-lived break. I hear you're already in trouble again. I just hope you had time to find a lawyer."

"You're going to need one," sneered Sergeant Unwin, also taking a seat.

Dotty shook her head and replied dully, "No, I didn't."

There was a tap on the door, and Sergeant Unwin rose to his feet and opened it a fraction.

Dotty heard the voice of the duty sergeant from reception say, "Mrs Sayer's lawyer is here. And he's asking for some time alone with his client."

Sergeant Unwin turned and shook his head at Dotty. "Do you lie about everything?"

"But I haven't contacted a lawyer," she pleaded. In a dull voice, she added, "I don't know any." She shrank back in her chair.

Chief Inspector Ringrose stood and collected his papers from the table. "I hope he is your lawyer." For the first time, she saw the briefest look of sympathy in his eyes. "And if so, I can't complete this interview until he's spoken to you."

The two police officers left and Dotty was alone for several minutes until the door opened again and Ryan entered, leading a young man with mousy brown hair, a round face and large round glasses. He wore a brown corduroy jacket and a bow tie with a yellow shirt.

Nervously, the man placed a soft brown leather briefcase on the table and stood back, his shoulders hunched as he wrung his hands. Was this her lawyer? Dotty wasn't filled with confidence.

She was still staring at him, her eyebrows drawn together, when Ryan said, "Dotty, this is my friend Gerald Wood. He may not look like it, but he's a brilliant solicitor and has argued, or should I say persuaded, the police to drop charges when some of our friends have got themselves into trouble after a few too many drinks."

Dotty glanced from Gerald to Ryan. She couldn't imagine either of them having friends who drank too much in pubs and got into fights or disturbed the peace.

Ryan continued, "I called Keya when I was at Barnton Manor and told her you needed legal representation, and I suggested Gerald. She spoke to Aunt Beanie, who confirmed she knows one of the partners at Gerald's firm, Mr Briggs, and he's agreed to oversee your case, but Gerald will deal with it on a day-to-day basis."

Dotty flinched. Ryan made it sound so serious. She looked down at the table. It was serious. She was in a lot of trouble.

She heard Ryan say, "I've filled Gerald in on the bare bones of this case, and I'll meet him later to give him the history of the robe and everything else."

Dotty looked up and gulped. "Thank you. But did you find the missing painting?"

Ryan leaned against the closed door. Was he making sure nobody else could come in?

"No," he admitted.

"Although there were scraps of brown paper beside one of the bookcases. I also found a back door at the end of a passage between the tower and the main house, and it was unlocked. There was a flagstone path leading into the garden, but I only had time to inspect it briefly and I couldn't tell if anyone had used it recently or could have escaped that way with a painting. Sergeant Unwin called me back inside and told me to stop wasting my time. We already had our culprit."

Ryan smiled sadly at Dotty.

Seizing the chance to actually discuss the case with one of the officers who'd been there, and who was on her side, for the moment, Dotty sat up and said, "So we've no idea how Tariq escaped. That painting looked bulky and possibly heavy. I don't think he could have carried it far."

Ryan nodded. "I agree, and I'll try to go back later for a better look, but it'll probably be dark by the time I finish work."

"Thank you," Dotty said again. Her debt to Ryan was growing.

"I better leave you to speak to Gerald."

As the door closed behind Ryan, Gerald sat down and removed a notepad and three pencils of equal length from his briefcase. He spent a minute arranging the pencils precisely, side by side, next to his yellow legal pad.

He closed his eyes, and Dotty wondered if he was praying.

Suddenly, his eyes flew open, and he stared intently, studying her. Dotty stared back, unsure whether or not to speak.

"Good," announced Gerald.

"Good?" Dotty repeated. She didn't think anything about the current situation was good.

"I can't defend anyone unless I know they're innocent or truly remorseful for the crime they've committed."

Were his unruly mates always sorry for the trouble they caused? wondered Dotty.

"It's not a particularly useful trait in a solicitor, as we're supposed to allow the guilty, as well as the innocent, the opportunity to put their case forward."

Gerald attempted to straighten his perfectly aligned pencils. "I also dislike police interview rooms."

"So do I," agreed Dotty. At least they had something in common.

"But it's another limiting characteristic for a solicitor." Gerald picked up a pencil and wrote neatly at the top of a fresh sheet on his pad, 'Miss Sayers'.

Dotty could discern his neat writing and said, "Actually, it's Mrs."

Gerald's face tightened as he ripped off the sheet and screwed the paper into a tight ball. As he wrote 'Mrs Sayers' on a fresh sheet, he apologised, "I did know that. It's just that you're young to be a widow. Now tell me exactly what happened this afternoon."

Dotty explained her version of events as she watched Gerald make tidy notes on his pad.

Without looking up, Gerald asked, "How did you know it was Tariq Kazem?"

"I've met him a few times," replied Dotty. "David Rook introduced us at an antique fair in Bath. And then I met him with Keya, Sergeant Varma, at a meeting in Lemington. He was at Cotswold Airport when the police discovered the stolen Middle Eastern robe in my suitcase, which Ryan referred to earlier."

"Ryan can give me those details later, but returning to Mr Kazem, did you feel for a pulse?"

Dotty shook her head. "I should have done, I know. But it was the blood on his face. I panicked."

"Where was the blood?" asked Gerald.

"Under his nose and around his mouth. And a smear across his white shirt. But it couldn't have been blood, could it?"

"It certainly could have been. From a knock or a nosebleed."

"I suppose so. But Ryan told me he found spots of red ink on the floor and a smudge, but no red ink on the desk."

"I'll also ask him about that. And did you see the painting?"

"Yes. No. That is, I saw a painting-shaped parcel propped up against a bookcase. Part of the brown wrapping paper had been ripped away and the edge of a gilt frame was visible."

"But you have no idea if it was the painting of Jesus' betrayal," pressed Gerald.

"No," conceded Dotty. "But what else could it have been?"

Gerald aligned the pencil he'd been using with the other two against the legal pad. "There are several points I want to raise in your defence with the police. Firstly, you were the one who called in the crime, albeit you rang them about a death rather than a missing painting. Secondly, you remained at the scene, and thirdly, the police searched your car and house, but they didn't find the painting."

Dotty gasped and exclaimed, "They've searched my house?" She prayed they hadn't left too much of a mess. When she finally got out of here, the last thing she wanted was to return home and find her drawers emptied and her possessions scattered across the floors of her cottage. But why would they be searching her cupboards for a large painting? Maybe it wouldn't be too bad.

Gerald interrupted her introspection as he conceded, "But you could have passed the painting to an accomplice."

"Accomplice? This is starting to sound farcical." Her voice began to rise in pitch, as she continued, "First, I find a dead body which disappears. Then I'm accused of a crime I didn't commit, and when it's obvious I don't have the painting, instead of clearing me, the police think I have a mystery accomplice."

Gerald held his hands up in a conciliatory gesture. "I'm not saying that is what they think."

"But I bet they do," retorted Dotty, red in the face.

CHAPTER FIVE

Ryan was sitting at his desk in the team room he shared with Nick, Sergeant Unwin, and another constable, who was off duty.

He pressed the print button and sat back as the printer whirled and produced a paper copy of the document he'd put together for Nick, detailing the history of Sir Reginald Spencer's painting.

He accepted his place as the junior member of Inspector Evans' team and didn't mind that Nick was ambitious and always pushing his way to the front of any interesting or potentially high-profile cases.

Although Nick had only joined the team six months before Ryan, Keya had told him that Nick had received a commendation for apprehending a murderer and exposing an antiques scam on his very first case. She'd also said the praise had gone to his head, and he'd ignored the fact that Dotty was the one who'd worked it all out and had physically stopped the culprit escaping.

Dotty had also worked out who had killed Roger Dewhirst, an antique dealer, in the team's most recent case, which was the first one Ryan had been involved in. It was clear to him that she was no criminal as she was too honest and candid and wore her heart on her sleeve, as he knew he often did.

It wasn't a particularly beneficial trait in a police officer, and he was having to learn to keep a straight face and an even tone when something surprised him. He stood up and as he walked to the printer, beside the partition which separated the room from Inspector Evans' office. He reflected that helping Dotty clear her name would require more practice with his poker face, especially if he stepped over his professional line, as he was planning to do this evening.

He collected the printed sheets, wondering if Nick was interviewing Dotty again, or perhaps he was still upstairs in Chief Inspector Ringrose's office. Nick was spending as much time, if not more, with the chief inspector than with his own team at the moment.

Keya thought Dotty had disappointed Nick, getting caught a second time trying to smuggle antiques out of the country, but was it necessary to show her such contempt? Ryan could see how much it hurt Dotty.

And Dotty and Nick had been getting on so well, working on the Roger Dewhirst case together. Nick had even let Dotty drive his precious car, and Ryan had thought their relationship might lead to something more intimate. Actually, Nick's behaviour was like that of a spurned lover. Had something else happened besides Dotty's arrest?

And was there another reason Chief Inspector Ringrose was now targeting Dotty? He'd always appeared to like her and he worked closely with his consultant, Aunt Beanie - as Keya and Dotty called her - who was Dotty's landlady and her most vocal supporter.

"Why are you standing there, staring into my office, Constable?" Ryan started as Inspector Evan's baritone Welsh voice interrupted his internal musing.

"I was collecting a report I've printed off for Sergeant Unwin about the missing painting."

Inspector Evans grunted. "Is our ambitious sergeant still holed up with the chief inspector? I sometimes wonder whose team he's actually on. And to arrest young Dotty Sayers for stealing a painting. It's ridiculous."

Ryan's eyes bulged in surprise at the inspector's words.

The inspector wrinkled his nose. "I know, I have not always been an advocate of Mrs Sayers, and she has a habit of poking her nose into police business, but I can't deny the cases she's solved and the help she's given us. And if she says she saw a body in the library, then I for one, believe her."

The inspector tapped his nose, before continuing, "I smell something else here. Something much bigger than you, me, or Mrs

Sayers, but the trouble is, I'm not sure I can do anything about it."

Ryan and the inspector were still standing by the printer as the inspector checked his watch and instructed, "Get yourself home, lad. No need to worry about Sergeant Unwin if he can't make time for our department. Give those papers to me. I'll have a read through them and then leave them on his desk."

"Thank you, sir," replied Ryan, handing over the printed sheets.

"Doing anything interesting tonight?" asked the inspector, trying to sound casual.

Ryan checked his watch. Just after six. "Not much," he lied, and felt his cheeks flush. He was going to have to control that.

"Ahh," said the inspector in a knowing tone. "There's a woman involved."

Ryan nodded. That at least was true, but not in the way the inspector thought.

Inspector Evans slapped Ryan on the back as he said, "Go and enjoy yourself."

Ryan changed out of his black and white police uniform and left the station at a quarter past six wearing jeans, trainers, and a green parka jacket with a fur-lined hood over his sweatshirt. Sticking out of the deep pocket of his jacket was a roll of papers. They were additional, unofficial evidence which he'd collected about the missing painting. He knew that, technically, he shouldn't be removing them from the police station.

He stopped under a streetlight and tapped his phone. His call was immediately answered by a breathless Ozzie Winters. She was a young, only nineteen, ambitious reporter for the local Cirencester Times, who'd followed and written about Roger Dewhirst's case. Ryan had been introduced to her at a charity tabletop sale Keya had organised.

"Are you still on for tonight?" asked Ozzie, unable to conceal the excitement in her voice.

"Yes," replied Ryan resolutely. He knew he could get into trouble for what he was about to do, but he needed help from someone outside the police force. Someone he could trust. But could he trust Ozzie? "I'm leaving work now and should be in Barnton in twenty minutes."

"Great, I'll make my way back and meet you outside The Village Pub."

"Back?" queried Ryan.

"Yes. You didn't think I'd wait to visit the scene in the dark? Who knows what I would miss. I went this afternoon, as soon as you called me, and I've a few things to show you." She hung up, ending the call with, "See you soon."

Twenty minutes later, Ryan pulled up behind a row of parked cars in what constituted the main street of Barnton. He locked his car - it might be a small, sleepy village, but he knew you couldn't be complacent - and walked towards The Village Pub, whose small windows illuminated the road outside with magnified rectangles of light.

As he approached, the front door opened, and he heard a murmur of voices as a shadowy figure stepped out. The figure turned and walked away as a voice startled him.

"Evening Constable," greeted Ozzie Winters dryly.

"Shhh," he whispered, "it's Ryan when I'm off duty."

Ozzie stepped out of the shadows. Her black spiky hair was concealed beneath a black knitted hat with a faux fur pom-pom, and she wore a long, black padded jacket. Ryan wondered if she had done this type of thing before, as she was certainly dressed for the part.

"So this is not official police business," she remarked.

"No, I'm helping a friend. But remember, you promised not to print a word until I give you the go ahead. I don't want to make matters worse."

She raised her hands - on which she wore black-fingerless gloves - in a gesture of surrender, before asking in a more businesslike tone, "Shall we start with my discovery this afternoon?"

Ozzie led Ryan back past his car before turning right down a street of period Cotswold-stone properties, intermingled with modern brick houses.

"Why did you call me this afternoon? I know you said someone stole a painting from Sir

Reginald Spencer, but why does that interest you? And why ask for my help?"

"As I said, I'm helping a friend, and I can't involve my colleagues. Except Keya, Sergeant Varma. And why you? Because I followed your reports on the Roger Dewhirst case and most of the time you knew what was going on before we did."

"But why the cloak-and-dagger approach?"

"I believe this is about more than just a painting. And you're good at digging and trying to make links. I don't think you were correct suggesting a connection between Ethel's death and Roger Dewhirst's, but it might be linked with other cases. If it is, you'll have a devil of a story to tell."

"So why here? Why Barnton?" Ozzie took another right and they entered a street with bungalows on either side.

"This is the most recent crime. And we have to start somewhere."

"But Dotty Sayers has been arrested. She was found at the scene."

"I know she was, and she hasn't been arrested. She's just helping police with their enquires. But the painting wasn't found at the scene, and if it didn't leave via the front of the house …"

"It had to have been taken out another way, which is why you suggested we look for an alternative way to access Barnton Manor."

"Precisely."

The bungalows on the right ended, and they passed a modern brick village hall. "Fair enough," accepted Ozzie. "It's not as if I have anything better to do on a Tuesday evening."

Ryan glanced across at her, but he didn't feel she was being ironic.

The village hall was the last building and a final streetlight illuminated its entrance.

Ozzie produced a black Maglite torch, but she didn't switch it on. She must have noticed Ryan staring at it as she said, "I prefer to use my night vision, but sometimes I need extra light to peer into dark corners, and something to protect me if I don't like what I find." She tapped the heavy metal torch against her palm.

"There's a playground and tennis courts on the other side of this hedge." She inclined her head towards a tall hedge with patches of brittle brown leaves. "And then there's a playing field. And that's where it gets interesting. An official footpath runs across the field to a wood. Here's the entrance."

Separately, they negotiated the metal kissing gate and entered the field beyond. Ryan had expected it to be dark, but lights penetrated the wood from the far side.

The wood must be narrow and merely separate the playing fields from other houses and, if his navigation skills were correct, one of them should be Sir Reginald's.

"I think you've guessed that we're looking towards the rear of Barnton Manor," explained Ozzie. "I'm not sure if you want to look now, but this afternoon I followed the footpath into those woods. The path actually turns away from the village and heads into the countryside. Some properties have gates or stiles into the woods, but not Barnton Manor. It has a hedge but in a gap a section of post and rail fence has been added."

Ryan considered his options before deciding, "I don't think we should be sneaking about at the back of Sir Reginald's house or flashing a torch. He's bound to be jumpy after today's theft, and the last thing I want is him calling the police."

He smiled thinly at Ozzie before asking, "Do you think it's possible that someone could have left the property that way carrying a large painting?"

Ozzie smiled and held up a piece of brown paper. "Not only do I think they could, I know they did."

Ryan reached out for the paper, but Ozzie closed her hand around it.

"Now, now," she chastised. "When you share, so will I. For now, this is mine. It's not as if you can officially test it for fingerprints."

Ryan narrowed his eyes as he asked, "Where did you find it?"

"Snagged on a splinter of wood under the bottom rail of the fence at the rear of Barnton Manor. And from the drag marks and flattened vegetation, I'd say that something heavy was dragged under the fence. I also found several footprints. Size tens would be my estimate, so most likely a man's. I can send you the photos if you want."

Ryan's distrust was replaced by relief, and he exclaimed, "That's great work, and it backs up Dotty's story. But I'll still need to find more substantial evidence before my colleagues believe she's innocent."

"So that's who this is all about. Dotty Sayers. Did she really try to smuggle an ancient robe out of the country?"

"No," snapped Ryan, annoyed he'd given Dotty's name away.

"Do you think she'll speak to me? Tell me her side of the story?"

Ryan sighed. "Not at the moment. She's in Cirencester Police Station."

CHAPTER SIX

Dotty was woken by Aunt Beanie's gentle voice. "Are you all right? Sorry it's so late but it's taken ages to persuade the chief inspector to let me take you home tonight.

"He was insisting on an electronic ankle tag until Keya got back from wherever she'd been and said he couldn't authorise that. Only a judge can, and the courts are closed. So as long as you promise not to run away, you can sleep in your own bed tonight."

Aunt Beanie smiled sadly down at Dotty from the partially open doorway of the police interview room.

Dotty realised she'd fallen asleep on the table and her neck was stiff as she lifted her head off her hands. "What time is it?" she mumbled drowsily.

"Seven o'clock," replied Aunt Beanie. "I called Norman, and he's picking up fish and chips before driving us home."

Norman Climpson had moved into Meadowbank Farm over a year ago to help Aunt Beanie look after her ailing husband, Uncle Cliff. But Uncle Cliff's dementia had worsened, and he'd moved to a local nursing home.

Norman remained at the farmhouse helping Aunt Beanie, looking after his Jersey cow, Buttercup, and working part-time with Dotty as the porter at Akemans auction house.

Norman was waiting in the farm's Land Rover Defender as Dotty and Aunt Beanie left the police station. As Dotty squeezed herself into the front seat beside Aunt Beanie, she smelt the vinegar from the fish and chips, and her tummy rumbled.

"Have you eaten anything today?" asked Aunt Beanie sharply.

"Ryan bought me some cake after I was released at lunchtime, but I couldn't eat it." Her stomach gurgled again.

Aunt Beanie stared down at the polystyrene boxes she held and asked, "Do you mind if we start Norman? There doesn't seem any point letting these get cold."

"Help yourselves," replied Norman as he grated the gears of the old Land Rover and it jumped forward. "But can you hand me a few chips once we're on a straight bit of road?"

The chips were a little soggy, but Dotty didn't care. The batter on the fish was crisp and tasted slightly malty. She needed to enjoy these little luxuries and her taste of freedom, as she had no idea how long they would last.

Chief Inspector Ringrose and Nick appeared convinced she'd stolen Sir Reginald's painting, and that she'd been involved with a mounting number of crimes.

She was looking forward to curling up with Earl Grey, her furry British blue cat. She must save some of her fish for him.

"Can someone please explain why Dotty has been arrested again?" demanded Norman as he negotiated a roundabout.

Dotty explained about her visit to Barnton Manor, the missing painting, and Tariq Kazem's body in the library.

"And you're certain it was this Tariq Kazem lying on the floor?" pressed Norman.

"Yes, although …" Dotty hesitated, "as nobody else saw it I am beginning to wonder if I made it all up."

"Don't be ridiculous," interjected Aunt Beanie. "You saw his body and then phoned the police. And as both he and the painting, which you also saw, are missing, the explanation is clear. Either he was dead, and the culprit hid his body and stole the painting, or he wasn't dead, and he stole the painting. Simple."

"It is to Chief Inspector Ringrose and Sergeant Unwin. They're convinced I made it all up and stole the painting. But my solicitor," she turned to Aunt Beanie and said, "Thanks for organising one."

"No, problem. It was Ryan's idea, when he called from Sir Reginald's. I know one of the partners in the firm, Mr Briggs, he helped us when some idiot walked across one of our fields and was chased by a bull."

Norman shook his head as the traffic lights changed from red to green and the Land Rover chugged slowly forward, and then he asked, "But I thought Chief Inspector Ringrose was on your side?"

"Not anymore," replied Aunt Beanie. "And neither is Sergeant Unwin. I can't understand where they're coming from. Maybe they have evidence I don't know about now they've kicked me off Operation Bumblebee."

"Really?" spluttered Dotty through a mouthful of fish. "What was that all about, anyway?"

"I can't tell you," snapped Aunt Beanie, clamping her lips together.

"It all sounds very fishy to me," remarked Norman. "Talking of which, can you pass me a couple of chips?"

"What we need is a council of war," proposed Aunt Beanie.

"It's not that bad, is it?" asked Norman.

Aunt Beanie sighed. "I'm afraid it is. There are a growing number of cases with links to Dotty, and I'm concerned that she's going to be framed for all of them."

"Like some master criminal?" exclaimed Norman. "Surely not."

"Oh, yes. The chief inspector is deadly serious, so we need to prove Dotty's innocence in at least one of the cases, to shake their resolve about charging her with the rest."

"But who's going to help me?" pleaded Dotty. "Everyone I know who could help, apart from Norman and my solicitor, are employed by Gloucestershire Police."

"You know Keya and I will assist you in any way we can, and so will Ryan." Aunt Beanie laid her hand on Dotty's leg. "Don't worry. We're going to get you out of this mess."

CHAPTER SEVEN

R yan pulled open the front door of The Axeman pub in Coln Akeman, the village nearest to Akemans antiques and auction house where Dotty worked.

He welcomed the warm, slightly stuffy atmosphere inside after the chill night air. A fire glowed in the large inglenook fireplace and the atmosphere was genial as regular drinkers mixed with couples and a family eating supper.

Poor Dotty. He hoped she wasn't still at the station. Worse still, he prayed she wouldn't be kept overnight and made to sleep in one of the cells.

He spotted his friend, and Dotty's new solicitor, Gerald, sitting uncomfortably at a table in the corner, arranging square beer mats into a neat row.

As Ryan approached the table, he apologised, "Sorry I'm late."

Gerald looked up and smiled weakly as he replied, "You're not. I was early."

Still standing, Ryan explained, "I called Keya, Sergeant Varma, and asked her to join us. She's Dotty's best friend. Can I get you a drink while we wait?"

Gerald glanced at the bar. "Just a sparkling water. Can you bring me the bottle, still sealed and …"

"Make sure the glass is clean. Don't worry, I know the routine." Ryan smiled at Gerald. He was used to his eccentricities.

As Ryan paid for the drinks, he saw Keya enter the rear snug, where most of the locals gathered. She must have parked at the back of the pub. She waved, and he waited for her to join him.

"I bought you an orange juice and lemonade," he said. "I hope that's OK? Can you carry it? Gerald's found a table in the far corner."

"Thanks," she replied and followed him, weaving between occupied tables to join Gerald.

"Gerald, Keya. Keya, Gerald," Ryan introduced them as he placed Gerald's bottle of sparkling water and clean glass on the table with his own pint of zero alcohol beer.

"Hi," Keya and Gerald said in unison.

Ryan was relieved Keya didn't try to shake Gerald's hand, as he'd only have refused.

"Thank you both for coming. Keya, Gerald is representing Dotty legally, so I thought it best we give him the whole picture. Since I joined the station, I've noticed lots of crimes which Dotty has been connected to, although I can't work out which are, or are not, relevant to her current predicament."

"But what about this stolen painting?" asked Keya. "It took all Aunt Beanie's powers of persuasion to make Chief Inspector Ringrose agree Dotty could go back to the farm with her tonight. But Dotty has to return for more questioning in the morning."

"Aunt Beanie?" queried Gerald.

"Your partner's friend, Bernadette Devereaux. Aunt Beanie is the nickname we've adopted for her. From Dotty." At least Dotty wasn't locked in a cell tonight, which was a huge relief.

"The painting?" repeated Keya.

"Still missing, as far as I know," replied Gerald, "And until it's found, or a witness comes forward who actually saw Dotty take it, there isn't much progress I can make with the case. But as Dotty called the police, and she was found by the owner sitting in her car, it'll be difficult to put together a strong enough case unless, as I discussed with Dotty, the police can establish she was working with an accomplice. Don't you agree?"

"An accomplice," squawked Keya, and several customers looked round at her in surprise. Abashed, she dipped her chin and continued in a quieter voice, "I've known Dotty for eighteen months and she doesn't have a lot of friends, and none of them are the criminal type."

"I don't know," mused Ryan. "I bet Aunt Beanie could talk her way into getting pretty much anything she wanted."

"Except Dotty's release," muttered Keya. "And I thought the chief inspector was on our side."

"But I thought Dotty had been released?" Ryan said in a confused tone.

"Only for tonight." Keya clarified.

"That's an interesting phrase, Keya," considered Gerald. "Why do you think there are sides?"

"Oh, it's just a figure of speech," dismissed Keya, but her eyes met Ryan's and he realised Keya was right, and they had already chosen sides. Dotty's side, whatever that meant.

Gerald twisted the cap off his bottle and poured the fizzing water into his glass as he reasoned, "Neither of you have actually known Dotty long. What about her earlier life? Could she have friends or associates from the past who she could be working with?"

Keya shook her head vehemently. "She was an army wife and lived in a totally different world. Besides, she left a domineering father for a controlling husband, and didn't have any friends outside the military community, and even then, none she could really call close."

"And what about in the antiques world?" pressed Gerald.

Keya answered again. "She knew nothing about it until she started working for Akemans, which is when I first met her. She was very shy and self-conscious, although it was clear she had a sharp mind and a knack for solving police cases." Keya smiled to herself.

"So the picture you're painting," confirmed Gerald, "is of a sheltered young woman, getting on with her life, with few close friends. But could she be hiding a secret from you?"

"No," responded Keya firmly.

Evenly, Ryan replied, "I haven't known Dotty as long as Keya, but secretive isn't a word I'd use to describe her. Quite the opposite. She's open and honest and often struggles to hide her feelings. She often blushes."

Still using a defensive tone, Keya added, "And she's not weak-willed or stupid. She's an honest, intelligent, and loyal friend. And like us," Keya once more looked up at Ryan, "she believes in justice and doing the right thing."

Gerald shrank back in his chair. "OK. OK. I get it, but I had to be sure. From my own point of view, as much as anything. If I'm going to defend her, I'll do it because I'm also seeking justice."

"Good," muttered Keya. "As long as we're on the same team."

Why was Keya preoccupied with sides and teams, Ryan wondered.

Gerald continued, "And, Ryan, I trust your judgement. It's never let us down in the past. So going back to the current case. Even if the police try the accomplice angle, they're unlikely to find any evidence to support it. Correct?"

"Yes," agreed Ryan.

Keya nodded her head.

"Then it looks as if we'll have to wait until the painting is discovered to confirm her innocence. Ryan, you mentioned other crimes. What are they?"

Ryan sipped his beer as he thought. Then he said, "There are those which Sergeant Unwin believes Dotty could be involved with, and others which we think may be linked, but nobody is currently blaming Dotty for."

"I agree," said Keya. "And we can prove Dotty wasn't involved with those linked cases, as the culprits have been arrested and, in most cases, convicted."

Gerald and Keya both looked at Ryan, as he scratched his chin and said, "Yes and no."

"What does that mean?" asked Keya sharply.

"Take the first time Dotty was arrested for attempting to smuggle stolen paintings out of the country," explained Ryan. "A man who admitted he was guilty was arrested, but was he working alone? And you're convinced there was someone behind the counterfeit furniture scam and that the craftsman you arrested was actually working under someone else's direction."

"Fair point," agreed Keya.

"I'm confused," admitted Gerald. "Can we start at the beginning?"

CHAPTER EIGHT

Ryan and Gerald both looked at Keya as she sipped her orange juice. Some of the diners had left The Axeman, but the drinkers, particularly those in the snug on the far side of the bar, were becoming louder with shouts, jeers, and some raucous laughter.

Keya appeared to be ignoring it all, lost in thought.

Finally she said, "The first two cases Dotty and I worked on have nothing to do with what's currently happening, at least I don't think they do. The previous receptionist at Akemans, Gail, was murdered and Dotty discovered her killer, although she received a nasty bang on the head and would have been killed if it hadn't been for the timely arrival of her late husband's dog."

Gerald raised his eyebrows.

Keya continued. "The next case, when Dotty had just started working at Akemans as the new receptionist, involved a man of multiple identities. He was a thief and, although he stole some valuable items, he also took some less valuable ones, and money didn't appear to be his motive, and it wasn't the reason he was killed. With me so far?"

Ryan and Gerald nodded.

"The third case I worked on with Dotty, and the first with Sergeant Unwin, did involve antiques, and the death of a celebrity expert on set at the filming of *The Antiques Tour*. And the reason behind the death was an antique scam, but I believe we caught all those involved."

Keya stopped to sip her orange juice before continuing, "Now the counterfeit furniture you mentioned was more complicated, and it didn't happen in isolation. At the same time, there were several break-ins at country houses and some valuable items were taken. As you said, Ryan, I caught the craftsman as he was dumping his materials and trying to make a run for it, but Dotty and I believe someone else was paying him and telling him what furniture to make."

Keya paused and bit her lip. "I think we should talk to an antique dealer called Didier Vogt about that. He seemed to pop up a lot in connection with it, and even convinced Dotty to buy an expensive counterfeit table. I remember David Rook was so furious he arranged for the table to be sold at an auction in London, so it wouldn't be seen at Akemans."

Keya smiled briefly, but became serious again as she remembered, "But Dotty was mortified for being duped into buying it. And then we get to the forged paintings. Paintings were either sent by their owners for repair or cleaning, or they were stolen.

"Then they were copied, and the originals sold abroad for loads of money, while the copies were returned to the original owners. Well, not the stolen ones. But it wasn't actually a new idea. A local expert admitted the gentry have been doing it for years to raise funds."

"Which expert?" asked Gerald.

"A man called Jarrod Willcox. He used to run a gallery in Cirencester, but he's closed it down and gone into business with Lady Stanley-Rudd and a young artist called Finn Andrews. They still hold art exhibitions at her ladyship's house, or in a barn at Jarrod's place, but their main business is assessing painting collections.

"They identify which pictures are originals and which are copies. And as a side business, they arrange for owners of valuable paintings who need cash to have a painting copied, so they can continue to hang it, or at least the copy, in their house, and discreetly sell the original."

"He might also be worth talking to?" Gerald suggested.

"Certainly," replied Keya. "He's not particularly forthcoming, but I bet he knows far more about what's happening in the antique world, particularly in relation to paintings, than he lets on."

"Do you think he's worth approaching about Sir Reginald's missing painting?" asked Ryan.

Keya's eyes widened. "Of course. Why didn't I think of that? I'm out and about in the Cotswolds tomorrow, so I'll try to track him down."

"Good. And hopefully we can make some progress with the current situation. Anything else?" enquired Gerald.

"Yes," replied Keya.

"Those paintings Ryan mentioned, which were hidden in Dotty's luggage. They were some of those stolen as part of the copying scam. And someone was arrested and convicted, and he admitted he'd organised the whole fraudulent scheme. But I've always wondered how he put the scam together and where he found the forgers, as the copies were excellent. It needed someone brave and willing to take huge risks, which didn't match his character. He was more of the front-of-house type, happy to follow orders. And I bet deep down, Dotty had the same misgivings."

Gerald pressed his lips together as he listened to Keya. When she finished, he said, "So you think there's someone else involved? A Mr Big character? And that breaking into country houses and stealing their contents, creating counterfeit furniture, and copying valuable paintings was all his work. That's a lot for one person. Wouldn't it take a huge amount of organisation? And to what end? Money? One scheme I can understand, but three different ones? Surely that's too much for a single individual to dream up and manage?"

"I don't disagree with your logic," admitted Ryan.

"It's to keep us on our toes," insisted Keya. "As soon as we get close to working out one scheme, he or they, as it could be an organisation, move on to something else. And we only catch the small fish. Not the larger sharks."

Ryan leaned towards Keya. "You really believe there is some higher force at work?"

Keya shrugged her shoulders. "Sometimes I do, but at other times I don't see how there can be. But I'm sure Dotty does, but like us, she can't work out how all the pieces fit together. And since she's been accused of orchestrating the more recent crimes, she may be more convinced than ever."

"Yes, moving onto those," said Gerald, glancing at his watch.

Ryan answered. "I met Dotty while investigating the case of a dead stallholder at an antique fair. With Dotty's help …"

"She was the one who solved the case!" exclaimed Keya.

Luckily, the table closest to them was now empty, so Ryan continued, without worrying about being overheard, "OK. Dotty discovered who the killer was and why the stallholder had been killed, and that case seems self-contained. But at the next fair, an elderly lady, well-known on the antique fair circuit, was also found dead.

"That investigation is with Worcestershire Police. My contact there told me the case will be closed soon unless evidence can be found to contradict the pathologist, whose findings are that she died of a heart attack."

"That seems a reasonable explanation," considered Gerald.

"Except Dotty found her with a scarf wrapped around her mouth, and when I removed it, there were clearly marks on her neck," countered Keya.

"Which the pathologist concluded happened when her scarf caught on something as she fell," explained Ryan.

"Caught on what?" demanded Keya.

"I don't know." Ryan leaned back in his chair. "I'm just passing on the information I was given."

"Sorry. I didn't mean to shout at you," Keya apologised. "It's just so … frustrating."

"What has the dead woman to do with Dotty? I thought you said Worcestershire Police think she died of a heart attack. So they're not blaming Dotty for her death?"

"No, but my chief inspector and Sergeant Unwin are," claimed Keya. "And we think the old lady was murdered, don't we, Ryan?"

"It fits the evidence from the crime scene, but we don't have a suspect. Which leads to the other crime at the fair, the theft of the ancient robe, which Dotty is accused of stealing and trying to smuggle out of the country."

"And it's not the only valuable item which has been stolen and shipped abroad," added Keya. "At the same fair where the antique dealer was killed, what turned out to be a valuable copper jug was stolen and reappeared in a museum in Baghdad."

"Baghdad? Now I am getting lost." Gerald shook his head as if to clear it.

"You see how complicated this is?" insisted Keya.

"And there's the death of Bernard Ingram," remembered Ryan.

"Who?" asked Gerald.

"A member of the ground crew at Cotswold Airport whose body was washed up on the side of a lake at Cotswold Water Park," Ryan explained. "And I discovered that before his death, £5,000 was paid into his bank account."

"And Cotswold Airport was where Dotty's suitcase was stored before it was loaded into the private jet." Keya screwed up her eyes. "I bet Bernard Ingram hid the robe in it."

"Unfortunately, as he's dead, we can't confirm that with him," Gerald pointed out.

Keya looked glum as she replied, "I know."

"Is that everything?" asked Gerald in a resigned tone.

Ryan looked at Keya, who nodded. "I think so."

"It's certainly complicated, but for the moment, the only crime Dotty has actually been accused of is stealing Sir Reginald's painting," reasoned Gerald.

"That's right," confirmed Ryan.

"But she is under suspicion for the recent thefts and deaths," responded Keya. "And I can't just sit around and wait for the evidence to mount up against her. But there again, I'm not sure what I can do. I've been shut out of all my department's investigations and I'm spending my time at primary schools conducting road safety talks, or I'm tied up with disputes between local villagers."

"And Sergeant Unwin hasn't included me in the relevant cases recently," admitted Ryan, "or Inspector Evans for that matter. Chief Inspector

Ringrose and Sergeant Unwin are keeping their cards close to their chests."

"I suppose as Dotty is a friend of yours, they're trying to prevent a conflict of interest. Do you have anything against the two police officers?" asked Gerald.

Ryan shook his head as he replied, "Sergeant Unwin is ambitious, but he's straight and he doesn't cut corners."

"And the chief inspector has always been fair," reasoned Keya, "and he appointed me to his team when not everyone would have done."

Ryan gave Keya a sympathetic look. "Don't put yourself down. You're an enthusiastic and dedicated police officer."

"Without the brains and the drive of Sergeant Unwin, and the contacts of the chief inspector," protested Keya, smiling weakly.

"So at the moment, there isn't much either of you can actively do," concluded Gerald.

"I'll work on having the charges against Dotty for the stolen painting dropped, but you need to keep your eyes and your ears open and compile as much evidence in Dotty's favour as you can, in case she's implicated in any of these other cases in the future.

"But as you're both convinced she's innocent, I'm sure matters will work themselves out, and that'll be the end of her troubles."

CHAPTER NINE

"Dotty, are you awake?" Aunt Beanie called.

Sleepily, Dotty opened her eyes, staring straight at the large furry grey ball curled up on top of her duvet. It must be early if Earl Grey hadn't left for his breakfast.

She'd been relieved to find her home relatively tidy when she'd returned the previous evening. Clearly the police had only searched the places they thought a large painting could have been hidden.

"I promised the chief inspector I'd return you to the station by half past seven," Aunt Beanie shouted. "Norman's cooking breakfast when you're ready."

At the word breakfast, Earl Grey stretched out his front legs before slowly lifting himself into a standing position. He gave Dotty a quick glance before jumping off the bed and trotting out of the open door.

She turned and looked across at her daisy-print curtains penetrated by a soft light.

Time to get up.

When she'd showered and dressed, she joined Aunt Beanie, Norman, and Earl Grey in the kitchen. Earl Grey's cat bowl was empty, and he was staring greedily at Norman, who was frying bacon.

"Sorry to wake you so early," apologised Aunt Beanie. "Did you sleep OK?"

"Wonderfully. As if it was the last night in my own bed."

"Now don't talk like that. Today's a new day, so let's see what it brings."

"Being accused of more crimes I didn't commit," replied Dotty dully.

Norman pulled the frying pan off the hot plate and said, "Stay strong, lass. I know what it's like sitting in one of those interview rooms waiting for someone to return and ask you more questions about something you don't know anything about. And the worst thing is the look in their eyes. When I was interviewed by Inspector Evans, he seemed convinced I was a morally corrupt criminal."

Norman had been arrested the previous year when a local man had been killed. He'd taken Earl Grey with him to the police station, as there had been nobody to look after the cat.

When Dotty arrived to collect him, Earl Grey had been meowing and interrupting the interview, much to the inspector's irritation.

Norman had remained stalwart throughout, despite Inspector Evans' attempts to intimidate him, but he hadn't protested his innocence for fear of passing the blame onto others. Principally Aunt Beanie.

Dotty looked up from her seat at the pine kitchen table as the older woman placed a cup of tea in front of her and said in a sincere voice, "We're going to get you out of this."

After the past few days of cold weather, Dotty couldn't help feeling uplifted by the warm sunshine on her face as she looked up at the grey-blue sky with its scattering of puffy white clouds. Standing outside Cirencester police station, she took a deep lungful of air.

She could do this. She was innocent and just needed to remain calm. And when asked, she should describe exactly what happened, even when she repeated herself. As Norman had told her, she needed to stay strong.

Dotty followed Aunt Beanie towards the entrance and was surprised when her solicitor, Gerald, stepped into her path. Despite his padded blue jacket, he looked cold and Dotty wondered how long he'd been waiting.

"Dotty, there you are. The station told me you'd be coming in early," greeted Gerald, shuffling from one foot to another.

Aunt Beanie stopped before entering the station and retraced her steps.

"This is Gerald, my solicitor," Dotty told Aunt Beanie. "Gerald, this is Aunt Beanie."

"Bernadette Devereaux, an honour to meet you," enthused Gerald.

"Well I don't know about that. But I am pleased to see you, and so early in the morning. Why didn't you wait for Dotty inside?"

Gerald looked down at his feet as he replied, "I'm not a fan of police reception areas."

"I see," although Dotty doubted Aunt Beanie knew about Gerald's phobias. "And do you have any new evidence to secure Dotty's release?"

"No, but it's the lack of police evidence which is important. I'll argue that as the painting is not in her possession, she remained at the scene, and there are no witnesses who saw her take it, she should be released."

"That sounds logical. Let's hope the police haven't found anything else overnight which they can use to keep her here," Aunt Beanie said as she opened the door to the police station.

This time, Gerald stayed in the interview room with Dotty, and he requested drinks while they waited, which Dotty thought was for her benefit as he produced his own bottle of water.

"I met your friends last night, Ryan and Keya. They wanted to explain the background to your case, and everything else that has happened over the past year. Keya is convinced you're embroiled in some complex antiques racket being run by a Mr Big character."

"Keya does have a flair for the dramatic. I'm sure she's wrong … but …" Dotty trailed off as she gave Keya's theory some thought. It was something they'd both discussed before, but without wanting to believe it. As if it were a game. But this was no game. And the stakes were rising.

The door opened as Ryan entered, carrying a paper cup and bottle of water. He looked disappointed when he noticed Gerald's bottle on the table.

"Thank you," said Dotty when he handed her the paper cup.

"I didn't know you'd be the tea boy," apologised Gerald, as he pocketed his bottle and took the one Ryan held. "Anything we should know about?"

Ryan looked out into the corridor and quietly closed the door. "Sergeant Unwin is busy reading emails and making phone calls trying to locate the painting. Chief Inspector Ringrose is at Akemans, checking if you've hidden it there."

"Oh no," groaned Dotty. "But at least George is away in France, and there isn't much to look through, as we haven't had many deliveries yet for this month's auction."

George, whose full name was Georgina Carey-Boyd, ran Akemans auction house, but she and her husband, Marcus, were currently away in Paris.

When she was a student, George had lived there, but after an affair with a married artist, she'd returned home in disgrace. George's sister, Gilly Wimsey, had persuaded her she hadn't done anything wrong, as she had been young and impressionable at the time.

So George and Marcus were laying George's ghosts to rest and searching for a nude picture of her which the married artist had painted.

Ryan brought Dotty's thoughts back to the current situation. "His team is also searching the antiques centre."

"What? The stallholders won't like that. But I suppose it's a blessing the painting is large," conceded Dotty, "as most of the stalls won't have room to hide it."

"I hope the search doesn't take too long. I've an appointment back at the office at ten," stated Gerald.

"I better go." Ryan left and Dotty and Gerald sat in silence.

Dotty sipped her tea, thinking about the search and the events of the past few months.

After ten minutes, Gerald stood up and left the room. He returned some twenty minutes later with Sergeant Unwin. The sergeant looked frustrated as he ran his hand through his short, dark hair.

"You're free to go, Dotty," was all Sergeant Unwin said before he turned on his heels and left the room.

"Is that it?" asked Dotty.

"For now, yes," confirmed Gerald.

"I told the sergeant he didn't have enough evidence to hold you. He protested and said he needed to speak to the chief inspector, which I think he did. As you saw, he wasn't exactly happy with the decision to release you, but he knows they can't take the case to the magistrate without more proof you committed the crime.

"But we need to be wary. I didn't get the impression they are looking for other suspects, so be prepared to return for further questioning. I'll tell Ryan to keep me updated. Can I give you a lift anywhere?"

"I'm not sure. Is Aunt Beanie still here?"

CHAPTER TEN

Aunt Beanie drove Dotty back from Cirencester police station to Meadowbank Farm. "I'm working from home for the rest of the day," she explained, as Dotty carried a cardboard box into the farmhouse.

"Those are files from old cases the chief inspector has asked me to work through. I think he's deliberately keeping me away from current ones. What are you going to do with yourself?"

"I can't hang around here all day," replied Dotty, as Earl Grey brushed against her legs. "I've admin to catch up on at Akemans from yesterday. And I need to organise more deliveries and start preparing the catalogue for this month's sale."

It was half past ten by the time Dotty entered the reception-cum-office area at Akemans auction house. It was empty, but someone had been sitting at the reception desk. Probably Marion Rook, judging by the fragrance of cardamom from the empty coffee cup.

Marion helped out when they were busy, particularly during the week of an auction, and when Dotty was away or working in the antiques centre. Marion's husband, David, a well-known and respected expert in the antiques world, also worked for Akemans, as a consultant.

Dotty found Marion in the main auction room, supervising Norman and two delivery men as they off-loaded some interesting pieces of furniture from a white van parked outside the double doors, halfway down the room.

"Dotty, what a relief to see you. Have the police finally seen sense and let you go?" asked

Marion. She wore grey jogging bottoms underneath a white tennis skirt, and a matching grey sweatshirt. Usually immaculately turned out, her hair looked slightly dishevelled and her normally impeccable make-up was lacking, making her look all of her sixty-something years.

"David was furious. Not only about your arrest, which he said was preposterous, but also for Sir Reginald and his stolen painting. But he was curious. Did you really see Tariq Kazem on the library floor?"

"It all seems rather surreal now, especially after spending so much time in a police interview room, but yes, I'm sure I did." She had seen him. She was certain.

Dotty watched as Norman carried a golden-coloured oak tilt-top side table into the room. He placed it close to Marion, who stepped across and caressed it as she said admiringly, "Isn't it absolute perfection? Look how the timber patination of the Pollard Oak catches the light. It's glorious."

The table was certainly attractive, but they'd had other beautiful pieces in auctions before and Marion hadn't been so emotional about them.

"Where is it from?" Dotty asked.

Marion gulped before replying, "A private collection. All these items are, and there are some ornaments, clocks, and lamps. I wondered if you'd help me catalogue them?"

"Of course." Dotty looked around the auction room before asking, "Did the police create much of a mess?"

"Not in here, but Gilly was moaning about them upsetting stallholders in the antiques centre."

"I hope she isn't annoyed with me."

"Why should she be? It's not your fault the police are inept and think you walked out of Sir Reginald's house with a large painting, which then vanished into thin air."

When the van left, Dotty found the company tablet, which she used to photograph and write descriptions of each auction Lot before transferring the information into the auction catalogue template. But the process took longer than usual as Marion fussed about, rearranging items and asking her to retake photographs until she was completely satisfied.

The seller must be very important if Marion was giving the collection such personal attention.

"Hello," a voice called from the reception area.

Relieved, Dotty handed the tablet to Marion and left the main auction room. She was surprised to find Didier Vogt waiting for her in reception.

"Didier, how are you? And the girls?" asked Dotty.

Didier had sole parenting responsibility for his young twin girls.

"It's not been easy for them … since their mother went away. And after a recent incident … well, I've decided to move them back to France. My parents own a large farmhouse, so there's plenty of room for us, and the girls can attend the local school. They're not exactly bilingual, but they know some French."

"And I'm sure they'll pick the rest up quickly. Children are like that. And it'll be wonderful to spend time with their grandparents, and it'll give you a break. Will you come back to the UK for work?"

Didier shook his head. "I've had enough of the antiques world. I'm going to help my father on the farm and expand the small vineyard he has. I feel I'm ready to get my hands dirty again, in the right sort of way."

That was a strange phrase, but Dotty didn't dwell on it as she said, "It sounds idyllic. So how can I help?"

"I've some furniture to enter in this month's auction, which I can't take with me." He handed Dotty a list.

She glanced at it as Didier continued, "The girls and I leave tonight, but the removal company has been instructed to bring these pieces to you. Can you check everything when it arrives?"

"Of course," although Dotty wasn't sure what she could do if the wrong pieces were sent, or those on the list didn't turn up, as she presumed the rest of Didier's possessions were being shipped to France.

"Excellent." Didier smiled sadly at her. "And of course, you must come and visit."

"I'd like that." Although Dotty doubted she ever would.

Didier turned to the reception desk and scribbled on a piece of paper. He tore off the written section and handed it to her as he whispered, "This will be my address in France. Promise you won't give it to anyone else. However much they insist."

Uncertainly, Dotty looked into Didier's eyes. He looked scared as he still hung onto one side of the scrap of paper.

"OK," Dotty replied, but Didier continued to stare at her. "I promise."

Didier let go of the paper, and slowly smiled. "Thank you."

He turned, and left Dotty standing in the reception area, gazing after him.

"Hiya, what are you staring at?" asked Keya a few moments later as she stepped through the same door.

"Oh. Hi. I was just thinking about Didier Vogt," replied Dotty, still rooted to the spot.

"Well that's a coincidence, as Ryan and I were discussing him with your solicitor, Gerald, last night. I think we need to speak to him about the counterfeit furniture scam last summer."

"You'll need to be quick. He's moving to France with the girls. That's why he came in, to enter some furniture into this month's auction."

"He was here? When?" Keya's eyes widened.

"Just now. Didn't you pass him in the antiques centre?"

Without responding, Keya turned and rushed out of the reception area.

CHAPTER ELEVEN

Dotty returned to Akemans auction room to help Marion catalogue the private collection they'd received that day.

"Was that someone wanting to buy or sell at the auction, or just a salesman trying to sell Akemans something we don't need?" asked Marion as she handed Dotty the company tablet.

"Actually, it was Didier Vogt. He's moving to France and wants to sell the items he can't take with him in this month's auction."

Marion nearly dropped the vintage Oriental bronze table lamp she was holding. "Didier? Has he left?"

"I'm not sure. He went into the antiques centre, but Keya ran after him as she wanted to speak to him as well."

Marion scraped her hand through her hair as she glanced across at the door leading into the reception area. "Carry on here," she blurted as she pushed the lamp at Dotty and hurried from the room.

Why was Didier so popular today?

Dotty placed the lamp on an attractive walnut table beside a vase of flowers which had materialised from somewhere. Had Marion brought them specifically to photograph with this collection?

Dotty took several photographs of the lamp and was about to start writing the sales description when a puffing Keya entered the auction room. "I was too late. He jumped into his car and although I waved frantically, he didn't see me and drove off."

"Marion won't be happy."

"Why?"

"She wanted to speak to Didier too. Didn't you see her? She left soon after you to find him."

"No. Anyway, how are you?" Keya asked, staring more intently at Dotty.

"I'm fine. Just relieved it's all over. For the moment, at least. But Sergeant Unwin is like a dog with a bone. I don't think he'll give up until he's pinned at least one crime on me."

"Or proves that you weren't involved in any of them."

Dotty was unsure how to respond and only mumbled, "Er ..."

"Don't you see? He's attracted to you, and he was really impressed with your deductions in the Roger Dewhirst case. But then you were caught smuggling. Again. He has to be sure you're as innocent as you claim to be, and you can see his point. You are mixed up with a lot of antique-related crimes."

"But ..."

Keya raised her hands in submission. "I know. It's your job to be at antique events, and you can't help getting involved in police cases, but perhaps, just until this blows over, you'll leave the investigations to us. I do believe Sergeant Unwin is only seeking the truth, even though his current version is rather warped. But Ryan and I, and Aunt Beanie, will keep digging."

"But …" Dotty repeated.

Keya interjected again. "Don't worry, we're not going to leave you out altogether. But you have a lot to do," Keya glanced at the furniture in the auction room, "so it might be better to concentrate on this month's auction and keep your head down for a while."

After Keya left, Dotty tried in vain to concentrate on writing a description of the lamp. It wasn't just what Keya had said, it was the way she'd said it. Her friend had always carried out the work she was given happily and compliantly.

Lately she had seemed frustrated and had hinted that she was being left out of more important cases, but Dotty had never seen her so

... assertive. It was a new side to Keya. To Sergeant Varma.

"Are you still cataloguing that lamp?" asked Marion in a sharp tone.

"Sorry," apologised Dotty. "I think the last couple of days must be getting to me."

Marion's face softened. "That's completely understandable. Let's break for lunch and we can discuss the remaining items still to be listed. I have to leave in an hour for my tennis match. The first of the season, and I've even persuaded David to play. You finish that lamp and I'll bring our lunch boxes and hot drinks."

Dotty forced herself to consider the lamp, and tapped out a brief description on the tablet. She put her own reserve value guesstimate at £500.

She wandered around the remaining items. They were a strange mix. A private collector usually concentrated on a particular historical period, or a specific category, such as glassware or porcelain ornaments, but these items were a complete mixture.

Attractive and valuable, but more likely to be seen in someone's house. That was it. These looked loved and, well, used.

"Anything in particular catch your eye?" asked Marion as she appeared, a jute bag hanging from her arm and a cup in each hand.

"It all looks too expensive for me."

"Yes, it is valuable, and has been meticulously collected over many years. A shame to see it sold, but there we are." Marion placed the cups on the plastic table they usually used for photographing smaller items, and removed her plastic container and Dotty's metal sandwich tin, with pictures of chickens on it, from the bag.

Dotty frowned. "I didn't have time to make my lunch this morning."

"I know. Norman brought this in." Marion handed Dotty her tin. "He apologises if they're not up to your usual high standard."

Gratefully, Dotty opened her lunch box and removed a bacon, lettuce, and tomato sandwich. "Thank you, Norman," she whispered.

"So of the furniture still left to catalogue, there's this oak bookcase, the pair of vintage French bedside tables, the Edward Rundell Norton St Phillip grandfather clock, and that group of occasional tables," instructed Marion.

Dotty ate her lunch as she listened to Marion describe the furniture and other items still to be catalogued. They were nearly finished when Marion's phone rang.

"David, yes, I'm still at Akemans. I'm just running through pieces for Dotty to itemise this afternoon." Marion finished speaking and as she listened, her forehead wrinkled.

"Really. Does it have to be this afternoon?" Marion asked. "Half past three, at Lemington Hall."

She listened for another minute before finishing the call with, "I'll see you soon." She turned to Dotty and once again ran her hand through her hair. It was strange to see Marion with even one strand out of place, never mind her current ruffled appearance.

Marion explained, "David would like you to pick up a painting ..."

Dotty felt the colour drain from her face.

"From Tariq Kazem, at Lemington Hall."

Dotty's legs trembled and as they began to buckle, Marion grabbed her and manoeuvred her across to a Georgian mahogany armchair.

"Thank you," mumbled Dotty. Not again. She wasn't going on her own to collect another painting, and not from Tariq. "What if he's dead?" she muttered to herself.

"I really have no idea what you saw in Sir Reginald's library, but I can assure you Tariq Kazem is very much alive. Indeed, we had dinner with him last night at Lemington Hall. David must want you to collect the portrait of one of the previous owner's relatives which was found in a cupboard at the hall. He thinks it's by an artist called William Salter Herrick and, if he's right, it's rather valuable."

She looked around the auction room and added, "And it'll complement this collection superbly."

"But do I have to go on my own?" Dotty asked.

Marion laid a hand on her shoulder. "Don't worry, you'll be fine. And you don't need to go anywhere near the main house. Tariq will be in his office, which he's converted from one of the buildings in the stable yard. As you approach the hall, take the first turning on the left."

"But what if Tariq isn't there?"

"David assured me he'll be ready and waiting for you at half past three. I think he has an appointment before that, at his office, so he will be there."

"I'm still not sure. Not after last time," protested Dotty.

"I'll tell you what. Why don't you call me at three, just before you leave? We usually have a break around then, and our tennis match is only fifteen minutes away from the hall, so if you have any problems I can pop over."

"Thank you," replied Dotty, only partly reassured. But was she being silly? She and George often visited people's houses collecting items for auctions, and so did Gilly, for the antiques centre. It was part of their business. But she knew people ... Nick, Sergeant Unwin ... thought her stupid for being caught a second time trying to smuggle a stolen item out of the country. She didn't want him to think the same if she visited another house and a painting went missing.

And more than that. She didn't want to be arrested again.

She'd call Keya.

Marion glanced at her watch. "I have to go. Now you know what you're doing here, and you'll call me at three, when you leave?"

Dotty nodded and watched Marion stride out of the auction room.

Taking her phone out of her pocket, she called her friend.

"Hiya, has Didier Vogt turned up again?" Keya asked when she answered Dotty's call.

"I'm afraid not. Look, I know this sounds silly, but I've been asked to pick up a painting from Lemington Hall ..."

"From the Kazems?"

"From Tariq, actually. And the thing is, I don't want a repeat of yesterday. I wondered if you'd come with me?"

"Sure. When do you want to go?"

"I've been told to be there, at Tariq's office in the stable yard, at half past three."

Keya was silent. "I'm handing out road safety certificates at Sherborne Primary school, but it's less than fifteen minutes away, so I'll be there as soon as I can after half past three. Is that OK?"

Dotty pursed her lips. Surely Tariq wouldn't mind if she was a bit late. And if she waited in her car and he brought the painting out to her, all the better. "Yes, that's fine," she replied. "I'll see you there."

CHAPTER TWELVE

Dotty glanced at her watch. It was five minutes to three. She put the tablet down and looked around, thinking she'd done a good afternoon's work, even if she hadn't quite finished.

There were still two standard lamps and some clocks to catalogue, but she should be able to finish them later, when she returned from collecting the painting.

The painting. She gulped. Why was she so concerned about collecting it?

Because of the last time. Because it was Tariq.

But wasn't this the perfect opportunity to find out what had happened last time, and speak to Tariq about it? On his own. Maybe he'd been playing a game, or messing with her and he'd reveal all today.

Feeling more positive, she called Marion Rook. "How's the tennis?" she asked. "Are you winning?"

"No. David isn't concentrating and he keeps missing shots. He's taken himself away for a good talking to."

"But it's the first match of the season. Why is he so hard on himself?"

"He likes to win. So do I, but if I'm playing the best I can and I'm beaten by a better opponent, I can accept that. Anyway, are you calling to say you're leaving for Lemington Hall?"

"Yes," replied Dotty resolutely.

"Good. Call me back when you've collected the painting. I'm not sure if we're playing anymore, or if David is too embarrassed about our near love defeat."

"Thanks, Marion." Dotty finished the call, collected her coat and bag, and left Akemans for Lemington Hall.

It really was a lovely day and made her feel that spring was truly on the way. As the narrow lane she drove along passed through a wood, she smelt the sharp tang of wild garlic and noticed a scattering of yellow-green leaves budding on the trees.

As she slowed to drive through a village, the honey-coloured Cotswold stone was warm and inviting, and so were the tubs of yellow daffodils.

She approached Lemington from the south and before she reached the village, took a left turn between newly constructed stone pillars and through open black-metal gates. Again, she was greeted by daffodils, some yellow and others white, which covered the verges on either side of the drive.

Slowing, she peered out of her windscreen looking for the turning into the stable yard. The house had just come into view when she saw it and turned left.

The stables looked abandoned, as if they hadn't been used for many years, but a single-story building to the right of the entrance had a new roof, windows, and doors.

She parked, facing the office door, and checked her watch. It was only twenty-five past three. Tariq might still be in his meeting, and she'd told Keya she'd wait for her, so she remained in her car.

Dotty wondered if Tariq found it lonely working on his own, and slightly spooky with the old buildings. But maybe he had a secretary or PA, and perhaps he had plans to convert the rest of the stable yard. I

t would probably be popular as a small office space for local businesses, or for those people who didn't want to commute to London each day but weren't comfortable working from home.

She continued her musing as she waited.

The next time she looked at her watch it was 3.40.

Where was Keya? And surely Tariq had heard her arrive and had spotted her car. If he was expecting her, why hadn't he come out to investigate?

After another five minutes, she became restless. She couldn't sit around here all day. Besides, she was bored with sitting in her car. She climbed out and stretched her back, noticing the light from a lamp on a desk through the office window.

But she couldn't see Tariq.

This was ridiculous. What was she scared of? All she was doing was collecting a painting. It wasn't as if she was going to find Tariq dead again.

She strode across to the office door, constructed in two halves like that of a stable, knocked loudly and waited.

Nothing.

Nobody opened the door, and she didn't hear anyone inside.

That was strange. Perhaps Tariq was in a back room.

She pulled on the door handle and pushed the door. It swung open, and she stood on the threshold staring in.

Still nothing. This was strange. Perhaps she should wait for Keya.

But a voice inside urged her forward. She was a strong young woman. She didn't need to wait for the police to enter a room. Tentatively, she took a step inside. Then another.

When she was parallel with Tariq's desk, she stopped and looked around.

It was eerily quiet.

Another step. And she froze.

Tariq Kazem was lying on his back. The handle of a dagger protruding from his chest.

Oh no! Not again.

Dotty heard a car approach, and she turned and rushed to the office door.

Keya's Ford Focus skidded to a halt and her friend jumped out calling, "Sorry I'm late. The presentation overran. What's wrong with you? You look as if you've seen a ghost."

"I have." Dotty turned back to the office and pointed. "Over there."

Dotty stepped out of the office, allowing Keya to enter. She saw her friend crouch down on the far side of the desk before speaking into her radio.

Returning to the door, Keya confirmed, "It is Tariq, and this time he is definitely dead. But the body is still warm. What time did you arrive?"

"Twenty-five past three, but I stayed in my car as we agreed. I haven't seen anyone else since I got here."

Keya looked grave. "I've had to call this in and no doubt your not-so-favourite Sergeant will arrive. So before he does, talk me through exactly what happened."

"I waited in the car until a quarter to four. I was bored, and stiff, so I got out and stretched. When I saw the light from a desk lamp, I thought he must be here, and maybe it was a chance for him to explain what had happened at Sir Reginald's house.

"After knocking on the door, I slowly entered the room, not hearing or seeing anything, until I spotted Tariq lying on the floor. And you're right. This time was different. I knew he was dead."

"Why was it different?"

"There was a chilling stillness, lifelessness about him. And the blood around his mouth and nose, well ...". Dotty turned and gulped in mouthfuls of fresh air.

Keya laid a hand on her arm and reassured her, "It's OK. You don't need to say any more. What about the painting you're here to collect?"

Dotty turned back to her friend. "I've no idea. I haven't seen it, but then I'd only just found Tariq when I heard you arrive."

"Let me have a look."

Keya entered the office and Dotty watched her move slowly around. There was the desk near the window, with the lamp still on, and a second desk facing it.

There was a door beyond where Tariq lay, and beyond the second desk a two-seater leather sofa facing two armchairs. Against the back wall, there was a semi-circular table with a vase of fresh daffodils.

"I can't see it. What was the painting of?" called Keya.

"Marion said it was a portrait of one of the people who used to live in the hall."

"No, I still can't find it."

Dotty pressed her lips together. Should she call Marion and explain about the painting? About Tariq?

She stepped away from the open office door as Keya continued her search and dialled Marion's number.

"Hi," answered Marion. "We've just finished, and although David's talk to himself worked and he played magnificently after the break, we still lost. Have you finished? Are you on the way back to Akemans?"

Dotty hesitated, unsure where to start.

"Dotty, are you there?" Marion asked, a note of concern in her voice.

"Yes, yes, I'm here. It's just that …"

"Oh, no. Don't tell me the painting wasn't there. It hasn't been stolen, has it?"

"Yes, well, I think so, but that's not the worst of it. It's Tariq. He really is dead this time."

"What? Wait there. We'll be straight over."

CHAPTER THIRTEEN

Marion and David arrived at the stable yard at Lemington Hall just before Sergeant Unwin's metallic grey Mercedes cruised in and braked to a stop.

As David parked behind Dotty's Skoda, Marion jumped out and rushed across to Dotty, who was sitting in her car with the door open. Marion squatted down and stared at Dotty with concern as she asked, "Are you all right?"

"I'm not sure," Dotty replied truthfully. She didn't know what to think. Tariq was dead. Who had killed him, and why? And what game had he been playing at Sir Reginald's house? Had he been trying to scare her again, but something had gone wrong?

Yet they hardly knew each other, and the few times they had met, he'd been charming and the epitome of politeness. No, he wasn't one to play such a macabre game.

She felt Marion move away and when she focused again, she was staring at David, who was regarding her with … pity.

She stood up and he walked towards her, muttering, "Terrible. Terrible. And I was so looking forward to working more with Tariq. In business, and as a friend." He slowly shook his head of short grey hair and his large dark eyes, which were usually so watchful, watered as they focused inwardly.

David's tanned face seemed a shade lighter than normal, and his high, prominent forehead wrinkled in concern. He wore grey tracksuit bottoms and a white knitted V-neck cable-knit jumper.

"Mrs Sayers," called Sergeant Unwin as he strode towards her. "So we meet again. And at another crime scene."

David drifted away as, wearily, Dotty concentrated on the young sergeant. His face was grim and his tone polite but cutting.

"Now, now, Sergeant. No jumping to conclusions," admonished the deep, melodic Welsh voice of Inspector Evans. Dotty couldn't believe how relieved she was to hear it.

Sergeant Unwin gave her a disgruntled look as he left to join Keya at the office door.

Inspector Evans joined Dotty and murmured, "But this doesn't look good for you, lassie. I'll do what I can, but my hands might be tied. The young sergeant over there is convinced you're tied up in some fiendish plot, and he's determined to stop you. At any cost."

"Oh dear," replied Dotty, which she thought was rather a weak response considering the predicament she was in. But she must stick to the facts. To the truth.

She heard another vehicle, and a few moments later, an ambulance entered the courtyard and Keya directed the driver as he reversed up to the office door.

Marion joined Dotty as, together, they watched the moss-green uniformed ambulance crew load Tariq's body into the vehicle.

"I simply can't believe it," Marion said in a baffled tone. "Last night he was so charming and extolling the virtues of being an English gentleman. He was considering making the Cotswolds his permanent home, and there were several ladies whose names he mentioned, including you."

"Me?" cried Dotty in surprise. "But I hardly knew him."

"Still, you must have made an impression, and he felt guilty for the trouble at Cotswold Airport and your subsequent arrest. He was all for sending his father's lawyer to represent you, but David persuaded him you were better off with a local solicitor for the moment. You do have one, don't you?"

"Yes, Gerald. Aunt Beanie and Ryan, Constable Jenkins, found him for me."

"Then may I suggest you call him? I overheard Sergeant Unwin speaking on his phone and," Marion turned to Dotty and placed a hand on her arm, "I think there's no doubt he's going to arrest you, whether or not there is any evidence linking you to Tariq's death. You were found alone with the body and that'll probably be enough to charge you. I'm so sorry to drag you into this. And all for a painting of a dead man. Talking of which, where is the painting?"

"That's what I'd like to know," said Sergeant Unwin as he joined them, followed by a reluctant-looking Keya. "Sergeant Varma has searched the victim's office, but there's no sign of it there. Are you sure you didn't pick it up?"

"Certain," replied Dotty, stepping towards the young sergeant and meeting his gaze. "If you don't believe me, search my car."

"You shouldn't have said that," murmured Marion.

"I've nothing to hide," insisted Dotty.

"Thank you," smirked Sergeant Unwin. "Sergeant Varma, search Mrs Sayers' car."

Keya looked uncomfortable as she stared at Sergeant Unwin without moving.

Sergeant Unwin turned round and repeated, "Sergeant Varma. Search Mrs Sayer's car."

Inspector Evans said something to the ambulance driver before turning and walking towards the group.

The ambulance pulled out of the stable yard.

"Sergeant Unwin," declared the inspector as he reached them, "Sergeant Varma is not actually in our team and as she's the same rank as you are, she does not have to follow your orders. Why don't I search Mrs Sayers' car?"

Sergeant Unwin only looked slightly put out as he replied, "Yes, sir."

Dotty watched the inspector approach her car and peer through the still open driver's door as Sergeant Unwin asked her, "You came to collect a painting? That's a familiar story."

"There's no need to take that tone, Sergeant," chided Marion. "I asked her to come here, on David's instructions. We had dinner with Tariq last night and he showed us a painting he'd found in the hall. He didn't want it, but David thought it might have some value and suggested he enter it into this month's auction."

"Was it large?"

"Not particularly."

"So it would be easy enough to pick up and carry away. Can you describe the painting?"

"It was a portrait of a man, one of the family who used to live in the hall. Nineteenth century, David thought, and possibly by William Salter Herrick. It was very dark and the man looked sombre. It wasn't to my taste."

"Nor mine," agreed Inspector Evans as he stepped out from behind Dotty's car, holding up a painting.

Dotty's heart sank as Sergeant Unwin turned to her with a self-satisfied smile and said, "Dorothy Sayers, you're under arrest …"

"No!" cried Keya.

CHAPTER FOURTEEN

Keya stared at her colleague, Sergeant Unwin, as he arrested her friend, Dotty, for the murder of Tariq Kazem and the theft of a painting.

She thought she yelled something as she remained rooted to the spot in the abandoned stable yard at Lemington Hall. This was a mistake. Dotty had no reason to harm Tariq. Surely one of her disgruntled villagers had finally had enough of the newcomers in the hall and taken their revenge.

Just before she'd left Sherborne Primary School, she'd received a message from the groundsman at the hall complaining about motorbikes in the wood again. Had the feud between those at the hall and the inhabitants of Lemington reached a new level? A lethal one?

She checked her watch as a shadow fell across her.

"Somewhere else you need to be, Sergeant?" asked her old boss, Inspector Evans, in a kinder tone than he usually used.

"Er, yes, sir. I've arranged to meet Jarrod Willcox about Sir Reginald Spencer's missing painting."

The inspector raised his eyebrows. "Does he know where it is?"

She shuffled her feet feeling foolish. "No, sir. But he's actually quite knowledgeable about the art world and I thought, well, he might know where to look."

"Good thinking, Sergeant. Why don't you take this painting with you? See what he can tell you about it before you submit it as evidence."

Keya's eyes widened as she grasped the painting firmly, so as not to drop it.

"And Sergeant ..."

"Yes, sir."

"Let's keep this between the two of us. Although if you feel the need, you can pass on your findings to Constable Jenkins and Bernadette Devereux."

Keya felt her mouth fall open. How did he know they were helping Dotty?

Inspector Evans turned away and walked across to Sergeant Unwin's car as the sergeant ushered a compliant Dotty into the rear seat.

Keya lifted her hand to wave at her friend, but stopped, and let it flop back to her side.

What a mess!

Dotty hadn't killed Tariq. Even though she was alone in the old stable yard when Keya arrived.

Hopefully the pathologist would confirm that the time of death was too early for Dotty to have done it. But would Dotty be able to provide witnesses to her movements this afternoon? And the body had still been warm when Keya had touched it.

Keya shivered and, conscious she still held the painting, she returned to her car and placed it in the back, securing it in place with her police coat and fluorescent jacket.

Keya found a key for Tariq's office on the inside of the door and locked it securely, pocketing the key. She'd try to return, and maybe bring Ryan, to search it thoroughly, but not now, she was too distracted.

She was the last to leave the stable yard, and she glanced at Dotty's abandoned little Skoda. Maybe she could use collecting the car as an excuse to bring Ryan to help her search the crime scene.

Driving through Lemington, she was relieved all was quiet. The last thing she needed was more trouble from the villagers.

She left the village with Lemington Hall's wood on her left and a stone wall on her right, beyond which were grass fields and in the nearest, a flock of sheep with young lambs. March was peak lambing season, so these little ones must have been born early and only recently released from their lambing barn.

The grass fields gave way to open areas of heath with gorse bushes and patches of rocky ground as she entered Eaton Common. It was more hamlet than village, with a few scattered houses and none of the usual community facilities.

She drove on and twenty minutes later arrived at Low Moor Barn, Jarrod Willcox's house. There were actually two traditional Cotswold barns, which she presumed had once belonged to the farm next door.

The larger, double-height barn had been converted into a house and the second, single-storey one was where she'd been told Jarrod now ran his business, after closing his Cirencester gallery.

It was one of Jarrod's business partners, Finn Andrews, who appeared from the smaller barn to greet her.

"Hi, it's good to see you again. How's Dotty?" Finn asked, a grin spreading across his boyish face. He was a young, aspiring artist of average height and build and slightly too long, brown hair.

Keya hesitated, unsure how to respond.

Finn's face fell. "She's in trouble, isn't she? Is that why you've come? And to ask about paintings? We heard she'd been arrested after one of Sir Reginald's paintings disappeared."

"You know about that?"

"Of course. There's not much in the art world that escapes Jarrod. But come in, he's expecting you."

Keya took a step forward and stopped. "Just a sec. Can you carry a painting I brought with me?" It was easier to ask young Finn rather than risk damaging it through her own clumsiness.

"Interesting," considered Finn as he picked up the portrait. "Mid to late nineteenth century, but you'll have to ask Jarrod for his opinion of the artist."

They entered the barn, which was bright inside from the high-level VELUX roof windows. Jarrod stood up behind his desk, which Keya suspected had come from his previous gallery and was out of place in the minimalistic modern surroundings.

Jarrod walked around the desk as he said, "Sergeant Varma, have you brought me a present?"

Keya handed him the painting and he took it back to his desk and examined it under a desk-top magnifying glass with its own ring of light.

"It's dark, partly from the colours used, but also because it's so dirty. If you'd like to leave it with me, I could clean it up for you and we could take a better look at it."

Keya smiled apologetically. "I'm afraid I can't. It's evidence in a current case."

"Really?" asked Jarrod, glancing up enquiringly. "Involving stolen paintings?"

"Not exactly." Keya paused, before revealing, "It's evidence in a murder case."

Finn gasped.

Jarrod remained calm as he asked, "And would I know the victim?"

Keya drew her lips together as Jarrod continued to stare at her in a composed but intense manner.

"I suppose you'll find out soon enough. Everyone will." Keya took a deep breath before revealing, "It's Tariq Kazem."

Finn gasped again behind Keya, but Jarrod considered the news as if he was tasting a new type of food and he wasn't sure if he liked the flavour.

Finally, he remarked, "That is interesting, but it does rather change things."

Keya frowned. "It does?"

Jarrod sat down and indicated for Keya to do the same on a modern orange velvet-covered chair.

"It looks like this could take some time," said Finn as he stepped forward. "Can I make you a drink, Sergeant? We have an espresso machine if you'd like a proper coffee."

"I'd love a cup of tea, if that's possible?" replied Keya.

"Of course. I'll leave you to Jarrod and I'll be back shortly."

As Finn left them, Jarrod asked, "What do you know about the Kazem family?"

"That they're from the Middle East, and they're wealthy. Wealthy enough to buy Lemington Hall and undertake extensive renovations, much to the annoyance of the local villagers who are constantly complaining about the newcomers." Keya took a breath and, returning to the point, added, "Tariq was the son, and he has a sister called Nadia, and the head of the family is Ahmad. I don't know if there's a Mrs Kazem. I've never seen her."

"Very good," acknowledged Jarrod, bringing the palms of his hands together in front of him as if he was praying.

His quiet, almost philosophical manner reminded Keya of her old history teacher.

"There is a Mrs Ahmad, and several younger sisters, but they've remained in Jordan. I've no idea where the family originated from, but they came to prominence during the rule of the Iraqi monarchy in the 1930s. Ahmad's father must have been astute as he moved the family to neighbouring Jordan in the early 1950s, retaining his wealth and surviving the coup that killed young King Faisal II in 1958."

Finn reappeared and handed Keya a chocolate brown mug with a gold rim and two colourful birds on it. He placed a similar, turquoise coloured one on Jarrod's desk.

"Ahmad continued to quietly build on his father's wealth. But Tariq was an interesting character. More of a playboy figure in his youth, chasing after beautiful women, you know the thing, but then he changed. He returned to university and completed an economics degree, followed by a job at a prestigious London accounting firm. I encountered him when he was in his mid-twenties, when he first entered the antiques world.

"At first, I thought he was just another collector, seeking to own beautiful things but astute enough to see them as investments. But he started visiting Baghdad and his tastes changed as he began searching for items with Iraqi heritage. He was particularly interested in those items looted during the 2003 Iraqi War. I suspect that's why he persuaded his father to buy a house in the UK, and another in the US."

That was news. Keya didn't know the Kazems also owned a property in America, but was it relevant to this case? And Baghdad? Dotty was often mentioning the city, so perhaps it was significant.

"Why did you say Tariq's death has changed things?"

Jarrod leaned back before answering, "Because I thought you'd come to talk about Sir Reginald's painting of the Betrayal of Jesus, which went missing earlier this week."

She'd forgotten that was the initial reason for her visit. "Do you know where it is?"

"Not at this precise moment. But I do know someone offered it to a … how can I put this? … less than reputable buyer I sometimes deal with in Holland."

"When?" asked Keya, regaining some enthusiasm.

"Last week," replied Jarrod.

Keya's brow furrowed. "So before it disappeared from Sir Reginald's house."

"Yes, it was stolen to order, and I don't think Dotty has those kinds of contacts."

Keya's shoulders slumped. "That's not how my colleagues see it. Sergeant Unwin's convinced she's mixed up in a web of shady dealings, and it wouldn't surprise me if he suspects she's part of a larger gang of art thieves and scammers. And my boss, Chief Inspector Ringrose, is going along with it."

"You work for the chief inspector?"

"I do, although at the moment I see very little of him, or my desk, as he's always sending me out and about into the community."

"And what's your opinion of him?"

"Fair, open-minded, forthright, and intelligent. He and Aunt Beanie were excited about returning to cold cases that were shelved when his previous unit was closed down." Keya paused, thinking that her boss's interest in old cases had waned. "But I think he's bored with them, as Aunt Beanie generally works alone now."

"And his financial status?" probed Jarrod.

What an odd question. "He's always seemed well off. He drives a smart Land Rover, and his ties all represent sports and old-boy clubs. That hasn't changed."

"Very well, back to Sir Reginald's painting," directed Jarrod. "The other sergeant is right about one thing. There is a web of shady dealings, but I'm not sure about a gang."

An image of Tariq popped into Keya's head. "A big boss?"

"I don't want to say any more at the moment," conceded Jarrod, "But don't worry, I think we are on the same path, and searching for the same people. I will let you know if and when I find anything significant."

Keya sipped her tea. In a previous case Jarrod had provided crucial information, but only when he was sure he had the whole picture. "Don't put yourself in danger, Jarrod."

He smiled warmly at her. "Thank you for your concern, and your warning. But I'm used to it. I don't always work on the right side of the law, for my own reasons. And please, don't start looking into me. You won't find anything but a slightly crazy old man."

Jarrod had a twinkle in his eye as Keya stared at him, her mind taking in what he was saying, and wondering if appearances could be that deceiving.

Jarrod's tone became serious as he looked at the portrait on his desk and asked, "What else can you tell me about this painting?"

"Marion told me Tariq showed it to her and David at supper last night at Lemington Hall. He'd found it in a cupboard and presumed it was of an ancestor of the family who used to live there. As Tariq didn't want it, David suggested he enter it in Akemans' auction. So David told Marion to ask Dotty to collect it this afternoon. Dotty was worried about going on her own, after what happened at Sir Reginald's, so she called me to go with her, but I was late."

Keya sighed. If only the presentation hadn't overrun.

"When I arrived," she continued, "Dotty told me Tariq was dead. She said she hadn't seen the painting but when her car was searched by Inspector Evans, it was found in the back of it." Keya looked up at Jarrod's intense gaze. "Dotty said she didn't put it there and I believe her. So how did it end up in her car, especially when there were so many people about?"

"Which people?" asked Jarrod in a serious tone.

"Sergeant Unwin and Inspector Evans. The ambulance crew while they collected Tariq's body. Me, Dotty, Marion, and David."

Jarrod drummed his fingers on the top of his desk.

"Do you know what happened?" asked Keya.

"Perhaps, but it's not for sharing."

"But what about Dotty? She's been arrested again. What if she's sent to prison?"

Jarrod's look was grave as he said, "Perhaps that's the safest place for her."

CHAPTER FIFTEEN

Dotty slumped in the back of Sergeant Unwin's Mercedes. It wasn't that long ago he'd trusted her enough to drive it. But look at her now, a criminal being transported to Cirencester police station.

She caught Inspector Evans' occasional glance in the rear-view mirror and was surprised by his sad smile and sympathetic look. Neither he nor Sergeant Unwin spoke until they arrived at the police station.

"Drop me here, Sergeant," directed the inspector. "I'll leave you to process Mrs Sayers."

Inspector Evans gave her a simple nod before he turned, and Sergeant Unwin drove around the back of the station.

She felt strangely reassured by the inspector's simple action.

"Please get out of the car," Sergeant Unwin instructed in an unemotional voice as he opened the car door for her.

She stepped out into a concrete yard where several police vans and squad cars were parked.

"Follow me." Sergeant Unwin unlocked a metal security door with a plastic card and once inside, he gestured for Dotty to sit on a hard plastic bench attached to the wall at the back of a tiny room.

"This is a holding cell. Wait here while I find the duty sergeant."

Sergeant Unwin closed the holding cell door and Dotty was relieved she wasn't claustrophobic as the door brushed against her knees. There was a small observation panel near the top of the door, which let in some light. For the police to look in, rather than for her to look out.

She drew her legs up to her chest and hugged them.

How could she be so stupid? If only she'd waited for Keya, but would that have made a difference? She would still have been found on her own at the crime scene.

Would anyone have believed her if she'd told them she'd stayed in her car, as she'd done at Sir Reginald's, and had no idea Tariq was dead? She was sure Sergeant Unwin wouldn't, and he was the one calling the shots at the moment.

The door opened and Sergeant Unwin stood before her. "Come with me."

He used the plastic card to open two more metal security doors as he led her along a corridor and around a corner to an open area with several doors leading off it and a counter with a Perspex screen on top.

An older police officer, with a weary, I've-seen-it-all-before face and grey hair, regarded her from behind the screen through his black-rimmed glasses. He said, "I just need a few details from the arresting officer before we start the check-in process."

He stood in a small office space beside a computer monitor and keyboard. Two more police officers sat behind him, one with his back to them.

The older officer looked across at Sergeant Unwin and asked, "Arrest time?"

"16.25," replied Sergeant Unwin.

"Arrival time?"

"17.10."

"Location of arrest?"

"The old stable yard, Lemington Hall, Lemington."

The older sergeant tapped Sergeant Unwin's responses on the keyboard. When he finished, he looked up and said, "Thank you, Sergeant. We'll process the suspect. Do you wish to detain her overnight?"

Sergeant Unwin's eyes were cold and his face expressionless as he replied, "Of course. She's been arrested for murder."

The old sergeant's brow wrinkled but, wordlessly, he held Sergeant Unwin's stare.

"I'll let you get on with your work," conceded Sergeant Unwin. "I believe the suspect already has a solicitor, from when she was in for questioning this morning." These were Sergeant Unwin's final cutting remarks before he turned and left the custody area.

The old sergeant watched him leave and said, "One minute, Mrs Sayers."

He tapped his keyboard and stared at his monitor while Dotty waited silently. There was an uneasy tension in the air.

Finally, the old Sergeant rocked back and sighed. "It's all right, Ryan. Sergeant Onion has gone upstairs to see the chief inspector."

That was interesting, thought Dotty. She would have expected Sergeant Unwin - did all the officers in the station call him Sergeant Onion? - to discuss the case with Inspector Evans first, as he was at the crime scene and his unit dealt with serious crimes.

Just a minute. Had she heard the old sergeant correctly? Did he say Ryan?

She stared through the Perspex screen as the officer who'd had his back to her stood up and turned around. His eyes met hers and as he walked towards the screen, he asked, "Are you OK?"

"I think so. But I'm not sure reality has caught up with me yet. And what are you doing here?"

"Keya called and gave me the heads up, so I persuaded Sergeant Rowbottom to let me process you."

"Lad, it's no skin off my back if you want to work unpaid overtime, and I'm always short-staffed down here."

"I can't believe what's happened," admitted Ryan. "Well, actually, I can. Especially as I think Tariq stole Sir Reginald's painting."

"You do? Everyone else is convinced I made the whole thing up."

"I returned to Barnton with Ozzie Winters and …"

"The reporter?" interjected Dotty. "Why is she involved?"

Ryan looked put out, but in the pause Sergeant Rowbottom suggested, "You better start processing Mrs Sayers. If Sergeant Onion returns and …"

"Yes, of course." Ryan returned to the desk he'd been sitting at and pocketed his phone and other items before leaving the office by a side door. As he crossed to a room on the opposite side of the corridor, he said, "Come with me. We'll talk while I work."

"And I've phoned the duty nurse. She'll be here in twenty minutes," called Sergeant Rowbottom as they entered a room which resembled an office with large pieces of electronic equipment.

With an apologetic smile, Ryan asked, "Can you sit on the stool so I can take your photograph?"

A lone plastic-topped stool was positioned against a blank wall.

When she'd sat down and was facing Ryan, he indicated to a black ball on the side of a grey metal box which was attached to the wall. "Look at the camera."

"That's done," Ryan confirmed.

"So why did you invite Ozzie Winter back to Sir Reginald's and how did you persuade him to let her in his house?"

"We didn't go to Sir Reginald's. When I was searching for Tariq and the painting, I noticed a door at the end of a corridor next to the library, which opened onto a flagstone path at the back of the house.

"I didn't have time to search it as Sergeant Unwin called me back, so I asked Ozzie to help me look round. She went in daylight, while I was still at the station, and found a wood behind Sir Reginald's house and a fence between it and his garden. And she said it looked as if someone had dragged a large item under the fence. She even found scraps of brown wrapping paper snagged on it."

Dotty sat up. "So you think Tariq was there? And that he stole the painting while I was sitting in my car at the front of the house, and he escaped through the garden?"

"Yes, and there's a footpath from the woods across the village playing fields to a road."

"Did anyone see Tariq? I mean, a man carrying a large parcel across a field would look suspicious."

Ryan bowed his head. "I haven't had a chance to find out, and now Tariq is dead ..."

"You're not sure you'll have the opportunity," finished Dotty. "But what about Ozzie? And why have you involved her? Can she be trusted?"

Ryan looked up, nodding his head fervently. "She can, I'm sure. And she's just as keen as we are to get to the real truth, not the version others want us to believe."

"That's certainly a good start."

CHAPTER SIXTEEN

Dotty sat down beside a machine which looked like an office photocopier with a computer monitor on top, in a room at the back of Cirencester police station.

"This is our new, state-of-the-art fingerprint machine," explained Ryan. "Please place the fingers of your left hand on the pad in front of you."

As Dotty did so, she asked, "But now Tariq's dead, how can we prove he stole Sir Reginald Spencer's painting?"

"I'm not sure," Ryan conceded. "But Keya was arriving at Jarrod Willcox's place when she called. He might have heard about the painting and know where it is. Now your left thumb."

"Let's hope so." Dotty placed her thumb on the pad.

"Please repeat with your right hand." Dotty placed the fingers of her right hand on the pad as Ryan watched and announced, "But the more pressing matter is your detention. You heard Sergeant Unwin say you'll be kept here tonight. He may interview you later or wait until the morning. I'll call Gerald and explain what's happened while you're with the nurse."

"Nurse?" asked Dotty in surprise.

"Yes, it's part of the procedure. You have to be passed medically fit before you can be locked up in a cell."

"Charming," muttered Dotty under her breath.

Ryan didn't appear to notice as he continued, "As you've been arrested for a serious crime, you can be held for up to ninety-six hours before you're either formally charged or allowed to go home. And even if you do go home, it might be on bail and on condition that you return for further questioning."

Dotty removed her right thumb from the fingerprint pad and looked up at Ryan who was bent over the machine. "This isn't going away anytime soon, is it? At worst, I'll be charged with murder and imprisoned, and, at best, I could be under suspicion for months."

"Not if we work out who killed Tariq."

"We?" implored Dotty. "How can I when I'm stuck in here?"

"You're allowed to request a pen and paper, so why not make notes? Do you think Tariq's death is an isolated incident or is it linked to the other cases Sergeant Unwin and the chief inspector have been interviewing you about? Why not use your time to go back and work through each case?"

As Ryan removed a packet from a cupboard, Dotty thought he was right. There was no point feeling sorry for herself. It wouldn't get her out of jail, but trying to work out what was happening in the antiques world, with stolen and counterfeit items, and the rising body count, might. Or at least set her, Ryan, and Keya on the path to discovering who did kill Tariq.

Her shoulders slumped. She thought that only another suspect with a motive and opportunity to kill Tariq would satisfy Sergeant Unwin. And finding one would be almost impossible from a locked cell.

"Finally," said Ryan, holding out a long cotton wool bud, "a DNA swab. Open wide."

Ryan bent down and rubbed the swab around the inside of her cheeks before placing it in a plastic tube and screwing on the top.

"Am I allowed a phone call or is that just in the movies?" asked Dotty.

"As well as contacting your solicitor, you are allowed one other phone call. Do you mind me asking who you'd like to speak to?"

"Aunt Beanie. If Keya hasn't called her, she'll be wondering where I am."

"Let's check if the duty nurse has arrived and then I'll sort out the calls to her and Gerald." Ryan led Dotty to another room and knocked on the door.

"Come in," answered a pleasant female voice.

Dotty entered a room which was like any found in a doctor's surgery.

"I'll make those calls," said Ryan from the corridor before the nurse closed the door behind Dotty.

As well as examining Dotty, the nurse asked her to remove her scarf and belt and empty her pockets.

She gathered everything together, including Dotty's phone, and explained, "I'll hand these over to the duty sergeant, and you can collect them on your release. You're in excellent physical shape. While you're with us, you'll have access to a room with fresh air pumped into it so you can stretch your legs and perform any exercises you might like.

"You're also entitled to three meals a day and water, juice, or hot drinks between meals. There is a dedicated female toilet, shower, and sink. The rest of the time, apart from when you're being interviewed, you'll spend in a cell which you'll have to yourself. Do you understand?" the nurse asked sympathetically, but in a tone she might use to talk to a child.

Dotty nodded.

"Excellent. I'll call the constable back and he can show you to your cell." The nurse made it sound as if she was staying in a room in a five-star hotel.

As Ryan walked Dotty down another corridor, he said, "I called both Gerald and Aunt Beanie. Gerald said he'll try to find out if the police have any evidence on you, apart from the painting and finding you at the scene. And Aunt Beanie thanked me for the call but said Keya had already dropped round with some books from Jarrod Willcox and explained the situation. She's coming straight over."

Ryan stopped outside another metal door, which had a small observation panel at eye height. His face softened as he said, "I'm so sorry about all this, and I feel helpless because there's nothing I can do."

Dotty placed a hand on his arm. "You've been a great help. Imagine what it would have been like if Sergeant Unwin had processed me? As you said, I've got the pen and paper you've found for me, so instead of moping about in my cell I need to get to work."

Ryan opened the door and stepped inside.

Dotty followed him.

The cell was covered in off-white tiles and at the far end, a moulded-plastic bed, which resembled a large shelf, was attached to the wall. On top of it was a thin blue mattress and a smaller thin rectangular blue shape, which she presumed was a pillow. There was a pile of blue fabric.

"I asked Sergeant Rowbottom to give you an extra blanket. No sheets, duvets or down-filled pillows, I'm afraid. But Aunt Beanie is bringing you a change of clothes and some toiletries." Ryan turned to two blue coloured tiles near the door and explained, "Press the one on the right if you need the toilet, and the one on the left if you want to see someone from the custody desk."

Ryan stepped forward and gave Dotty the sheets of paper and pen he'd been carrying. "I hope you'll be OK, and that this is only temporary. I could stay ..."

"No, it's better for you to find out what's going on and help secure my release," insisted Dotty.

Ryan nodded and left the cell, closing the door behind him with a loud clang.

Dotty was all alone.

She sat down on the thin mattress and touched its cover. Foam covered with polyester, she thought. And the sheets were also polyester but quilted. She wrapped one around her and felt comforted.

She'd been sitting in her cell for some time - she had no idea exactly how long - when she was aware of raised voices in the corridor. The cell door opened as Sergeant Rowbottom said, "I don't have to allow you down here, Bernadette. And it's not my fault Mrs Sayers has been arrested." The old Sergeant entered the room but as he started to say, "You have ..."

Aunt Beanie pushed past him and exclaimed, "My poor girl! How are you?"

Dotty had stood up when the cell door opened and now found herself being tightly squeezed by Aunt Beanie's embrace.

"I'm fine, thank you," she gasped.

Aunt Beanie let go and apologised, "Sorry, I didn't mean to hurt you." She turned to Sergeant Rowbottom and demanded, "Can we have some privacy?"

"Not in here," he countered. "But the consulting room at the end of the corridor is free."

"Thank you," replied Aunt Beanie, calming down. "And any chance of a cup of tea?" She wore what she probably thought was an innocent expression.

"I guess so." The old sergeant shrugged his shoulders. "After all, it's a quiet evening and I have an extra pair of hands as young Ryan is still hanging around."

He led them to a room smaller in size than the interview rooms upstairs and painted cream rather than grey. There was no recording equipment on the grey topped Formica table, on which Aunt Beanie dumped her heavy bag and said, "Thank you, Sergeant Rowbottom."

When they were alone and sitting opposite each other, Aunt Beanie reached across the table and gripped Dotty's hand. "I'm so sorry it has come to this. Are you really OK?"

Dotty nodded. "I'm fine, or at least I am at the moment. But I've been thinking, we need to find the real culprit if we're to persuade Sergeant Unwin I'm innocent."

Aunt Beanie sighed. "You're probably right. But I'm not sure it's that simple. Not with you locked up in here, and no witnesses to the crime. And the painting that was found in your car. How did it get there? Are you sure you didn't see anyone in the old stable yard?"

"I'm certain, but there would be plenty of places to hide and I doubt I would have noticed while I was sitting in my car as my mind was wandering. And once I entered Tariq's office, my car was out of sight. Someone could have hidden the painting and then disappeared on foot. My car was the only one in the stable yard."

"But someone could have parked near the house. I'll see if Keya or Ryan can ask if anyone at the hall saw another vehicle," suggested Aunt Beanie.

"And now you've plenty of time on your hands ..." Aunt Beanie reached into her bag and removed a book. "Jarrod gave Keya some 'light' reading for you. This one is about the history of Iraq, ancient and modern." She removed a second book. "And this is entitled *The Art of the Con: The most Notorious Fakes, Frauds and Forgeries in the Art World.*"

Dotty picked the second book up and turned it over. "Interesting that Jarrod chose these particular books, but this one does look interesting." She returned it to the table and picked up the book on Iraqi history. "Baghdad. Why do so many paths lead to that city?"

"Do they?" asked Aunt Beanie as she removed an Ordnance Survey map of the Cotswolds from her bag and several guidebooks. "I thought these might help if you want to look at different locations, or just want to find out more about the area. And finally."

She removed a pack of plastic mechanical pencils and a brand new pad of lined paper.

"I wasn't sure what you were allowed, but Sergeant Rowbottom agreed you could have those pencils because they don't need sharpening. But please don't try to stab yourself, or anyone else, with them," Aunt Beanie added in a practical tone. "I wasn't sure about food, so

I put some sandwiches and snacks in another bag with some fresh clothes and toiletries, which I had to hand over to Sergeant Rowbottom."

The door opened and Ryan appeared, balancing two cups of tea on a tray with a plate of biscuits. "Here you are. I borrowed some tea bags from upstairs as the ones down here are pretty awful."

"You can't borrow tea bags, Ryan." Aunt Beanie chided before sipping her tea. "But I appreciate the gesture."

"I also bumped into Keya. She's handed the painting in as evidence and was on her way to see Chief Inspector Ringrose." Ryan looked from Aunt Beanie to Dotty and back again. "And she suggested we hold a council of war, at your farmhouse."

"A council of war?" repeated Aunt Beanie.

Ryan smiled apologetically at Dotty. "Yes, to discuss Dotty's … predicament."

CHAPTER SEVENTEEN

Ryan checked on Dotty before he left the police station. "I can smell chicken tikka masala, so I presume you've been fed?"

"Yes, I have, thank you." Dotty pushed at a nearly full plastic container, containing a bright orange sauce, on a plastic tray.

Ryan tilted his head to one side as he cautioned, "You need to eat to maintain your physical and mental energy."

Dotty sounded lacklustre as she replied, "I know but ..."

Ryan shook his head. "I'm afraid I can't offer you anything else. Believe it or not, that is the most popular meal amongst detainees."

Dotty closed her eyes before asking, "Is there any chance you could find the sandwiches Aunt Beanie put in the bag with my spare clothes?"

Ryan was grateful for an opportunity to help Dotty, but while smuggling food into cells wasn't exactly against the rules, it was frowned upon as it was felt all detainees should be treated equally. It also prevented drugs, weapons, and anything else being brought in.

He returned to the custody room, which was empty. An angry but slurred voice shouted, "Get off me," from the room with the fingerprint machine. Sergeant Rowbottom was probably helping another officer obtain a saliva sample.

Ryan took the opportunity to find Dotty's bag, which was clearly labelled and placed in the corner for detainees' possessions. He was squatting down beside the open green canvas bag with his hands inside it when Sergeant Rowbottom asked, "What are you doing, lad, searching through a lady's bag?"

Ryan touched a fleece and pulled out a navy-blue sleeve. "Mrs Sayers asked for another jumper." As he removed the other sleeve, he spotted a packet of sandwiches and an apple. He wrapped the jumper around them and pulled the entire bundle free of the bag.

"Take that to Mrs Sayers and then it's time you went home. My shift ends soon, thank goodness, as the drunks are already being brought in, but I doubt the night shift will appreciate your help."

Ryan returned to Dotty's cell.

"Thank you," she said in a relieved tone when Ryan handed her the sandwiches, apple, and her fleece. She wrapped the fleece around her shoulders and tore open the packet of sandwiches.

"I'm leaving now. Will you be OK?" Ryan asked.

"Yes," nodded Dotty. "Although if all the inmates tonight arrive as noisily as the last one, I won't get much sleep." She smiled weakly as Ryan closed the cell door behind him.

Upstairs, Ryan found Keya loitering outside his team's office. "Where have you been?" she hissed.

"Smuggling Dotty some sandwiches Aunt Beanie brought. She wasn't enamoured by our Indian ready meal supper."

"Tell her to ask for the vegetarian option next time. They're much better, although I hope there won't be too many next times. I'm heading to Meadowbank Farm now. Are you coming?"

"Yes," Ryan replied. "As soon as I've changed out of my uniform."

Half an hour later, Ryan walked into the warm, inviting kitchen at Meadowbank Farm. He was met by a rich aroma of meat and spices.

He heard Norman hail, "Excellent, you're here, Ryan. We can serve my chilli con carne." Norman was standing beside the Aga stirring the contents of a large, tall, aluminium pan.

"I've nearly finished slicing the crusty bread I bought on the way back from the station," called Aunt Beanie.

Keya squatted by the Aga and opened the bottom door of the oven. "I'll grab my veggie pasta."

"Is this enough chopped tomatoes?" asked Gerald, who was standing by the worktop with a sharp knife in his hand.

Beside him, spiky-haired Ozzie Winters replied, "Yes. I'll find a bowl for them and the cheese I've grated."

Norman yelled above the hubbub, "Ryan, can you grab the knives and forks next to Gerald and lay the table?"

Ryan felt disorientated by the frenetic activity, but he set the table as Norman requested.

"Here, take these," Ozzie instructed as she handed him two bowls. One was filled with finely diced tomato and the other with thin slivers of cheddar cheese.

The bustling activity continued until everyone had a bowlful of chilli, apart from Keya, who sprinkled cheese over her pasta.

Aunt Beanie rapped the end of her knife against the table and, when everyone stopped talking, announced, "Before we start, I'll say a short prayer."

Ryan bowed his head.

"Dear Lord, bless the food on our plates. Watch over Cliff and Dotty and keep them safe ..."

"Meow," interrupted Earl Grey.

"Amen," finished Aunt Beanie before looking down at Dotty's large, grey cat. "I think this is too spicy for you."

"Meow."

"Oh, all right. I know you're missing your mistress."

Aunt Beanie pushed back her chair, stood up and walked across to the fridge. Searching inside, she found a bowl of something which she placed on the terracotta-tiled floor. Earl Grey strode majestically across to it before sticking his nose into the bowl.

Aunt Beanie sat down again at the head of the table and considered everyone as they ate their supper with only minimal chatter.

"Excellent. Everyone is here. Although my niece Gilly and her husband, Dr Peter, have also offered their assistance should we need it."

Keya placed her fork on her plate and proclaimed, "As have Finn Andrews, the young artist Dotty helped, and his business partner, Jarrod Willcox. They're already searching for Sir Reginald's missing painting."

At the far end of the table, Norman finished his mouthful. "I took a call from Jay Newton this afternoon. He offered his and Tracy's help and asked if there was anything we need. He's already transferred £10,000 to Beanie for what he termed 'Dotty's war chest'."

"Wow, that was generous of him," enthused Keya. "And Kuki said if Dotty, or those helping her, need any food, we're just to ask and she'll bring it round. And," she paused dramatically, "Inspector Evans said to count him in."

Keya looked around the table at the open mouths and astonished expressions. She was delighted so many of Dotty's friends had offered their support.

Ryan was less surprised after the remarks the inspector had made to him beside the office printer.

Keya continued, "But he has to be careful and not be seen to be interfering with the case."

Norman broke the silence that followed Keya's remarks as he asked, "But surely, Keya, you and Ryan will be involved with the case?"

"I certainly won't be," interjected Aunt Beanie. "It's strictly cold cases for me at the moment."

Keya shook her head. "I barely have time to sit down at my desk and write a report before Chief Inspector Ringrose is sending me back to attend to some rural misdemeanour or community commitment."

Ryan smiled as he said, "And Sergeant Unwin is giving me a wide berth."

Fair-haired Gerald had remained silent, following the conversation with an interested expression, but he now added his thoughts. "At least I'll have access to most of the police's notes and evidence. Dotty hasn't been interviewed yet, but I'll be with her tomorrow when she is."

"Good," nodded Aunt Beanie.

"At least I have my contacts," Ozzie smiled sweetly. "What exactly do you need?"

Aunt Beanie answered, "Dotty thinks she'll only be released when the real killer is found."

"And how does she suggest we go about finding them?" asked Ozzie.

"We start with the painting," asserted Keya, from the opposite side of the table.

"Exactly," agreed Aunt Beanie, "and work out how it ended up in the back of Dotty's car."

"And you're certain Dotty didn't put it there herself?" pressed Ozzie.

"Certain," echoed Keya.

Aunt Beanie sat back as she considered, "Dotty told me there were no cars in the stable yard when she arrived, so whoever planted the painting left by foot. But they wouldn't get far walking, so they must have parked a vehicle close by. We need to find it. The Lemington Hall estate would be the best place to start."

"I need to speak to the groundsman," Keya volunteered. "He's been complaining about motorbikes in the woods again. So I'll ask him if he saw anything or anyone unusual."

"What about other members of staff at the hall?" asked Aunt Beanie, turning to Ryan. "Will you be asked to question them?"

"Probably, if the officer in charge is being thorough. But in this case, as Sergeant Unwin is convinced Dotty is guilty, they may be overlooked," Ryan replied.

Ozzie wiped her plate clean with a chunk of crusty bread as she asked, "What's so special about the painting? Is it hugely valuable?"

Keya replied, "I showed it to Jarrod, and he estimated it to be worth between £15,000 and £20,000, so nothing to be sniffed at, but why kill Tariq over it? He's bought and hung paintings worth millions in the hall, apparently. Jarrod didn't think there was anything special about this particular painting."

From the far end of the table, Norman asked, "But what about Sir Reginald's stolen one?"

Ryan cleared his throat. "Ozzie and I think it was removed from his house via the back garden, dragged under a fence and carried through a wood and across the village playing fields."

Ozzie added, "But I've asked around and haven't found any witnesses in Barnton yet."

"So do you believe Dotty?" pressed Norman. "Did she see Tariq playing dead?"

"I don't see why not," confirmed Ryan. "It makes sense since she also saw the wrapped painting and both it and Tariq disappeared."

Norman continued, "So if Tariq stole the painting, and we find it, will that help Dotty?"

"Yes and no," replied Keya. "Finding it won't necessarily help Dotty's defence for killing Tariq, but it might reveal what else is going on, and the links we suspect there are to other cases."

Ozzie, who had finished her supper, looked around the group and said, "I've been researching that painting and it has a chequered past. Its subject is Judas Iscariot betraying Jesus for thirty pieces of silver. And Tariq isn't the only person linked with it who's ended up dead.

"In the 1870s a man died mysteriously and the painting disappeared. When it resurfaced, just before the First World War, the wife of a wealthy landowner committed suicide. The story is she was betrayed to her jealous husband by her lover's brother."

"That would make an interesting article," suggested Aunt Beanie.

Ozzie glanced at Ryan and replied, "But I promised not to publish anything without Ryan's permission. That was his condition for my involvement here."

Aunt Beanie regarded Ryan and asked, "Don't you think a piece about the painting of Jesus, accompanied by a large image of it, might help flush it out? It's amazing what people suddenly see when something is mentioned to them …"

"Or the current owner might panic and try to get rid of it," interjected Keya.

Ozzie frowned. "But what if Tariq kept it for himself? You said he has an expensive collection of paintings at the hall, so where's the best place to hide something?"

Gerald nodded his head and replied, "In plain sight."

Aunt Beanie pushed her plate away from her and asked, "Ozzie, do you write articles about influential people and places in the Cotswolds?"

"I'm sure I could persuade my editor it would be a good idea to start," grinned the young reporter.

Norman called down the table. "What are you two getting at?"

Ozzie looked back at him and replied, "I think Aunt Beanie," she turned to the older woman sitting at the head of the table, "If I can call you that?"

"Please do, everyone else does," agreed Aunt Beanie.

"… is suggesting I visit Lemington Hall with a view to writing an article about it."

"And you'll need a photographer," declared Aunt Beanie, her eyes searching the table.

Ryan said, "Someone might recognise me."

"And me," echoed Keya.

"I don't think it's strictly ethical," added Gerald.

All eyes turned to Norman at the end of the table. "Me?" he cried.

CHAPTER EIGHTEEN

After a soggy 'All-Day-Breakfast' and a cup of what Keya would describe as builder's tea - strong and over-stewed - Dotty was led by a custody sergeant she didn't know to the same small consultation room she'd met Aunt Beanie in the previous evening.

Gerald was already sitting behind the table, facing the door, lining up three pencils next to his yellow legal pad. "Thank you. And can we have a cup of coffee, white no sugar, and a cup of tea, not too strong?"

The sergeant grunted his response as he left the room.

When the door closed, Gerald reached across to the spare chair beside him and removed from his bag a banana, a pot of vanilla yogurt, a packet of ready-cut fruit, and a pack of mixed sandwiches. He added a small wooden spoon and a bar of chocolate to the mix.

When he finished, he looked up and explained, "Aunt Beanie's suggestion, and Keya recommends you order the vegetarian options in future as at least they're edible."

"Thank you," replied Dotty as she peeled the thin plastic cover off the packet of mixed chopped fruit. "I better eat what I can in case they stop me taking it back to my cell." She peeled off the foil lid of the yoghurt and poured it over the fruit.

"How did you sleep last night?" asked Gerald.

Dotty swallowed her mouthful of melon and yogurt before replying, "Badly. It was so noisy. But at least I was allowed a hot shower this morning, so I feel OK."

Gerald leaned forward and lowered his voice. "Everyone asked me to pass on their support."

"Everyone?" questioned Dotty.

"Aunt Beanie, Norman, Ryan, Keya, and Ozzie."

"Ozzie, as in Ozzie Winters, the reporter?"

"Yes, Ryan told you to trust her, and I agree. She's hoping, with Norman posing as a photographer, to persuade the staff of Lemington Hall to let her inside on the pretext of writing a piece about the family and the restoration work they've done. But they'll concentrate on the paintings and try to find Sir Reginald's missing one."

"I'm not sure they'll be allowed in. Not after what happened yesterday," replied Dotty sceptically. "But I'm grateful for their help, and I think the idea is an excellent one. I presumed Tariq would sell the painting, but what if he didn't and it is hanging up at the hall?"

"Exactly. It's worth a try. And Ozzie and Keya want to question the hall staff to find out if they saw another vehicle there yesterday, or anyone acting strangely. We're trying to discover how the assailant who placed the painting in your car just disappeared."

"I've been wondering that too," confided Dotty, "so I'd be very interested to know what they find out."

Gerald sat up.

"And you don't need to worry about my fees for the moment. Jay Newton is covering them."

"Really?"

"Yes, he's transferred money to Aunt Beanie for what he describes as your 'war chest'. I told you, a lot of people support you. They believe in you and your innocence."

Gerald touched the row of identical pencils before looking up and revealing, "I haven't received any reports or information from the police, so either they're playing their cards close to their chest, or they're struggling for evidence. I asked about your interview and they told me it would be between half nine and ten this morning."

Gerald consulted his watch. "It's quarter to nine now, so let's begin with your account of yesterday's events. Did Tariq arrange the meeting directly with you?"

Dotty shook her head. "I never spoke to Tariq. Marion Rook told me yesterday morning, when we were at Akemans preparing for this month's auction, that David had arranged for me to collect the painting in the afternoon."

"Was the arrangement for a specific time, or afternoon in general?" asked Gerald.

"Marion was very specific. Half past three, as Tariq had a meeting before that."

"But you didn't see anyone else when you arrived?"

"No. And I didn't pass a car when I drove up the drive or see any other vehicles or people, until Keya arrived."

Gerald returned to examining his pencils. "Which is unfortunate, as there is no one to back up your story." He seemed to be thinking and then asked, "Do you often collect paintings from private houses?"

"Oh yes," confirmed Dotty. "And art galleries. Furniture is usually delivered via van or truck, but we sometimes collect smaller items, if they are valuable or delicate, but they are also delivered. It depends."

"So the requests to collect this painting, and Sir Reginald's, are part of your work at Akemans."

"That's right," agreed Dotty.

Gerald paused and made a note on his yellow legal pad with the first pencil.

He looked up and asked, "Who else knew you were collecting the painting?"

"Marion and David. And I called Keya and asked her to meet me at Lemington Hall. I've no idea who else knew."

Gerald leaned back. "How well did you know Tariq Kazem?"

"I was introduced to him by David Rook at an Antique Fair in January, and I met him again with Keya when I drove her to a meeting in Lemington. The meeting turned hostile. Tariq's father had generously provided food for the event, but the villagers started throwing it at Tariq. Tariq and I had to make our escape from the village hall until Ryan and Chief Inspector Ringrose arrived to break up the fight."

Dotty smiled. "Despite the hostile welcome, Tariq remained calm and upbeat."

Her smile evaporated as she recalled, "And, of course, there was the incident at Cotswold Airport when I was arrested for smuggling the chapan robe. Tariq was the one who met David and I, and he was escorting us when the police dramatically made their presence known."

There was a knock on the door.

"Ah, our tea and coffee. Come in," called Gerald.

A smiling Ryan entered. "Morning Dotty. I hope our hospitality wasn't too bad."

His cheerfulness was infectious, and she smiled back. "You need to be a little more discerning with your clientele."

"You should be here on a Friday or Saturday night," retorted Ryan.

Dotty winced. "I hope not."

"Do you have news for us, Ryan?" asked Gerald.

"I do. Sergeant Unwin asked me to escort you both to the interview room."

All jollity evaporated, and Dotty felt a knot in her stomach. It was time to face the music. What happened in the next hour or so would affect the rest of her life. She took a deep breath before standing up and saying, "Lead the way, Ryan."

Dotty was less confident by the time she entered the small interview room, which was already occupied by Sergeant Unwin and Chief Inspector Ringrose. Gerald followed her in, and they stood side by side facing the seated policemen.

The chief inspector indicated for them to sit as he stood and approached Ryan, who was hovering in the doorway. "Thank you, Constable. Now I've a job for you. Can you return to the victim's office and undertake a more thorough search? We have the murder weapon." The chief inspector lowered his voice, but Dotty still heard him say, "but we don't know if our suspect brought it with her or found it in the office."

Clearing his throat, the chief inspector continued, "And while you're there, see if there is anything else you consider relevant to the case." He handed Ryan a key.

Ryan gave Dotty a final encouraging smile before closing the door.

Sitting down, Chief Inspector Ringrose asked, "How did you know the victim, Tariq Kazem?"

Dotty gave a similar answer to the one she'd given Gerald, and she also explained why she went to meet Tariq and confirmed she'd been the only one there.

"So this earlier meeting was fictitious," stated the chief inspector.

"Not necessarily. It could have been online," countered Gerald. "I believe the victim had many international contacts."

"Hmm," muttered the chief inspector, looking down at his notes.

First point to Gerald, thought Dotty.

Chief Inspector Ringrose slowly raised his head and, looking directly at Dotty, asked, "What was special about this painting?"

"I don't know. I didn't see it," replied Dotty.

"So you say," muttered Sergeant Unwin.

"I didn't!" insisted Dotty, her voice rising in pitch and volume.

"Then how did it end up in the back of your car?" retorted the sergeant.

"I don't know." Dotty's tone was defensive.

Chief Inspector Ringrose leaned back. "You've already told us you were the only person in the old stable yard and, while you deny taking the painting, it does link you to Tariq's death."

Gerald reasoned, "But does it? We know my client was sent to collect the painting, so whether it was in her car or in the office makes little difference, and she doesn't deny entering Mr Kazem's office. She might have thought the office was empty, seen the picture and picked it up. Then returned to wait for Mr Kazem or to leave him a message that in his absence, she'd collected the picture."

"That sounds plausible," conceded the chief inspector. "Is it what happened, Mrs Sayers?"

"No," replied Dotty truthfully.

Gerald nodded at her sympathetically. He'd given her a way out, but she wasn't going to lie. She knew that if she did, she'd have to continue to lie and, most likely, she'd tie herself up in knots.

"I didn't see the painting or touch it. Why not check to see if it has my fingerprints on it?"

"You could have used gloves," quipped Sergeant Unwin.

Dotty gave him a pained expression before continuing, "And I only entered the office once, when I found Tariq lying on the floor."

"Did you bring the murder weapon with you?" Sergeant Unwin shot back.

She knew from the chief inspector's comments to Ryan that this was a point the police were trying to clear up.

"No. I didn't kill Tariq, so how could I?"

"But you know what it is?"

"A dagger, or that's what I glimpsed before I rushed out of the office."

Sergeant Unwin reached down to the floor and picked up a large plastic bag, which Dotty presumed contained the murder weapon. She stared at it in fascination.

The dagger had a slight curve, and its blade was dark, iron if it was as old as she thought it was or, if it was more modern, steel. The hilt could be gold inlaid with precious stones.

"Wow, it's beautiful. Is the hilt gold or copper? It's difficult to see through the bag. And are those precious stones or just glass?"

Gerald broke into Dotty's musings as he declared, "In Greek mythology, a dagger represents revenge."

"As this one was used to pierce the victim's heart, it could also symbolise betrayal," considered Chief Inspector Ringrose. "Had Tariq betrayed your love, Mrs Sayers?"

"What?" Dotty started. "Do you think I was romantically involved with Tariq?"

"There are rumours he thought highly of you," the chief inspector replied.

"Did he seduce you, and then cast you aside for a younger, more attractive, or famous model?" asked Sergeant Unwin in a malicious tone.

"Don't be ridiculous," laughed Dotty. If the police were pursuing this line of enquiry, they clearly had no idea what was going on. They were clutching at straws. They had no evidence against her. No witnesses. And there would be no forensic evidence linking her to the murder.

But someone had killed Tariq, and she was convinced that until she worked out who it was, she would remain the prime suspect.

CHAPTER NINETEEN

K eya avoided Cirencester police station on Thursday morning and instead drove straight to Lemington Hall. The sun was bright but low as she carefully negotiated the winding country lanes in her Ford Focus police car.

At the hall, the lack of a police presence surprised her. Perhaps they were still searching Tariq's office and the old stable yard. As she parked in the cobbled courtyard to the side of the hall, a mud-splattered Toyota Hilux drove into the yard and stopped beside her car.

She climbed out as Bob Wicks, the estate groundsman, lowered his window and called,

"What you here for? I know nothing about Master Tariq's death. It's nowt to do with me."

Keya took a deep breath and replied politely, "You contacted me about trespassers in the woods again, particularly those on motorcycles."

"Right, you'd better come in then." Bob parked at an angle in front of a black painted door in one of the outbuildings, climbed down from his car, and unlocked the door with a key from a bunch which hung from his belt.

He didn't say anything else, so Keya followed him into his office. As on previous visits, the shelves lining one wall were crammed with cardboard and plastic files and stacks of paper. Other papers were scattered across the pine table behind which Bob sat down.

Keya removed a stack of magazines about countryside management from a stool and also sat down as she said, "I'm sorry about Tariq's death. Do you think the Kazems will sell the hall?"

"I don't know, but I doubt it will affect me. I was here for ten years with the previous occupants and continued for another five while the hall was empty. If the Kazems do decide to leave, it'll make my life easier, although I do think the villagers need to stop thinking they own the wood and can do what they like in it."

He paused before continuing, "I messaged you about them still riding motorbikes around it. I heard one yesterday afternoon, and several last weekend. I've repaired the boundary wall, so they must be riding along the footpath from Eaton Common."

"Is that why you've been blocking the footpath? You know it's infuriated the inhabitants of Lemington?"

"A footpath is for walking on. Not cycling, and certainly not for motorbikes." Bob leaned back and folded his arms.

"Then why not build a stile, or a kissing gate, or something," Keya suggested.

"I did build a stile, but all I received were complaints from people about having to lift their dogs over it. And then some vandal broke it, so I had to take it away. Those villagers have no respect. That's why the Kazems ordered me to block the path and access to the wood, but of course, as you know, someone sawed through the fence I built.

"I don't know what to do now, but as you say, if the hall is sold, I can leave well alone. As long as the villagers don't set fire to the woods, or start dumping bodies in it, I'm happy to let them use it as before."

"But if the Kazems decide to stay?"

"Then the war will continue." Bob Wicks sighed deeply.

This was her chance. "Do people ever drive up to the hall or park their vehicles in the grounds when they use the woods or walk along the footpath?" Keya asked.

"No, they know better than that." Bob shook his head.

"So you didn't notice any strange cars yesterday, or people for that matter?"

Bob narrowed his eyes at Keya. "What are you getting at?"

"I've been told to ask around for possible witnesses to yesterday's events." Which was true, but it wasn't her police bosses who had asked her to do it.

"I told you. What happened has nothing to do with me. Now have you finished? Or do you have any bright ideas on how to deal with the motorbikes?"

Keya shook her head. "I can only think about barriers to restrict the bikes but not the walkers, but if those are being removed … I'll ask the villagers for possible solutions. If they buy into an idea, then it might work."

"When have they ever agreed on anything?" muttered Bob.

"When the Kazems moved into the hall."

Keya left Bob's office and was surprised to find Ozzie Clark and a stony-faced Norman standing outside the side door to the hall, speaking to the housekeeper, Mrs Johnson.

"I know nothing about a reporter and article, even if it is for Country Life," said Mrs Johnson. She tucked strands of her dyed copper-brown hair behind her ear, exposing grey roots.

"Good morning," said Keya cheerfully, as she approached the group.

Norman made as if to speak and she gave him a slight shake of her head.

"Is everything OK?" Keya asked.

"Constable," greeted Mrs Johnson gruffly, standing guard in the doorway.

Keya did not correct her.

"This lady says she's a reporter and she arranged a visit with Master Tariq to view the house and his collection of paintings for an article she's writing."

Keya nodded, and replied, "I've met Miss Winters before, and she is a journalist."

"But I don't think I can let her in ... not after what happened yesterday."

Ozzie turned and raised her eyebrows at Keya.

"Mrs Johnson, after what happened yesterday, don't you think an article would be a nice way to remember Master Tariq? And I understand he was very proud of his art collection."

Mrs Johnson nodded her head. "Oh, he was. I'd hate to say how much money he spent on it. Some of those paintings are worth more than my husband and I'll earn in a lifetime. And you see, that's another reason I can't just let this reporter and her photographer in the house. I can't stay with them. The rest of the family are arriving this evening."

Keya's eyes widened. If the family were returning later today, this was their only chance to search the house.

Keya smiled warmly at Mrs Johnson and suggested, "What if I escort them? I'll make sure they don't touch anything, and you can get on with your duties."

Mrs Johnson straightened her apron. "Well, I'm not sure, what would Master Tariq say?"

"I met Tariq, and he was a proud but polite man. He always looked after his guests and these two are his guests."

"You're right about that. Very good with visitors, he was. I made chicken pie for two of them only the other night. Mr Rook, very polite and knowledgeable he is, and his wife is always well dressed."

She leaned forward and lowered her voice. "They came to discuss the painting I found when clearing out a cupboard on the second floor. Said it might be worth something. Ever so proud I was. Mr Rook came back yesterday to discuss it but when I met him, as I was cycling in from the village with some eggs from Mrs Benson, I asked if he was going to sell it.

"And he told me he was sending a girl from a local auction house to collect it and that it would be entered into this month's sale. So exciting. I suppose he has people to do these things for him and he could hardly take the painting himself."

"Why not?" asked Ozzie before Keya could.

"Well, he was dressed in a grey tracksuit and told me his wife had persuaded him to play tennis again this year. Joked he needed to after my cooking the other night." Mrs Johnson smiled smugly and moved her head like a preening hen.

"I like a good homemade chicken pie," Norman piped up.

Mrs Johnson stood a little taller as she looked at him and replied, "So does my husband." She looked around the group. "Oh, I'm sure it can't do any harm you coming in and looking around. But mind you don't touch anything, and you'll stay with them, Constable?"

"I will," agreed Keya, as Mrs Johnson stepped inside. She led them down a narrow corridor, up a set of worn concrete steps, and through a door under the central staircase into the main entrance hall.

Ozzie stepped forward to view the large paintings of horses and landscapes on the walls and Norman followed her. Ozzie whispered to Norman, and he lifted his camera and pointed it at the painting of the river scene, with cows grazing in the foreground and the glimpse of a country house between trees on a hill in the background.

Mrs Johnson remained standing beside Keya.

"Did you see anyone else besides David Rook yesterday?" asked Keya.

Mrs Johnson pondered the question before replying, "There was an attractive Frenchman, or was that the day before? Asking for directions to Tariq's office."

Keya's senses were alert as she asked, "Did he give his name?"

"Xavier or something like that."

"Could it have been Didier?"

"Oh yes, that's the one. Long wavy hair down the collar of his immaculate white shirt."

What business did Didier Vogt have with Tariq?

"Anyone else?" asked Keya, not expecting there to be.

"Only that young lad who ran errands for Master Tariq. Don't trust him myself. Too smooth by far."

"And what was his name?"

"Billy Edwards."

Keya's mouth fell open in surprise. Composing herself, she asked in a slightly shrill voice, "And did you see him yesterday?"

"I did. When I went to collect Master Tariq's lunch dishes. Oh!" Mrs Johnson gasped.

"What is it?" pressed Keya.

"I think he and Master Tariq had been arguing."

CHAPTER TWENTY

Keya, Ozzie and Norman continued to look round the ground floor rooms at Lemington Hall. Although antiques were Dotty's area of expertise, Keya had picked up a few tips from being around her and spending time at Akemans.

As they entered the dining room, she asked Ozzie and Norman, "Is it me? Or have two different people decorated this house?"

The elegance of the entrance hall had given way to what she could only describe as 'bling' in the dining room. The walls were dark cream with mirrors and large gilt patterns.

Heavy green velvet curtains, with gold tassels, adorned the two windows, and the same material covered the opulent dining chairs. There was an elaborate gold monogram on the back of each chair, presumably Tariq's father's initials.

The table was cream coloured with gold edging and decorations. Two large chandeliers hung from the ceiling, but at least that was white.

"No paintings in here," observed Norman drily.

He was about to return to the entrance hall when Ozzie asked, "Can you take a few photos, anyway? You never know when we may need images for future articles. It's not every day I get access to such expensive interior design."

The main drawing room was also overpowering with its use of dark-cream and gold. The sofa and chairs were pink satin and the floor marble, like the dining room.

"Not somewhere to relax in," commented Norman, but he duly took several photographs for Ozzie.

Keya stepped into the next room, with a large snooker table in the centre, and smiled. In complete contrast with the dining and drawing rooms, it was what she expected from a country house. The walls were covered with an elegant dark-green wallpaper and the heads of stags with impressive antlers hung above paintings of distinguished looking gentlemen.

"This is more like it," murmured Ozzie. "I wonder who all these men are?"

"This one's Winston Churchill, but it's not the most flattering image of him," observed Norman.

"And next to it is one of his paintings. The plaque says it's The Tower of Katoubia Mosque, 'the most beautiful place on earth'," Keya read.

From the snooker room they entered a wood-panelled library with more paintings, which Norman dutifully photographed.

"No sign of the Betrayal of Jesus," commented Ozzie as they climbed the stairs to the first floor. The bedrooms and their ensuite bathrooms were all beautiful but ostentatious, following the design of the living and dining rooms, and there were no paintings.

"Come on, we might have more luck on the second floor," called Ozzie as she climbed a narrower wooden staircase.

Keya had expected the second floor to feel cramped with low ceilings, but that wasn't the case. They entered an elegant bedroom with rich purple curtains, oriental rugs, and antique mahogany furniture. The art in the room was modern, with abstract images and portraits.

"I think I've found something," called Ozzie. Her voice sounded faint.

Keya entered a corridor running along the back of the building, passing a rack of coats and tweed caps, and even a baseball cap with 'Cotswold Airport' printed on it.

"Where are you?" shouted Keya.

"In here." Ozzie sounded closer.

The rooms leading off the corridor were smaller with low ceilings, and the first one she came to was undecorated, with exposed plaster walls.

Keya found Ozzie in the third room along. It had been painted white and the bare floorboards varnished. Ozzie stood beside a stack of canvases of various sizes. Beside her, propped against the wall, was a painting of the Betrayal of Jesus.

"Is that Sir Reginald's painting?" asked Keya.

Ozzie nodded. "I've just checked my research, and this certainly looks like the missing painting, although we'll need Sir Reginald, or an expert, to confirm it."

"Well done," praised Keya. "Although I'm not exactly sure how I'm going to explain where we found it."

"Stick to the story," insisted Ozzie. "Who's going to deny that Tariq arranged for me to view his art collection? And as the housekeeper didn't have time to show me around, you volunteered to escort me and my photographer. Where is Norman, by the way? We should take pictures of all these paintings."

"You called," grunted Norman as he entered the room. He clenched his jaw when he saw the stack of paintings.

"Here, pass me the camera," Ozzie held her hand out to Norman. "I'll photograph these, but can you help me, Keya?"

Keya supported the front of the stack as Ozzie flipped through it, photographing each picture in turn. There was a huge variety of old and modern art, landscapes, portraits, and abstract images in a variety of frames, and a few were just canvases.

"Finished. What shall we do with this painting?" Ozzie pointed at the one of the Betrayal of Jesus.

"I better take it," replied Keya, "but I'll need to tell the housekeeper, Mrs Johnson, and it might be best to inform Bob Wicks as well. I don't want anyone accusing us of stealing it."

"And the others?" asked Ozzie, looking down at the stack of pictures.

"I'll contact Jarrod and see if he and his team can come over, preferably before the Kazem family arrive tonight."

After checking the remaining rooms, and taking photographs of more paintings they found, they descended the stairs to the entrance hall.

"I feel I should write something about the hall or Tariq, but Ryan won't forgive me if I print anything which impacts on Dotty's case," reasoned Ozzie.

"The news has already broken about Tariq's death," confirmed Keya.

"And I heard on the radio that they know a suspect is being held for questioning. As long as you don't name Dotty, or mention the painting, you should be OK. The higher profile the case, the more pressure to arrest someone and while that person is currently Dotty, without evidence, we'll be forced to let her go. I think Sergeant Unwin was hasty arresting her."

"I agree," muttered Norman.

"And why don't we visit the old stable yard on our way out and you can photograph Tariq's office? That would annoy Sergeant Unwin." Keya grinned.

"Have you finished?" called Mrs Johnson as she appeared through the door below the staircase.

"Yes, thank you for your help," replied Ozzie politely.

Mrs Johnson stepped forward and asked, "Is that one of Master Tariq's pictures, Constable?"

"It was found in his collection, but I believe it was recently stolen," replied Keya.

Mrs Johnson gasped.

"I'm taking it to the station to check its authenticity."

Mrs Johnson smoothed down her apron. "Surely not. Master Tariq didn't need to steal pictures, not with all the money he had. And what will Mr Kazem say if I just let you walk out with it?"

"I'm not accusing Master Tariq of stealing it, but we have a register of stolen paintings and antiques, which I need to check it against. It's the law." Which was partly true, thought Keya.

"Oh, in that case. But should you give me a receipt or something?" pressed Mrs Johnson.

"If you want to know more, or your employer does, I'll be happy to speak to him down at the station, once an expert has examined the painting."

"That's not necessary, I'm sure," replied Mrs Johnson, taking a step back.

"Thank you for your time," said Ozzie politely.

Mrs Johnson was biting the inside of her cheek and looking at each of them in turn.

"Time to leave," whispered Norman.

"We'll show ourselves out." Keya picked up the painting and strode past Mrs Johnson down the corridor they'd come in through and into the cobbled courtyard. Bob Wicks' Hilux was absent.

"I'm pleased to get out of there," admitted Ozzie.

"Poor woman," sympathised Norman. "It can't be easy working for a family who are away half the time, and then one of them dies mysteriously and the police and reporters start sniffing around."

"Talking of sniffing around," said Keya, "let's visit the old stable yard, and then I really should take this painting to the station."

Keya drove her Ford Focus away from the hall and turned off the main drive towards the old stable yard. Ozzie followed with Norman in her small, old-style VW Golf.

Keya braked sharply as she emerged from the stone entrance arch and spotted a police squad car next to Dotty's green Skoda Fabia. She breathed out when Ryan stepped out of Tariq's office.

She parked next to Ryan's car and as she climbed out, she remarked, "I see Dotty's car is still here. I thought Sergeant Unwin would want to impound it as evidence."

"He hasn't said anything about it, and I'm not sure what to do. We can't just leave it here, can we?" Ryan looked at Keya for direction.

"Where are the keys?" asked Norman as he joined them.

"In the car," confirmed Ryan. "I checked. And I had a quick search, but there are no other hidden paintings or stolen items."

"Why don't I drive it back to the farm?" suggested Norman. "And then if you do want it again, you'll know where to find it. But it'll also be ready for Dotty when she's released." Norman spoke the last sentence with conviction.

"Sounds reasonable to me," confirmed Keya.

Ryan nodded his agreement before looking across at Ozzie, who was standing apart from the group. He asked, "Did you get inside the house?"

"Yes, thanks to Keya, who persuaded the housekeeper by saying she'd escort us. And see what we found."

Ozzie looked across at Keya, who reached into the back of her car and pulled out the Betrayal of Jesus painting.

"Sir Reginald's?" asked Ryan.

"I think so, but you better ask an expert to confirm it is," suggested Ozzie.

"Talking of which, will you excuse me?" Keya walked away from the group, tapping the keys on her phone.

"Good morning, Sergeant," Jarrod greeted her. "Any news on Dotty? Did she appreciate the reading material I sent her?"

"I'm afraid I don't know. I haven't had a chance to visit her as I've been working on her case, which is why I'm calling. I'm at Lemington Hall and we've found a collection of paintings including, we think, the one stolen from Sir Reginald. The Kazem family is due back this evening so I know it's a long shot, but would you be able to come to the hall today and examine the collection? We might not have access to it once the Kazem family is back, and who knows what might happen to the paintings."

Keya heard Jarrod speak to someone else, presumably Finn, "Call Violet and ask her to meet us at Lemington Hall as soon as she can."

So he was requesting back up from his business partner, Lady Violet Stanley-Rudd.

Jarrod confirmed this as he said, "Sergeant, my team will be with you shortly."

"Thank you."

Keya returned to Ozzie and Ryan, who were discussing Tariq's death. Norman, still in his role as photographer, was snapping away at the outside of Tariq's office.

"Jarrod and his team are on their way," declared Keya.

"I'm not sure how happy Sergeant Unwin will be about this," remarked Ryan.

"He and I are the same rank," countered Keya, "And part of my role is discovering and dealing with stolen and forged paintings and antiques. I have the authority to authorise the search ... I think."

"I always find it easier to apologise afterwards, having achieved what I need to, than ask first," Ozzie remarked.

Ryan wrinkled his forehead as he considered her. "That isn't the approach we take in the police force." He turned to Keya. "But I think it's the right call. I'm not sure we'll persuade Sergeant Unwin or the chief inspector to authorise a search in time and, if Tariq was involved with stolen paintings, it could be vital to Dotty's case."

Ozzie looked from Ryan to Keya and asked, "Can I have a sneak peek inside Tariq's office?"

Ryan turned to Keya for direction.

"OK, but just from the doorway, and Norman can't take any photos."

They all walked towards the open office door, stopping a few metres away. Norman joined Ryan and Keya as Ozzie stepped forward and stared into the office.

Keya saw a flash. "I said no photos."

Ozzie rejoined them and clarified, "You said Norman couldn't take any photos."

Keya scowled.

"Anyway, I need to get back to the office and decide what to write. But first, Norman, I think you and I deserve a good lunch, on expenses."

Norman brightened and replied, "I wouldn't say no to pie and chips."

CHAPTER TWENTY-ONE

K eya and Ryan stood in Lemington Hall's old stable yard and watched Ozzie drive away in her old VW Golf, with Norman following in Dotty's Skoda.

"What was it like inside the hall?" asked Ryan with boyish enthusiasm.

"A contrast of old English and modern opulence. My family would love all the bling, but it's not to my taste. And what have you been sent here to do?"

"Sergeant Unwin wants me to find out if Tariq owned the dagger which was used to kill him, and if it was already in the office, or if his assailant brought it with them." Ryan glanced across at Keya before adding, "The sergeant and Chief Inspector Ringrose were about to interview Dotty when I left."

"How was she?" asked Keya. "I feel guilty for not visiting her, but I thought trying to prove her innocence was more important."

"And I'm sure she'll agree. The chief inspector also asked me to search for anything in Tariq's office I think might be relevant to the case."

"Would you like me to help until Jarrod arrives?"

"Thanks." Ryan paused and looked down at his feet.

Keya laughed. "I know, as long as I'm careful and try not to break anything."

Ryan smiled back ruefully and handed Keya a pair of blue latex gloves, which she put on.

The office was neat and tidy. Ryan started searching Tariq's desk while Keya approached the second one. It was clear of papers and the drawers were empty apart from a tall black chess piece. She hadn't spotted a chess set.

"I guess Tariq was considering a partner," mused Keya.

"Or a PA. He must have done everything himself, but there are only a few papers on his desk."

"Do we know what work he did? I presumed he was a man of leisure, or helped run the estate or family business."

"He was working as an accountant in London until two years ago. Since then I've discovered him on the board of several companies with interests ranging from oil exploration to diamond mines and a vineyard."

"A man of means, I think the term is." Keya was drawn to a bookcase behind the second desk. There was a wooden stand on top of it holding a gold scabbard encrusted with jewels.

"I think I know where our murder weapon came from," Keya announced.

Ryan, who was peering at the screen of Tariq's open laptop, stopped and joined Keya beside the bookshelf. "Is that real gold?" he asked.

"I think so. The inscription on the base says, 'Presented to Tariq Kazem by the Government of Iraq, in recognition of his services'."

"What services?" queried Ryan.

"I've no idea, but I doubt the Iraqi government would have presented someone of Tariq's standing with a fake gold item, or an empty sheath, for that matter. Would the murder weapon fit in it?"

"I don't know. I haven't seen the dagger, but let's bag this as evidence and take it back. And I'll do the same with Tariq's computer, although I'm not sure I'll be able to access it, as I've no idea what his password is."

As Ryan returned to Tariq's desk to continue his search, Keya examined the contents of the bookshelf on which she'd found the gold scabbard. Most of the books looked old, and she wondered if there were any rare first editions.

A battered red leather case caught her eye, and she removed it from the middle of the top shelf. Carefully, she opened the leather flap and tipped the contents into her hand. A beautifully decorated edition of the Qur'an slipped out, and with it several sheets of paper.

"Oh toda!" she exclaimed as the sheets fell to the floor. She bent down to pick them up and realised they were covered in numbers and letters. "Hey, Ryan, what do you make of these?" She placed the papers, together with the copy of the Qur'an and its leather case, on the second desk.

Ryan joined her, glanced at the ornate book, and picked up one of the sheets. "Were these inside the case?"

"Yes, or at least they fell out when I removed the book."

Ryan carefully opened the Qur'an. "This looks old and valuable. Maybe it had some significance to Tariq, which is why he used it as a hiding place. I'm not sure what this means, but let's return the papers and the book to the case and bag them. I'll have a closer look at everything when I return to the station."

Ryan collected two plastic boxes from his car. In the first he placed the laptop, scabbard and leather case, and in the second a stack of paper and files.

Keya checked the other books for more hidden papers but didn't find any.

"Hello, anyone home?" called a familiar voice.

Keya stood up and found Aunt Beanie hovering in the open office doorway. "Find anything which will help Dotty?" she asked.

"I'm not sure," replied Ryan as he carried out a plastic box.

Aunt Beanie stepped aside to let him pass and when he had, she whispered to Keya, "Jarrod called me, and asked if I'd help with your inspection of the paintings in the hall."

"Great," replied Keya, but she wasn't so sure it was such a good idea anymore. What if Mrs Johnson refused to let them in? She hadn't thought of that.

She heard another car and called across to Ryan, "That might be Jarrod. Are you OK finishing here and locking up?"

"Yes, I'll only be a few more minutes. When will you be back at the station?"

"I'm not sure. It depends on whether Mrs Johnson, the housekeeper, lets us back in the hall."

"Mrs Johnson, you say ... I wonder," muttered Aunt Beanie.

Keya drove back to the hall and Aunt Beanie followed her in Meadowbank Farm's battered Land Rover Defender. They met Jarrod, Finn, and Lady Violet Stanley-Rudd in front of the hall.

"Good morning, Bernadette," greeted Lady Violet as Aunt Beanie climbed down from the Land Rover.

"Thank you for joining us," said Jarrod. "I fear that our time here may be limited, so an extra pair of eyes and expert opinion is most welcome."

"I just hope Mrs Johnson will let us in. I've already looked round with Ozzie Winters and Norman, and I think we found Sir Reginald Spencer's painting. I put it in my car."

"Can I see it?" asked Aunt Beanie hopefully.

"Later, Bernadette. Our current mission is the paintings inside the hall," explained Jarrod, but Keya was already lifting the painting out of the back of her car.

The front door of the hall opened, and an irritated Mrs Johnson stood on the top step, looking down at them. "We don't need no reporters hanging around today," she shouted.

Lady Violet stopped her discussion with Jarrod and stepped away from the group, towards the entrance steps and the front door. "Mrs Johnson, how are you? And Mr Johnson?"

"Oh, your Ladyship, I didn't see you there. We're both well. Thank you kindly for asking."

"My colleagues and I are helping the police," Lady Violet pointed towards Keya, "with their enquires. It's a delicate matter, which is why I'm here and we don't want to cause a fuss, or advertise our interest by seeking a warrant …"

"Oh come in, come in. I'm sure Mr Kazem wouldn't mind your ladyship and your friends visiting, and we all want to do what we can to help catch Master Tariq's killer."

Keya raised her eyebrows. Mrs Johnson hadn't appeared so keen to help earlier in the day.

Aunt Beanie followed Lady Violet and Mrs Johnson inside the hall and Jarrod, Finn and Keya followed them.

"Where do you suggest we start?" Jarrod asked Keya, who glanced across at Mrs Johnson.

"It's been lovely seeing you again, Mrs Johnson, but we should get on," declared Lady Violet.

"Oh, of course, and I've plenty of work of my own, with the family returning this evening."

Keya waited until Mrs Johnson departed by the door under the central staircase before suggesting, "The second floor. There are a couple of rooms stacked with canvases and plenty of art on the wall. But first, is this Sir Reginald's painting?"

The others stepped forward as Keya held the painting up in front of her.

"Not my type of thing," she heard Finn say.

"But so full of emotion," countered Lady Violet.

"But is it the one stolen from Sir Reginald's?" Keya asked, her arms tiring from holding up the painting.

"Most definitely," confirmed Jarrod.

With relief, Keya lowered the painting to the floor and said, "There's no point carrying it upstairs. I'll leave it here, against this wall, but can you make sure I don't forget to take it back to the police station with me?"

The group made their way upstairs, with Aunt Beanie trailing behind as she'd insisted on 'having a quick look' at the dining and living rooms. When she caught up with Keya, she whispered, "Not exactly my style of decoration. What did Norman think?"

"He didn't say much. I'm not sure he was happy about being Ozzie's photographer."

"Poor Norman. He's still muttering about finding his meaning of life."

"Where now?" asked Jarrod from the landing on the second floor.

"The corridor over there leads to smaller rooms where paintings are stacked, but you'll also find some on the walls in the front bedrooms," Keya directed.

"Ladies," Jarrod spoke to Lady Violet and Aunt Beanie, "Why don't you start in the bedrooms and Finn and I will tackle the storerooms?"

Keya followed Aunt Beanie and Lady Violet into the elegant bedroom with purple curtains. She felt rather useless as she listened to the two older women discuss paintings with knowledge and enthusiasm.

"A varied collection," Aunt Beanie said as she left the room, "but tasteful."

Aunt Beanie and Lady Violet studied the paintings on the walls of the other front bedrooms before Lady Violet announced, "Everything I've seen so far is authentic, as far as I can tell, although I would be interested in examining a couple of Lucian Freuds.

"They are certainly subjects he painted, but they're not ones I've seen before. And one looks very similar to a painting the Duchess of Devonshire bought of the rear end of a skewbald horse."

Keya thought back the snooker room and said, "I'd be interested in your opinion of some paintings we found in the snooker room."

Lady Violet and Aunt Beanie followed Keya back down the stairs and into the snooker room.

"This is a man's room," enthused Aunt Beanie. "So what interested Norman?"

Keya led them to the portrait of Winston Churchill, under a stag's head, and the landscape painting beside it. "Did Winston Churchill really paint this?"

Aunt Beanie peered at the picture. "I thought this was in America. Is it a copy, Violet?"

There was no reply.

Aunt Beanie and Keya looked up at Lady Violet, who was transfixed by the portrait of Winston Churchill.

"What's the matter?" asked Aunt Beanie.

"I can't believe it," replied Lady Violet. "This painting was supposed to have been destroyed by Lady Spencer-Churchill. Her husband, the man himself, remarked that it was "a remarkable example of modern art," and he didn't mean it as a compliment. He hated the picture, which was presented to him by both Houses of Parliament on his eightieth birthday. And his youngest daughter, Lady Soames, even persuaded the Carlton Club not to hang a copy in their Churchill Room."

Lady Violet leaned towards the portrait. "I'd love to find out if this is authentic."

They all returned upstairs and found Jarrod lining up paintings along a wall.

"Just a minute," cried Aunt Beanie. "Those first two are in one of my cold case files. They were stolen from a house in Oxfordshire five years ago."

Jarrod smiled and suggested, "And I think you'll find these two were taken from a small gallery in Cambridge last year."

Finn appeared, carrying two more paintings.

Jarrod pointed to them and continued, "And I've seen these hanging on the wall at The Grand Hotel in Cheltenham, which means one set is a copy. And I'd wager it's not these."

"So what's your conclusion of the collection?" asked Keya.

"That there are some impressive pieces. In particular, a couple of Andy Warhols, which would both make over a million pounds at auction, and a Damien Hirst worth several million pounds. But I do question the provenance of some of the paintings. If they are genuine, then I doubt they were acquired legally."

"Would you impound the entire collection?" asked Keya. Her head was starting to spin. What had started out as a simple search for a missing painting had grown into a possible multi-million pound art scandal.

"That's not my call, Sergeant. Nor yours. It's for those well above your pay grade to decide."

Keya took a deep breath and called Chief Inspector Ringrose.

CHAPTER TWENTY-TWO

R yan returned to Cirencester police station with the evidence he'd collected from Tariq Kazem's office.

It was quiet when he carried in the plastic box containing the gold scabbard, the leather case with the Qur'an, and Tariq's laptop. But when he returned with the box of files and paperwork, he found Chief Inspector Ringrose and Sergeant Unwin standing beside his desk, examining the scabbard.

Sergeant Unwin held up a plastic bag containing a dagger and, as Ryan placed his box on the floor, he noticed light sparkle on the hilt.

"The scabbard is gold, and decorated with precious jewels, just like the hilt of the dagger," remarked the chief inspector. He turned to Ryan and said, "Well done. We can now confirm the murder weapon was already at the crime scene."

"Which means what?" asked Ryan.

"That our suspect didn't bring it with her," replied Sergeant Unwin. "So either she knew it was there or this murder was spontaneous. Perhaps she and the victim had an argument. She saw the dagger and in the heat of the moment grabbed it and stabbed Tariq."

"It doesn't sound like something Dotty would do," muttered Ryan. Clearing his throat, he countered, "But wouldn't the victim have defended himself? Surely he would have seen Mrs Sayers pick up the dagger and, even if she'd threatened him with it, could she really overpower and stab him?"

"A woman scorned," responded Sergeant Unwin. "If they'd had a lovers' tiff, and our suspect was filled with anger or jealously. She's not much shorter than our victim and if he'd turned his back on her and she'd surprised him."

"But he was stabbed in the heart," pressed Ryan.

"As I say, a crime of passion." Sergeant Unwin crossed his arms.

Ryan realised there was no point in arguing. Sergeant Unwin had clearly made up his mind that Dotty was guilty and was making the evidence fit his version of the crime.

Chief Inspector Ringrose was examining the scabbard, on its stand, through the evidence bag.

Ryan asked him, "Do you want me to send that and the dagger to Gloucester to be tested for fingerprints?"

"The lab has a two-week delay, but Sergeant Unwin tells me you did an excellent job extracting and identifying Billy Edwards' prints from a Coke can in the Roger Dewhirst case. So I thought you could examine these. Gold is a relatively easy surface on which to identify fingerprints," the chief inspector explained as he handed the evidence bag over to Ryan.

Ryan glanced at Tariq's laptop, which was what he really wanted to get his hands on to see if he could crack the password and find out what information was hiding on it.

"Let me know how you get on," said Chief Inspector Ringrose dismissively as he turned his back on Ryan.

As Ryan placed the box with the laptop and leather case on the one with the files beside his desk, he heard the chief inspector say to Sergeant Unwin, "So you'll visit Akemans and see if anyone saw Mrs Sayers leave, and then speak to Marion and David Rook again." He didn't catch the sergeant's response as the two men left the room.

Ryan picked up the evidence bag containing the dagger that Sergeant Unwin had left on his desk, and compared it with the scabbard. The two items certainly looked as if they belonged together, but he would check if the knife fitted the scabbard after he'd dusted them both for fingerprints.

"At last, I can have my room back," grumbled Inspector Evans as he stepped out of his office.

The inspector's door had been open when Ryan carried in the first box and he'd presumed the inspector was out.

"Sir?"

"Did I startle you? Sometimes keeping one's head down has its advantages."

Was the inspector speaking literally or metaphorically?

The inspector eyed the evidence bags Ryan held and commented, "I heard you'd found the scabbard for the murder weapon. So now you've been tasked with testing them both for fingerprints. I doubt you'll find the killer's prints on either, but as long as Mrs Sayers aren't on them, we're a step further to proving her innocence."

"You still believe she didn't kill Tariq?"

"I do. Now, what else is in those boxes you're hiding beside your desk?"

"I found Tariq's laptop, but it's password protected. I'd like to get to work on it immediately, but …"

"Start with the fingerprints," instructed Inspector Evans, "and then I'll make sure you're not disturbed or tasked by Sergeant Unwin for the rest of the day. Use my office and pull the blinds down. I won't be needing it for a while as I'm going to visit my favourite auction house."

"Akemans? Isn't that where Sergeant Unwin was going?"

"Is it?" asked Inspector Evans in an innocent voice.

Ryan carried the dagger and scabbard in their evidence bags to the rear of the building.

Sergeant Rowbottom was back on duty at the custody desk.

Ryan greeted him. "Afternoon Sergeant, how is Mrs Sayers?"

"Bright enough. I don't think Sergeant Onion and the chief inspector made much progress during her interview this morning, and her solicitor seemed pretty convinced she'll be released soon. Although I'm not sure Mrs Sayers is as optimistic. Anyway, she ate all her vegetarian lunch, so I'm happy with that."

Ryan's stomach grumbled. He hadn't had time for lunch.

"I'm sending a young PC out for sandwiches," remarked the older sergeant. "Would you like him to grab you something? You look as if your hands are full."

"Yes, please. I have to analyse these for fingerprints."

Sergeant Rowbottom stared through the Perspex screen at the evidence bags and said, "Let's hope you don't find any."

"Why do you say that?"

Sergeant Rowbottom wrinkled his brow and replied, "Because if you find Mrs Sayers, her goose is cooked, so to speak."

Ryan carried the evidence bags into a room next to the one he'd used to collect Dotty's fingerprints and DNA sample.

After pulling on a pair of latex gloves and donning a set of plastic goggles, he covered the Formica worktop with a plastic sheet and tipped the dagger out of its evidence bag. Carefully holding the dagger by its blade, he gently dusted one side of the hilt with magnesium powder, which would stick to the grease of any fingerprints.

He wasn't sure if he was happy or not when several were revealed, but he dutifully manoeuvred the mounted camera into place and photographed all the prints together, and then each in turn. He repeated the process with the other side of the hilt and its top. Then he moved on to the underside and the blade.

Ryan decided to take a break from searching for fingerprints and, peeling off his gloves and pushing his goggles onto the top of his head, he turned on the computer, which was linked to the camera. Three clear fingerprints had been photographed and several others were blurred, but a similar pattern covered them.

Ryan switched to the images of each side of the hilt and arranged them side by side. He then lifted his hand and considered it. If he used the dagger to stab someone, he would clasp it in his palm. Was a palm print covering some of the fingerprints and what was that white thread stuck to one of them?

There was a mounted magnifying glass on the other side of the worktop. Pulling on another set of latex gloves, he held the hilt under the lens. There it was again. He picked up a pair of tweezers and delicately removed the thread. It was white, and not just from the magnesium powder.

As he placed it in a small evidence bag, his thoughts were drawn to a pair of cotton gloves in the evidence box for Roger Dewhirst's death. Some antique dealers wore cotton gloves when handling glass or other items they didn't want to leave marks on. Was this thread from a similar pair of gloves?

And Ryan had recently read an article in which Birmingham University claimed they could now identify fingerprints and palm prints on an object even when thin latex gloves had been used to handle it. Would they be able to do the same if thin cotton gloves had been used?

Ryan repeated the fingerprint examination process with the gold scabbard and its stand. The stand had a lot of fingerprints on it, probably because many people had held and admired it.

When all the fingerprints were loaded into the computer, and the duplicates discarded, he started a program which would check them against fingerprints already in the system. He set the program so it started its search with 'most recent' and 'local'.

It immediately pinged and with trepidation, Ryan checked the results. He hadn't realised he'd been holding his breath until he exhaled. It wasn't Dotty's prints that had been found, but the victim's.

While the computer continued its analysis, he searched on his phone for the article about Birmingham University's research into gloves and fingerprints. It gave him the name of a professor and, after a further search of the university's website, he found the telephone number he needed and called.

"Professor Watkin's office," answered a young male voice.

"Is the professor there?" asked Ryan. "I'm calling from Gloucestershire Police about his research into gloves and fingerprints."

"I'm sure the professor would love to speak to you, but he's currently in a seminar. Can I give you his email address?"

Ryan jotted down the address and thanked the young man.

The fingerprint machine continued its search without providing any more results.

Ryan composed an email asking if it would be possible to distinguish a palm print on an item where cotton gloves had been worn.

The computer pinged. The fingerprint match it found was for a Mari Cox. Ryan had never heard of her, but he searched the database for a photograph. The one shown was old, and of a woman in her early twenties. Ryan stared hard at it. Could it be of a young Marion Rook?

CHAPTER TWENTY-THREE

Keya stood beside the central staircase in Lemington Hall and answered her phone.

"Yes, Chief Inspector, I understand. I'll wait here until the team arrives." She listened again. "Yes, I'll make sure nothing is removed."

When she finished the call, Jarrod approached her and asked, "What's the verdict?"

Keya replied, "Apparently the collection is too large, too prestigious, and too valuable for our team, so the Chief Inspector has asked a team from London to come down. They're already on their way."

Jarrod nodded. "That's probably sensible, since you have your hands full proving Dotty's innocence, and dealing with other related crimes."

Aunt Beanie had joined them and added, "Besides, the chief inspector is running out of members of his team he appears to trust with such matters. I'd love to be involved with this collection and establishing where all the paintings are from. And I know Violet is obsessed by that portrait of Churchill."

Jarrod nodded his head in understanding but replied, "I would also relish the challenge of such a collection, but we have more pressing concerns closer to home. Besides, if it's the team I think it is, I know most of them and I'm sure they'd appreciate our help, but only once we're finished with current matters."

Keya wasn't sure what current matters Jarrod referred to, but she agreed that proving Dotty's innocence was her priority, and then catching Tariq's real killer.

Lady Violet opened the door under the central staircase and called, "Lunch time. I've helped Mrs Johnson prepare soup and sandwiches for us all. Finn told me you're a vegetarian, Keya, so we made leek and potato soup."

"Thank you," replied Keya gratefully. She'd thought she'd have to skip lunch … again.

Keya, Aunt Beanie, Jarrod, Lady Violet, and Finn enjoyed their lunch with Mrs Johnson in the large kitchen at Lemington Hall.

"Do you do all the cleaning and cooking on your own?" Keya asked.

"Not when the family is at home. They're very particular and bring a chef with them from London. I just cook for Bob, myself, and one of the girls from the village who comes to help with the cleaning and laundry."

"But you cooked for Master Tariq, and his guests?" pressed Keya.

"Oh, he was no bother. All his meat was delivered from Cheltenham, from a special halal butcher. And he didn't have many guests. Just Mr and Mrs Rook recently, but you know about them. It was nice to have another lady in the house."

Keya returned to her delicious soup, but Aunt Beanie asked, "Do you mean that it was usually men that Tariq entertained?"

"Yes. But they were always very polite. Before the family left, there were quite a few foreign gentlemen, including that Frenchman I told you about." Mrs Johnson turned to Keya. "And I remembered he was here on Monday."

"Which Frenchman?" asked Aunt Beanie.

"Didier Vogt," replied Keya.

Aunt Beanie narrowed her eyes and asked, "Who else visited this week?"

"David Rook also came on Monday, but he was often here. That was why it was so nice he brought his wife for supper."

A large bell on the wall rang as it rocked from side-to-side. Mrs Johnson looked up and announced, "That must be the people from London."

Keya handed over responsibility for Tariq's art collection to the team of police experts from

London and left Lady Violet and Jarrod discussing individual paintings with them.

Aunt Beanie had disappeared from Lemington Hall without saying goodbye.

Keya didn't feel like returning to the police station straight away and, when she saw a signpost telling her the next turning was for Coln Akeman, she instinctively turned off the main road. Akemans auction house and antiques centre was on the right-hand side, half a mile before the village of Coln Akeman.

The antiques centre occupied a three-storey, nineteenth century converted flour mill, and the auction house a single-storey stone building beside it. There were other stone outbuildings which continued to be used for storage.

As Keya parked in the gravel yard in front of the antiques centre, she spotted several vehicles of interest. First was Sergeant Unwin's metallic grey Mercedes, parked in a disabled parking space close to the entrance.

Aunt Beanie had parked her Land Rover further back, and over on the far side, she spotted

Inspector Evan's old Volvo. The windows were steamed up. Was the Inspector sitting in his car?

She strode across to the inspector's car and he lowered the driver's side window as she approached.

"Good afternoon, Sergeant. What have you to report from Lemington Hall?"

"How do you ..." Keya didn't finish her sentence.

"Young PC Jenkins brought plenty back with him. I thought he might need some privacy this afternoon to work on the victim's laptop. If you want to take him a cup of tea later, he's using my office, and there's a spare desk should you also need some peace and quiet away from senior police officers and other sergeants."

"Er, thank you, sir. But can I ask what you're doing here?"

"Observing and thinking for the moment. But I might join you inside in due course." Inspector Evans glanced across at Sergeant Unwin's car and then grinned at Keya.

"Why don't you find that ambitious sergeant who's supposed to work on my team and see if he needs any help?"

"Very good, sir." Keya wasn't sure what help Sergeant Unwin would need, but she was also interested in finding out what he was doing at Akemans.

There was no sign of Sergeant Unwin in the large, open-plan ground floor of the antiques centre, where rows of individual stalls sold a variety of antique and vintage items, as well as more modern pieces.

Keya pushed open the door into the reception-cum-office area of the auction house and found Sergeant Unwin standing in front of the reception desk, behind which Marion Rook was sitting. Marion did not look her usual cool, collected self and Keya, who was no fashion guru, didn't think her orange frilly shirt went with her green cardigan.

"So you left Akemans just after lunch and went straight to Eaton Common for your tennis match. What time did you arrive?" asked Sergeant Unwin.

"I had an early lunch with Dotty in the main auction room as we discussed items to be collated for this month's auction. Then I drove straight to the Tylers' and arrived just after quarter to two. They were already warming up with David, so I joined them."

Sergeant Unwin nodded. "And what time did you finish you match?"

"About ten to four. We initially stopped at about quarter to three, as we'd been well and truly beaten in two sets, but after a break of about half an hour, David suggested we play a third set. And we did much better, only losing by six games to four."

"And when did you speak to Mrs Sayers?"

"She called just before three to tell me she was leaving for Lemington Hall, and again just before four, which is when she told me Tariq was dead. David and I drove straight over."

"And how did she sound?"

"Nervous the first time. I know she was worried about collecting the painting on her own after what had happened at Sir Reginald's, but I didn't think she needed to be. We all collect pictures and antiques from private houses. It's part of our job description. But when she called me the second time, she sounded ... well, in shock."

"And what was the relationship between the deceased and Mrs Sayers?"

"Relationship?" queried Marion. "None that I'm aware of."

Marion glanced up at Keya, and Sergeant Unwin followed her gaze.

"Yes, Sergeant?" he snapped.

"I just wondered if you wanted any help," replied Keya, trying to remain civil. Had Sergeant Unwin forgotten they were the same rank?

"Why should I need your help?"

"I'll take that as a no, then." Keya turned and left the office, annoyed by Sergeant Unwin's attitude, but not completely surprised by it. He would see her as the opposition. On Dotty's side. She returned to Inspector Evans, who was still sitting in his car in the car park.

"Sergeant Unwin made it clear he didn't need any assistance from me, but from what I overheard, he won't learn anything new," divulged Keya.

Inspector Evans stared past her, at the antiques centre, and said, "Watch out. Here he comes."

The inspector wound up his window as Keya dashed round to the far side of his car and ducked out of sight.

CHAPTER TWENTY-FOUR

Several minutes later, Inspector Evans climbed out of his car and announced, "The coast is clear, Sergeant. I think I'll interview Mrs Rook myself. Would you like to accompany me?"

"Yes, sir," Keya felt obliged to say yes, although she was keen to see if the inspector could extract any additional information from Marion.

Keya found herself reflecting that it hadn't been so bad when she'd worked as a constable on the inspector's team. He'd been grumpy, and always kept her busy with tasks, some of which hadn't seemed important, but he'd always included her in investigations.

Something Chief Inspector Ringrose was no longer doing.

"Ah, Mrs Rook. Any chance of a cuppa for my Sergeant and I?" asked Inspector Evans when they entered the reception-cum-office area of the auction house. "I know Sergeant Unwin has already interviewed you, but I hope you won't mind answering some additional questions that I have."

"We're trying to help Dotty," added Keya.

"In that case, sit down over there and I'll bring us all drinks." Marion indicated to a grey sofa and tub chairs in the far corner of the reception area. "I could do with a drink myself, although I'd prefer something a little stronger than coffee." She smiled ruefully and turned towards the kitchenette at the back of the small office.

As Keya and the inspector sat down in the tub chairs, Keya checked her messages and emails. An email from Ryan caught her attention as it was titled, 'Is this Marion Rook?' Intrigued, Keya opened it and examined the old photograph Ryan had attached of someone called Mari Cox. She could be a younger version of Marion.

Marion placed cups of tea for Keya and Inspector Evans on the reclaimed-elm coffee table before carrying over her own aromatic coffee, which Keya knew contained cardamom.

When Marion was settled on the sofa, Inspector Evans asked, "How well did you know Tariq Kazem and his family?"

"I'd met Tariq and his father several times, usually in London for supper or at an exhibition or auction at Sotheby's, Christie's or Gainfords. But it was David who had the business relationship with them."

"With both the Kazems?" pressed Inspector Evans.

Marion considered the question before replying, "His relationship with Ahmad, Tariq's father, is more formal. I think Ahmad asks David to source particular pieces of artwork or antiques for him, but with Tariq, David had a more relaxed working relationship, although I don't know what business they actually conducted together."

"So David spent considerable time with Tariq?"

"I wouldn't say considerable, but I think they sometimes went on trips abroad together. And since Tariq has been living at Lemington Hall, I'd say they meet up once or twice a week."

"And was Tuesday evening the first time you'd been invited round for supper?"

"It was," confirmed Marion.

"Did you eat in the dining room?" asked Keya.

Marion looked at her and smiled. "You've visited the hall?"

Keya nodded.

"Yes, we ate in the dining room. It felt overwhelming at first, with all that marble, gold and green velvet, but I soon got used to it. David was at ease, especially playing snooker afterwards with Tariq."

"And there were no other guests? Nobody else who knew about the painting Tariq showed you?" continued the inspector.

"Nobody on Tuesday evening. I don't know if Tariq showed it to anyone other than us, but as he didn't think it was particularly valuable or important, I doubt he did."

The inspector picked up his coffee but didn't drink it. "So why that picture? What was so important about it that it led to Tariq's death?"

"But is the picture important?" counted Marion. "Your colleagues believe Dotty killed Tariq over it and then stole it, but why would she do that? She knew nothing about it. And if she was an international art thief, she wouldn't steal that painting, would she, Keya? You've been inside the house."

"You mean," considered Keya, "that any art thief who knew his stuff would have ignored Tariq's office and headed straight for Lemington Hall. I don't know if it's alarmed at night, but while Mrs Johnson is on duty, security is minimal, and a thief could soon get his hands on some very expensive paintings. Jarrod said there was a Damien Hurst worth several millions, and Lady Violet was fascinated by a picture of Churchill she believed had been destroyed."

"Exactly," agreed Marion.

Inspector Evans tilted his head back and stared at the ceiling.

Keya and Marion watched and waited.

"This isn't about the painting, is it?" the inspector asked, but didn't seem to expect a reply. "Although, why it ended up in Dotty's car is a conundrum."

"Maybe it was planted there," blurted Keya.

Inspector Evans turned and considered her. "I'm certain it was, and to lay suspicion at her feet. Was it someone who already knew my colleagues were interested in her in connection with other crimes and saw her as the perfect fall guy?"

"But that would implicate David and me." Marion's voice was shaky.

Inspector Evans turned and stared at her. "Yes, it would."

"But we were at the Tylers' all afternoon, and only drove to Lemington Hall after Dotty called me, and Tariq was dead by then."

"And the Tylers will be able to confirm that?"

"Certainly. I'll give you their number if you'd like to contact them."

"Sergeant," directed Inspector Evans.

Keya found her notebook and jotted down the number Marion gave her.

"Thank you, Mrs Rook. You've been most helpful," acknowledged Inspector Evans.

Marion stood, collected their coffee cups, and left Keya and the inspector.

Inspector Evans looked at Keya and instructed, "Follow up with the Tylers tomorrow. They live at Eaton Common, which is the next village on from Lemington. See how long it takes to get from the Tylers' house to the hall."

Keya's mouth opened into an O-shape.

"Yes, Sergeant. I want to find out if, during the break in their tennis match, David or Marion could have driven to Lemington Hall, stabbed Tariq, and returned to finish the match. And I agree with Marion. The painting found in Dotty's car is a distraction. I believe the murderer planted it there to throw suspicion onto her.

"I'll return to the station and see if I can persuade Chief Inspector Ringrose to release Dotty, even if it's on bail. As long as young Ryan didn't find her fingerprints on the murder weapon."

Keya remembered the email she'd received.

"Just a minute, sir. He sent me an email. Let me check if he said anything about fingerprints." Keya opened the email again and scrolled past the image of Mari Cox. "Ryan says the only fingerprints he's identified are the victims' and someone called Mari Cox."

There was a crash of breaking crockery from the back of the office.

Keya and the inspector exchanged glances before jumping up and dashing across the reception area. They stood in front of the reception desk, staring into the office area. Marion Rook stared back, ashen face.

Keya lifted her phone and, scrolling back through Ryan's email, showed the inspector the photo Ryan had sent her.

The inspector narrowed his eyes as he studied it before raising his head and asking, "Were you once known as Mari Cox, Mrs Rook?"

Marion was rigid and continued to stare at them, as if transfixed.

Keya studied the email again. "If you were, you're not in trouble. It's only that your fingerprints were found on a gold scabbard in Tariq's office."

Marion inhaled deeply and grabbed the edge of the sink.

"Tariq showed us a gift from the Iraqi government. It was a beautiful gold scabbard and dagger inlaid with previous stones. I did pick it up to examine it. Why is that relevant?"

"Because the dagger inside the scabbard was used to murder Tariq Kazem," stated Inspector Evans.

"No, that's not possible."

Keya rushed forward as Marion's legs buckled and she helped her across to the chair beside the spare office desk.

"Let's start at the beginning," suggested Inspector Evans. "You were once known as Mari Cox, your maiden name, I presume?"

Keya felt she should make Marion a sweet tea, but she didn't want to switch on the electric kettle and disturb the inspector's line of questioning.

"No, Cox was my first husband's name. Donny Cox."

It was the inspector's turn to gape. "You were married to Donny Cox?"

"I was, but I was young and impressionable back then, and Donny wasn't a bad man."

"Tell that to all the people trying to discover what became of their loved ones," countered the inspector.

"Who's Donny Cox, apart from your ex-husband, Marion?" asked Keya.

Marian looked up at her and explained, "He was part of the Kray brothers' gang in London's East End. But like the Krays, he was sent to prison. I've actually been helping to get him released so he can spend his last few years back in the East End, which he loved so much."

"I read about that. There was a petition or something," recalled Inspector Evans.

"That's right. A proper one. Not one of those online types. And his MP has promised to do what he can to persuade the authorities to at least hold a hearing. I just hope I'll be able to see him released."

"Is he ill?" asked Keya.

"Oh, no, it's not that ..." Marion's voice trailed off.

"So now we've established who you are, or at least were," concluded the inspector. "I presume your fingerprints were on file for some misdemeanour back then?"

"The police were always arresting us in clubs and pubs, and even at private parties. I was never convicted, although I was formally arrested on a couple of occasions. I guess that's why my prints are on file. From some forty years ago." Marion shook her head and smiled to herself. At least the colour was back in her cheeks.

"You say you handled the gold scabbard. When and where exactly?" asked the chief inspector, returning to his original line of enquiry.

"After supper on Tuesday night. Before Tariq showed us the painting. He was very proud to have been presented with it and David and I both admired it."

"Did your husband pick it up as well?"

"I'm not sure. No, I think he just watched as Tariq removed the dagger and demonstrated how sharp the blade was on a lemon." Marion's smile faltered, and she looked down at her hands clasped in her lap. Maybe she'd just remembered what the dagger had subsequently been used for.

"And did you visit Tariq's office on Tuesday evening?"

"No, I've never been inside it. David and I spent all our time in the house on Tuesday. Neither of us visited Tariq's office."

CHAPTER TWENTY-FIVE

"Thank you, Mrs Rook," said Inspector Evans politely, at the conclusion of his interview.

He turned to Keya and said, "I better return to the station and see what I can do about Dotty's release. Are you coming back?"

Keya regarded Marion and replied, "Soon."

"You and young Ryan can still use my office. I'll leave it free for you for the rest of the day."

"Thank you, sir."

As Inspector Evans left Akemans auction house, Keya rolled the reception chair across to Marion and sat down. "Are you OK?" she asked. "That was obviously a shock."

Marion turned her head and said, "I suppose we're never free of the choices we make. The consequences follow us wherever we go."

"But as you said, you were young and impressionable. And I'm sure you didn't do anything that terrible."

"I turned a blind eye. I didn't ask the right questions, because I didn't want to know the answers." Marion turned and stared down at the pieces of the cup she'd dropped, which were spread out across the office floor.

The connecting door opened and Keya swung round to face Gilly Wimsey, who was followed by a discerning looking man who was peering at a large tablet.

Gilly, whose unruly orange curls bounced as she moved, stopped suddenly when she saw Keya and Marion, and the man bumped into her.

"Sorry," he muttered before returning to his tablet.

Gilly's large smile faltered, and she asked, "Is everything all right?"

Marion gulped. "Fine. Fine. Inspector Evans has just questioned me about Tariq Kazem. His death is such a tragedy."

"It certainly is, and I know he was a friend of yours and David's, Marion. If there's anything I can do to help?"

Marion squared her shoulders and replied, "I need to keep busy, and with George in Paris and Dotty … away, I have plenty to do for this month's auction."

Gilly clasped her hands in front of her. "I wondered, if you are OK and before you start work, if you'd hear our plans for the antiques centre, and give me your view."

"Of course," replied Marion, standing up.

"Can I come?" asked Keya.

"Yes, of course," replied Gilly, her smile broadening. "The more ideas, the better."

Gilly turned and led the man, Keya, and Marion back into the antiques centre. They turned immediately right and walked towards the back of the building. Gilly introduced the man. "This is Fergal Blake, an architect from Cirencester."

"Hi," Keya said politely, but Fergal didn't reply. He seemed engrossed in the walls and ceiling of the antiques centre.

"As you know," remarked Gilly as they walked, "we're attracting an increasing number of buses to the antiques centre and they bring people, usually older in years, who are looking for an overall experience, and are not just searching for antiques."

"You're not planning amusements or animal attractions, are you?" responded Marion, a note of horror in her voice.

"No, nothing like that. But after the success of Dotty's temporary cafe during the pre-Christmas promotion, I really think we should have a permanent one. It would also save me setting one up every month for the auctions."

Keya recalled that Gilly's job on auction days was to run a small cafe in a corner of the auction room. Dotty often baked cakes and biscuits for her to sell.

"Fergal and I have looked at the first floor, but the structural alterations and access arrangements are prohibitively expensive, so an alternative we're considering is the rear of the ground floor. When we've been really full, I've set up stalls here," explained Gilly, coming to a halt, "But as you can see, it's rather dingy and the stallholders always complained about not doing well."

Keya looked up at a single light dangling from the ceiling. Turning her attention to the far wall, she asked, "What are those for?" and pointed to metal cogs on frames and wooden boxes attached to the stone wall.

"They're the mechanism for the old mill waterwheel," said Fergal, an Irish twang in his voice.

"Does it work?" The thought excited Keya.

"I'm not sure. I'd need to find an engineer who specialises in such contraptions to have a look at it."

"Wouldn't it be great if people could eat their lunch and watch the waterwheel turn?" enthused Keya. "I can see it now. The

Waterwheel Cafe."

"Hmm," mused Gilly. "That sounds expensive. It would need safety glass and everything."

"I don't know," considered Fergal. "I could look at it as an option, and it would be one way to brighten up this area."

"Where will the kitchen be?" asked Marion, practically.

"At the back here," confirmed Gilly, "with tables and chairs at the front and some sort of structure outside to provide shade for an outdoor seating area. And Fergal has suggested we build an extension for more seating, or a gift shop."

"That sounds wonderful," gushed Keya. "Just what I've always dreamed about running."

Gilly and Marion exchange surprised glances.

Keya's phone rang. "But back in the real world," she said regretfully, finding her phone. "Hi Ryan, just a minute." Keya looked at Gilly and Marion and said, "The cafe sounds like a fabulous idea. And I'm serious. If you're looking for someone to run it, I'm certainly interested."

And she was, but now she had other matters to deal with. She listened to Ryan before replying, "I'm on my way back to the station."

CHAPTER TWENTY-SIX

I t was late afternoon by the time Keya arrived at Cirencester police station, and she was relieved that many of the support staff and some of the police officers had already left.

When she glanced into Inspector Evans' team room, it was empty and glancing across at his office she noticed the blinds were drawn. Was Ryan still working in there? Quietly, she made her way across to the office door and knocked softly.

There was no reply, but she thought she heard movement from the other side.

"Ryan, is that you? It's Keya," she whispered loudly.

In response, the door opened and Ryan ushered her in before looking around the outer room, checking if anyone had seen them.

"Why are you hiding?" asked Keya inside the office.

"Shh. Not so loud. Sergeant Unwin has been stalking about and I heard him asking for me, so I can run errands for him." Ryan sat down again at the inspector's desk, Tariq's laptop open in front of him.

"But I thought you agreed with Inspector Evans to work on Tariq's computer."

"I did, but I'd rather not explain that to Sergeant Unwin, and I don't want any interruptions, as I'm struggling to crack the laptop's password."

Keya wondered if she was interrupting but asked, "Have you tried the obvious ones like his name, and that of his parents and siblings?"

"Of course, and variations of them, but none of them worked." Ryan looked up and asked, "Where do you keep your passwords?"

"At the back of one of my notebooks."

"I wonder if Tariq did the same, or at least hid his somewhere. I might need to go back to his office and search it again, but if he downloaded them onto a memory stick, it's so small it could be hidden anywhere."

"Talking about books and hiding things, did you work out what was on the pages hidden in the leather encased Qur'an?"

Ryan leaned back and replied, "To be honest, I haven't had a chance to look. As soon as I finished checking the dagger and scabbard for fingerprints, I got to work on this laptop."

"Where is the Qur'an?"

"In a box beside my desk, but if you go and get it, be careful nobody sees you."

Keya opened the office door an inch and peered out. The coast was clear. She dashed across to Ryan's desk, lifted the lid off the plastic box and was just reaching for the leather case when she heard Sergeant Unwin's voice.

She grabbed the case but as she did so, she knocked the box and heard it fall to the floor as she rushed back inside the inspector's office, closing the door behind her.

"Wh …"

"Shush," whispered Keya, placing the leather case on his desk, and returning to the closed door.

"What was that?" she heard Sergeant Unwin ask.

"Just that box falling on the floor," replied Inspector Evans.

Keya looked back at Ryan, who tugged his collar.

"On its own?" pressed Sergeant Unwin.

"Well, I can't see anyone else here. Now, Sergeant, about Dotty Sayers."

"You'll have to speak to the chief inspector," Sergeant Unwin interjected.

"I have tried, but he's out and nobody seems to know where, or when he'll be back. So, as his sidekick, I'll have to speak to you about it. I'm not sure what vendetta you have against Dotty …"

"I don't know what you mean." Sergeant Unwin sounded defensive.

Ryan's eyes had widened, and he was listening intently, the laptop forgotten for the moment.

"Sergeant, I'm not questioning your actions, even though I think them hasty. You did find Dotty at the scene of the crime and the missing painting in her car. But there is no other evidence. No witnesses, nothing to connect her to the victim, and no fingerprints on the murder weapon. I'm surprised her solicitor isn't pressing for her release unless … you haven't told him about the fingerprints."

Keya stood by the closed office door, but she was able to peer through a crack and saw Sergeant Unwin bow his head.

"The problem is, Sergeant, while you concentrate on compiling evidence against Dotty, you're missing vital pieces of information which could incriminate the real killer. That painting, for instance, what have you discovered about it?"

"Only what Sergeant Varma found out," admitted Sergeant Unwin.

"It's a red herring, lad, a misdirection, and it's working. Did Dotty have a motive to kill Tariq? Did anyone else?"

"I don't know," mumbled the sergeant, so faintly, Keya had to strain to hear him.

Keya couldn't see the inspector, but she could imagine him leaning back or rocking on his heels before he pronounced, "Sergeant, I don't want to interfere with the chief inspector's case, especially as he outranks me, but you work for me, and this is a homicide which brings it under my jurisdiction, not the chief inspector's.

"I've kept my nose out of his cases so far, but as the only suspect you have for any of them is Dotty Sayers, I think it's time to re-look at everything and let Dotty go. She is not a criminal mastermind. But she is a nosey and astute amateur sleuth and, at the moment, I'd like her on my side."

Impulsively, Keya opened the office door and clapped. "Well said, sir."

Sergeant Unwin's eyes widened, either in surprise, or confusion, or both. "What are you doing in there?" he asked in an uncertain tone.

"I gave PC Jenkins my office so he could quietly get on with some real police work and I presume Sergeant Varma was updating him after a busy day of investigation at Lemington Hall." Inspector Evans looked across at Keya and she nodded.

Sergeant Unwin took a deep breath and asked, "What have you found out?"

"All in good time, Sergeant," replied the inspector, turning his attention back to Sergeant Unwin. "For now, your task is securing Dotty's release. I don't care if it is with bail, and you set conditions for her return, if you think that will keep the chief inspector happy. Just let her go home."

"Yes, sir." Sergeant Unwin glanced at Keya, and behind her into Inspector Evan's office before turning and leaving the room.

Inspector Evans breathed in deeply and let out a long sigh. "I've allowed things to run off course for too long. Time to refocus these investigations."

Keya wondered exactly which investigations he was referring to but, before she had time to ask,

Ryan shouted, "I've got it."

Keya turned and stepped back into the office. "Got what?"

"The laptop password, and others, although I need to work out what they are for. And I think I've found various company and bank accounts. They were on those papers you found hidden in here." Ryan lifted up the empty leather case as Inspector Evans joined them.

Keya moved inside the office and perched on the spare desk.

"That sounded like a shout of progress. What have you found?" asked the inspector, eyeing the case Ryan held.

"Keya found this in Tariq's office and hidden inside it were some sheets of paper. I've discovered a list of his passwords, including the one which unlocks this laptop."

"That's good work. Do you want to continue this evening or start afresh in the morning?"

Ryan checked his watch. "I'll do another hour or so if Keya, Sergeant Varma, is happy to keep me company. I might need her help."

Keya wasn't sure what technical help she could provide, but she wanted to check her official emails and write up her report of the day's activities.

"Very well. I'll go and check on Sergeant Unwin."

Inspector Evans left his office, and Keya clicked open the computer on his spare desk and entered her account and password details.

"There were several messages asking her if she'd attend parish council meetings, or hand out prizes at local clubs and charities, or attend schools to give her road safety demonstration. She enjoyed working in the community with the local residents, but was this the pinnacle of her police career?

Absent-mindedly, she clicked open the next email and her attention was caught by a reference to an ancient headless limestone statuette. The report was an update from one issued the previous week about the statuette's theft from a private collection in Bristol. A young man had been caught on a nearby CCTV camera and the local police were asking if anyone recognised him.

Keya magnified the image of the man. It looked like Billy Edwards, who she'd first encountered with Dotty at the Cotswold Antique Fair. He made money by buying an object cheaply at one stall and selling it to another stallholder at a higher price. Sometimes, a considerably higher price.

"Ryan, would you mind having a look at this for me?"

Ryan stood up and walked the few paces to the desk where Keya was sitting.

"Do you recognise him?" Keya asked.

"It looks like Billy Edwards. What's he done?"

Keya returned to the article and showed him the image of the statue. "He's suspected of stealing that from a house in Bristol."

"Why? It doesn't look very valuable. The head's missing and it's cracked."

Ryan was about to walk away when Keya read, "It dates back to the earliest known civilisation in southern Mesopotamia, from around 2,500 years BC. Wow, that's old."

"Where is southern Mesopotamia in modern terms?" asked Ryan.

"I'm not sure."

Ryan leaned over Keya and tapped her keyboard, and a map appeared on the screen. "South-central Iraq," he confirmed.

"Is that a coincidence or …?"

"You mean, is another ancient object embarking on the long journey to The Iraqi Museum in Baghdad?"

"Exactly, but how did you know about that?"

"I've read the reports, and I've heard Dotty mention it several times."

Keya leaned back. "Mrs Johnson, the housekeeper at Lemington Hall, mentioned today that Billy Edwards ran errands for Tariq. Do you think this was one of those errands?"

"It could be," agreed Ryan. "Let me get back to the laptop. I might be able to find out more once I've worked through Tariq's files."

Keya considered calling Avon and Somerset Police but wondered if someone else from the station might have already contacted them. She checked the distribution list and found Chief Inspector Ringrose's email on it. Would he know about Billy after the Roger Dewhirst case, when Billy was one of the suspects?

Instead of calling, Keya sent an email to Somerset and Avon Police explaining who Billy Edwards was and that the theft of the statuette might be linked to other cases she was working on. Which was partly true. Then she decided it was time to write her report.

She was part way through it, at the point where Jarrod found Sir Reginald's stolen painting, when she realised she should have brought the painting back with her. "Oh no," she cried. "What if it's gone to London?"

"What if what's gone to London?" asked Ryan, looking up from the laptop.

"The painting of the Betrayal of Jesus, which we found at Lemington Hall."

"Really? So we were right. Tariq was at Sir Reginald's, pretending to be dead, and he did steal the painting."

"It looks like it."

"You should tell the inspector," suggested Ryan. "It's another piece of evidence against Dotty which no longer stands up."

"What is?" asked Inspector Evans as he entered his office.

"Sir Reginald's painting, which we found at Lemington Hall." Keya looked down at the desk as she admitted, "But I forgot to collect it and I'm afraid it'll have been packed up with the rest of the collection and moved to London."

"Just a minute." Inspector Evans left them and returned several minutes later carrying a brown paper package in the shape of a picture. "Jarrod Willcox left this at reception. Would you like to open it?" he asked Keya as he placed it on the desk in front of her.

"Can you? You know how clumsy I can be, and I don't want to damage it."

Using his pen knife, Inspector Evans cut off the wrapping paper to reveal Sir Reginald's painting. Leaning over, he considered it in silence for several minutes before stating, "Judas Iscariot betrayed Jesus for thirty pieces of silver. I wonder what the modern day equivalent is?"

He stood up and said to Keya, "I'll be back in a bit," and lifting the painting, he carried it away, leaving Keya and Ryan to their work.

After another fifteen minutes, Keya filed her report and yawned. "I'm finished. How about you?" She looked across at Ryan.

"I've accessed Tariq's files, but I don't understand their contents. I think I need to start again tomorrow with a clear head. But first, I need to send some images I found of smudged fingerprints to a professor at Birmingham University."

"Why?" asked Keya, her brow furrowed.

"Just an idea I had."

"Good news," announced Inspector Evans as he reappeared in the office doorway.

"Dotty is being released as we speak. She will be required to return to the station tomorrow afternoon, which was the condition Chief Inspector Ringrose placed on her release. Even with a complete lack of evidence, he was refusing to let her go until I showed Sergeant Unwin Sir Reginald's painting and explained that it had been discovered at Lemington Hall.

So well done for finding it, Sergeant, as it secured her release." He gave Keya a satisfied nod.

"That was down to Jarrod and Finn. They found the painting."

"But you asked them to assess the collection. I call it good teamwork."

Inspector Evans smiled proudly at Keya and Ryan. "But for a team to perform at its best, it needs rest and sustenance. I reckon you'll both receive phone calls shortly, which will deal with the latter, so pack up your things and we'll continue in the morning."

Inspector Evans stared at Tariq's laptop and frowned. "But I don't think we should leave that here, even if I lock my office. I'll take it with me, which I know goes against the rules, and you take the sheets of paper you found and keep them safe. Sergeant Varma, you take the Qur'an and its leather case. I may be paranoid, but for the time being, watch yourselves. Now go and enjoy the celebrations with Dotty."

"What celebrations?" Keya asked as her phone rang.

CHAPTER TWENTY-SEVEN

When her cell door opened in the late afternoon, Dotty expected her microwave ready meal supper to be brought in. She was grateful to Ryan for passing on Keya's suggestion about the vegetarian options, as her lunch had been far more palatable than the chicken curry the previous evening.

"I'm afraid there's a delay with your supper, so I brought you a cup of tea instead, and a Kit Kat from Inspector Evans."

Dotty's surprise must have shown on her face as Sergeant Rowbottom smiled as he handed her the cup and the chocolate bar. "I know the inspector can be a grumpy old so-and-so, but like I tell everyone, his bark is worse than his bite, and all he wants is to see justice done. You've been all right by yourself this afternoon?"

Sergeant Rowbottom glanced at the open books and jottings on the notepad Aunt Beanie had given Dotty.

Dotty gave a small laugh. "There are places I'd rather be, but at least I've had the opportunity to think without being disturbed."

"Apart from that lad we brought in earlier, but he seems to have calmed down now. I'll pop in again soon," Sergeant Rowbottom assured her as he closed the cell door behind him.

Her interview in the morning with Sergeant Unwin hadn't progressed her examination of Tariq's case and she doubted the sergeant had made much progress.

But at least she'd been shown the murder weapon. It looked very similar to a dagger she'd seen in the office of her late husband's regimental commanding officer. A dagger which she thought had disappeared and reappeared in the National Museum of Iraq.

She'd expected to be interviewed again this afternoon and wondered if it was a good or bad thing that she hadn't. Unfortunately, she was still stuck in her cell, and it didn't look as if she was being released any time soon.

She sipped her tea - fragrant and not stewed like the brew in the morning - and snapped a finger off her Kit Kat. As she leaned back against the cell wall and savoured the chocolate, she thought that the smallest things could be comforting when you were denied them.

She'd started reading the history of Iraq, wondering why Jarrod had given it to her, and had discovered a note he'd scribbled about the Kazem family. It explained how they'd come to prominence before the Second World War but moved to Jordan in the early 1950s with their accumulated wealth.

So as she expected, Tariq Kazem had a connection to Iraq, even if it was a historical one.

She'd been about to return the note to the book when she'd realised that on the other side there was an explanation about the use of the rook in chess. It explained that the rook was the second most important piece on the chessboard and could move any number of squares vertically or horizontally. It couldn't jump over pieces, but it could capture them. And rook is thought to originate from the Persian word Rokh, meaning chariot.

Dotty had picked up the pad of paper and scribbled notes about Tariq's family history. She'd also added a sentence about the rook as an important chess piece.

Then she'd picked up *The Art of the Con*, which had absorbed her attention for a couple of hours. Closing it, she cleared her mind and concentrated on all the cases she'd been involved with over the past year and a half, while working at Akemans.

On a fresh piece of paper she'd jotted down words and phrases which came to mind like antiques, forgeries, counterfeit furniture, auctions, Iraq, National Museum of Baghdad, smuggling, funds, stolen artefacts.

She'd then moved onto names and jotted down Tariq Kazem, Didier Vogt, Gilmore Chapman, The Fabulous Auction Boys, who ran an auction house in the Cotswolds, and Amanda Fernsby, who had been an auctioneer in Cirencester.

That was the progress she'd made when Sergeant Rowbottom had brought her the tea and Kit Kat. She wondered what her friends were doing and if they were trying to help her. Were they making any progress?

She continued her musing until the cell door opened and Sergeant Rowbottom reappeared. He was grinning. "I told you Inspector Evans is a good egg. He's spent the last half an hour persuading Sergeant Unwin and Chief Inspector Ringrose, wherever he is, that you should be released due to a lack of evidence."

The elderly sergeant stepped into the cell and lowered his voice as he revealed, "Young Ryan checked the murder weapon and your prints weren't on it. Of course, the sergeant argued that you could have worn gloves, but it means there is no physical evidence linking you to the crime, or at least that's what the inspector argued.

"I need to formally process you and you will be released on bail, a nominal amount of £100, and required to return for further questioning tomorrow afternoon."

"What further questioning?" asked Dotty. "I've been sitting here all afternoon."

Sergeant Rowbottom smiled weakly at her. "I think it's just a condition, so they can keep an eye on you, so to speak."

Dotty stood and gathered up the books, paper, and pencils. She was being released and should be grateful to Inspector Evans. And a lot could happen between now and the following afternoon.

CHAPTER TWENTY-EIGHT

"Welcome home," cried Aunt Beanie as she threw her arms around Dotty.

Standing in the warmth of the older woman's embrace in the kitchen at Meadowbank Farm, Dotty finally felt herself relax.

Norman entered the kitchen, carrying Dotty's green canvas overnight bag and a plastic bag containing the books Jarrod had lent her.

"Everything go smoothly?" Aunt Beanie asked Norman.

"It did. Although that young sergeant I thought I liked, Nick, looked at me as if I was a bailiff removing his treasured possessions."

"Thank you for putting up the bail money. I'll repay you as soon as I visit a cash machine," Dotty said.

"No need. The police will repay me soon enough. It's not as if you're a flight risk." Aunt Beanie raised her eyebrows at Dotty, who smiled weakly.

"Meow."

Dotty bent down and picked up Earl Grey. "Have you missed me?" she asked as she stroked him.

"Now, I've invited everyone over, and Keya and Ryan are collecting supper from Kuki, so you don't have to worry about cooking. How about a glass of chilled Prosecco? I put a couple of bottles in the fridge."

"Beanie," growled Norman.

"Thank you, that's really kind, but I don't feel like celebrating just yet," admitted Dotty. "There are still so many unanswered questions, including who killed Tariq, and it wouldn't surprise me if Sergeant Unwin hauled me back into the station tomorrow morning to question me about another crime he thinks I'm responsible for."

Aunt Beanie looked serious. "I don't think that's going to happen. Keya told me Inspector Evans has reined in Sergeant Unwin and he's taking over all the cases where there's been a death. I expect Chief Inspector Ringrose will continue to have responsibility for the antique thefts, but he'll be short staffed now he can't use Sergeant Unwin, unless he trusts Keya or me enough to work with him."

"I hadn't expected the inspector to be an ally," mused Dotty.

"Then you don't know him very well. I asked him to join us tonight, but he politely declined. I guess it is one thing securing your release, but quite another to be seen celebrating it when he has an open murder case. And Gerald also sends his apologies. He's war gaming, whatever that means."

"You're here," cried Keya as she rushed into the kitchen. "I can't hug you as my hands are full, but I'm so happy to see you. And I'm sorry I didn't visit you in your cell, but I was busy at Lemington Hall and …"

"Keya, slow down," interrupted Aunt Beanie. "We've all evening to discuss today's events. Hi, Ryan."

Ryan appeared, carrying a cardboard box.

"How many people did Kuki cook for?" asked Norman in a bemused voice.

"She said she made enough to fuel Dotty's brain cells for a few days," explained Keya.

"So we're just waiting for Ozzie," declared Aunt Beanie.

"I'm here," called Ozzie. "Can someone open the door for me?"

Ryan, who had deposited his box on the kitchen worktop, opened the door for Ozzie, who was carrying two bottles of wine. "To help us think," she grinned.

Aunt Beanie took charge. "Norman, can you and Ozzie sort out drinks, while the rest of us organise the food? We should tuck in while it's hot."

Dotty placed Earl Grey on the floor but refused Aunt Beanie's usual seat at the head of the table, preferring to sit in the middle, opposite Keya.

Ozzie sat between Keya and Norman, and Ryan opposite her, next to Dotty.

"Let us pray," proposed Aunt Beanie when they were all seated. "Dear Lord, thank you for your blessing and for ensuring that justice is done and Dotty is back with us to enjoy this fabulous meal. Bless and watch over Cliff. Amen."

"Amen," muttered the others.

Norman raised his glass of red wine. "A toast to welcome Dotty home."

The others raised their glasses and chorused, "Welcome home."

"Let's hope it's not as short-lived as the last occasion," joked Dotty, knowing it was no laughing matter.

"We've had a busy and productive day, haven't we, Keya?" declared Aunt Beanie. "Do you want to bring everyone else up to speed?"

Keya recounted her initial meeting with Bob Wicks, the groundsman at Lemington Hall, and then with Mrs Johnson, including the comments the housekeeper had made later in the day and at lunch.

"Norman did an excellent job photographing the paintings and interior of Lemington Hall," complimented Keya.

"He certainly did," agreed Ozzie. "And I'll be using some of them for an article I'm writing, now I have the inside scoop on the confiscation of Tariq's art collection. If it's OK to report on it?" Ozzie looked from Dotty to Ryan.

"Why shouldn't it be?" asked Dotty.

"Because I made it a condition of Ozzie joining us that she wouldn't write anything that might impact on you or the case."

Dotty placed her hand on Ryan's arm. "That's very sweet of you, but I don't see why Ozzie can't write about the art. I'm interested to know why it's been confiscated, and I can't see it will do me any harm."

"Quite the opposite," insisted Aunt Beanie, "since Sir Reginald's stolen painting was in the collection."

"What? Why did nobody tell me?" Wide-eyed, Dotty looked round the table.

"Because there's so much to tell you," replied Keya. "It was Ozzie who found the painting, and Jarrod confirmed it was Sir Reginald's. Although I left it at the hall, and he had to deliver it to the station for me."

"We've never doubted you, but Sergeant Unwin is a different matter," admitted Ryan.

"But even an idiot can work out that if Dotty saw Tariq, alive or pretending to be dead at Sir Reginald's with a painting, and that painting disappeared and was found hidden away with other paintings at Lemington Hall, then it was Tariq who stole it, not Dotty," proclaimed Ozzie.

"But why did he steal it?" asked Norman in a measured tone.

It was not a question Dotty had considered.

Keya asked, "Why were you picking it up, Dotty? Was it being sold at Akeman's next auction?"

That was another question Dotty hadn't asked herself. "I don't know. David didn't tell me."

"Do you mean, Keya, that if the painting was going under the hammer, Tariq could have bought it legitimately at the auction in two weeks' time?" asked Aunt Beanie. "But if David had lined up a private buyer, then Tariq would have lost his opportunity to acquire it."

"I think so, although I'm not sure why Tariq would want it. He seemed more into his modern art," replied Keya.

Dotty was impressed by her friend's observations on Tariq's collection.

"What about the paintings in the snooker room?" queried Ozzie. "They were all dark and formal."

"I know what Keya means. There were no other religious paintings," stated Aunt Beanie.

"Yes, that's it," agreed Keya.

"But the important point for me is that Sir Reginald's painting has been recovered from Lemington Hall, pointing the finger at Tariq as the thief and clearing me," declared Dotty.

"That's right," confirmed Ryan.

"So if you're no longer implicated, I can write about the theft," exclaimed Ozzie. "Which adds a fascinating angle to my article. I may even have to write two or three, depending on what else I find out about the collection."

"I can tell you that the Betrayal of Jesus wasn't the only stolen painting in it," announced Aunt Beanie.

"Really, what else was stolen?" Ozzie had removed her phone and placed it on the table. "You don't mind me recording this, do you?"

"Just the part about stolen paintings," cautioned Ryan.

"Do you have the photos Norman took?" asked Aunt Beanie.

"I can access them via my phone," confirmed Ozzie.

"You do that while I find the relevant files." Aunt Beanie left the table and searched through a stack of files piled on the armchair Uncle Cliff used to sit in. She eventually pulled out two of them.

Returning, she placed the thinner file on the table and opened it to reveal two landscape paintings.

Ozzie looked at them before scrolling through her phone. "These?" She pushed her phone towards Aunt Beanie.

"Yes, those are the ones," confirmed the older woman.

Dotty leaned across the table and picked up the phone, and she and Ryan considered the photos of the paintings.

"They were stolen five years ago from a house in Oxfordshire," explained Aunt Beanie. "Now this second folder is a list of all the paintings which have been stolen nationally during the past two years. Do any of them match the ones Norman photographed?"

Aunt Beanie slid the folder across the table to Ozzie, who took her phone back from Dotty and began swiping across it.

"This portrait," she tapped the image of a young woman, "and this horse," she tapped another image, "and this still life."

"Goodness!" Aunt Beanie grabbed the folder and looked at the last image Ozzie had tapped. "I think you and I should sit down later and run through this properly. And I have files of missing paintings going back ten years."

Ozzie grinned. "This is a real scoop."

CHAPTER TWENTY-NINE

D otty looked across the pine kitchen table at Keya and asked, "Have you found out anything else?"

"Oh, yes," Keya enthused. "So Tariq had a number of visitors before he died, including Didier Vogt, David Rook, and Billy Edwards."

"I think I told you, Keya, that I saw Didier Vogt yesterday morning when he visited Akemans." Was it really yesterday? So much had happened since she'd spoken to him.

"How is he?" asked Aunt Beanie, a note of concern in her voice.

"He put on a brave face, but I had the feeling he was rather sad and … what's the word? … disillusioned, although I couldn't say why exactly. Selling up and moving to France can't be easy for him or his girls."

"It's the sensible thing to do," reasoned Aunt Beanie. "So hard for him looking after the twins on his own and with all the memories his house holds. A fresh start will benefit them all."

Dotty glanced across at Keya, who was only just controlling her urge to speak, and apologised, "Sorry, I interrupted you."

"No, no. I wanted to hear about Didier, but you might find this interesting. Mrs Johnson said Billy Edwards had been running errands for Tariq. And this evening I saw a report from Somerset and Avon police about a stolen statuette and an image of Billy caught on a nearby CCTV camera."

"Are you still on the regional distribution list?" asked Aunt Beanie. "I seem to have been taken off."

"I am, and so is the chief inspector. I'm not sure if he's following the theft, as this was an update to the original report sent out last week."

"So you think," clarified Dotty, "that Billy Edwards stole a statue on Tariq's orders. Was there anything special about it?"

"Only that it was over four thousand years old, which is why, as Ryan pointed out, it is cracked and missing its head."

Ryan bowed his own head.

"But it's originally from a region which used to be part of Iraq. What's the betting it's currently on its way to the National Museum of Iraq, just like the copper jug stolen at Cotswold Antique Fair?"

"If you're correct," discerned Aunt Beanie, "then Tariq was linked to, or even organising, the smuggling of ancient artefacts back to Iraq."

"Which is what you and I, and I think Keya, have suspected for a while," voiced Dotty.

"I'm not sure I was with you at the beginning, but Ryan and I have both been wondering about the link with Iraq, since it's something you keep mentioning. But why is that?" asked Keya.

Dotty leaned back. "Do you remember the first case I was caught up with when I joined Akemans?"

"Yes, because the inspector asked Akemans to send someone to identify the victim's possessions, and they sent you," remembered Keya. "At the same time, you were helping David catalogue your late husband's regiment's assets."

"Exactly, and one object, which the commanding officer said he'd bought from a lady in Iraq who needed money to feed her family, was a Persian jambiya dagger."

"I don't remember that," admitted Keya.

"It was the first time I read about items looted in the 2003 Iraq War being returned to Bagdad and displayed in one of the museums. I think someone took that dagger and smuggled it back to Iraq."

"Who?" asked Ozzie, her eyes wide, and Dotty realised she sensed another story.

"You can't write about any of this. Not yet, anyway, as it's pure conjecture. But the article, where I read about the dagger, was in a magazine which fell out of Gilmore's coat pocket."

She remembered the night. It was a special viewing of the contents of a country house and the attractive Gilmore Chapman, an art expert from a prestigious London auction house, had given her that look over his champagne flute, and she'd blushed. But that was all in the past now.

"So you think Gilmore was involved?" Keya's eyes widened.

"It's possible, isn't it? Let's face it, he wasn't the man I thought he was," sighed Dotty.

Aunt Beanie scowled. "Gilmore was charming, but I don't think the painting scam he went to prison for was originally his idea. I suspect he copied it from someone else. Someone with more brains and shrewdness than Gilmore. Someone who Gilmore worked for." She paused before adding, "So Gilmore may have been instructed to steal the commanding officer's dagger."

Ryan cleared his throat, but his cheeks reddened as everyone turned to look at him. "Sorry."

"Go on, lad," encouraged Norman.

"Well, it's just that what you've said is just conjecture. But what if we find Billy, and he is involved in the same smuggling operation? Won't he be able to lead us to the ringleader?"

Norman looked confused. "But you said Billy was working for Tariq. So wasn't he the top man?"

"Oh," muttered Keya, "You mean that one of Tariq's underlings stabbed him in the back … or in this case the heart … to get control of his criminal gang."

"That's one possibility," agreed Aunt Beanie.

"The other being that Tariq was just a subordinate, and for some reason the leader wanted to get rid of him. But why would they?" asked Dotty.

Ozzie glanced at the folders still on the table. "Because he was stealing for himself. And Sir Reginald's painting was the final straw as you saw him at the crime scene, even though the police dismissed your claims."

"And that's why he had to be terminated!" exclaimed Keya.

Norman nodded. "That actually makes sense, you know."

"So now we just need to find out who the big bad boss is," enthused Keya.

"There are lots of files on Tariq's laptop," Ryan said. "I'll work through them tomorrow to see what I can discover."

"That sounds like a good plan, Ryan. Is there anything else you or Keya found today which needs following up?" asked Dotty.

"I'm looking into something after testing the dagger and its scabbard for fingerprints, but I doubt it'll provide any answers."

"What sort of thing?" asked Dotty.

"Birmingham University has been researching techniques for identifying fingerprints on objects even when thin gloves are worn. In the article I read they were using latex gloves, but I've asked them about cotton ones, like those used by some antique experts when dealing with items which easily mark."

"I know the ones you mean," Aunt Beanie confirmed.

"Do you think Tariq's murderer wore gloves?" asked Dotty.

"Yes, as several of the fingerprints were smudged. But the mark which covered them looked more like a palm print than fingerprints."

"It sounds like a shot in the dark to me," Aunt Beanie remarked.

Ryan's face fell.

"But still worth a try," she added hastily.

Dotty tapped the table as she thought about Ryan's comments. "So if the murderer did wear gloves, where are they? If we can find them, there is technology to extract fingerprints from inside them, isn't there?"

"Definitely, although the police lab in Gloucester has a two-week backlog," Ryan explained.

"Tackle that problem if and when you find the gloves," instructed Aunt Beanie. "Keya, why don't you and Dotty return to the crime scene tomorrow to look for the gloves and anything else of relevance? And what about the perpetrator's vehicle? Did anyone see a car parked at or near the hall?"

"I spoke to Bob Wicks and Mrs Johnson and neither of them saw one, or any strangers hanging around. But I haven't had a chance to speak to anyone in the village yet," explained Keya.

"That might be something else to follow up tomorrow," suggested Aunt Beanie.

Dotty was reticent about returning to the crime scene, but at least she'd be with Keya, and it might be a good thing to deal with her anxieties now, rather than let them fester. She might also suggest to Keya that they walk to the village to interview people, and enjoy the fresh air. Had Keya mentioned a path through the wood?

"By the way, how did my car get back here?" asked Dotty.

"Norman drove it," replied Aunt Beanie.

"Thank you," said Dotty, turning to Norman.

"Talking of cars," Keya commented, "Tomorrow I'll also need to check how long it takes to drive between Lemington Hall and the house in Eaton Common where Marion and David Rook were playing tennis."

"Is that where they were on Wednesday afternoon? Interesting," mused Aunt Beanie. "Was it your idea to check their alibi?"

Keya shook her head. "No, Inspector Evans suggested it. I think he wants to check up on everyone who had a connection with Tariq."

"Good luck finding Didier if he's already left for France," commiserated Dotty.

"It's another long shot, but I could ask George to keep an eye out for him in Paris," suggested Aunt Beanie.

"I suppose Didier might show his girls the sights before they go to their grandparents," considered Dotty. She didn't mention that she had the grandparents' address. She had promised Didier but she knew that if he became a serious suspect in Tariq's death, it was a promise she might have to break.

"Exactly," agreed Aunt Beanie. "And I'll also speak to some of my contacts in Europe and find out if any of them have seen, or know of, Billy

Edwards." Aunt Beanie looked around the table. "Does everyone have their tasks for tomorrow?"

"I don't, but then I have to help Marion at Akemans," Norman explained. "And she'll be needing your assistance too, Dotty. There's a lot to do with George away."

"Tell her I'll be in on Monday, but I need to work on the case tomorrow, even if it's only for my own satisfaction," Dotty replied.

"Now if you lot want to tidy away and continue your chat, I'd like to go through the files of missing paintings with Ozzie," declared Aunt Beanie.

As she and Ozzie commandeered the end of the table, Dotty helped clear supper away.

"What time do you want to meet tomorrow?" she asked Keya.

Keya glanced across at Ryan. "Can we make it early? Say eight o'clock. So that I can be in the station in the afternoon to help Ryan. Wait for me at the village hall and I'll drive us both to the old stable yard."

Dotty nodded. "I'll see you there."

CHAPTER THIRTY

The following morning was Friday. Dotty thought it had been a long week, but hopefully she and her friends could find the answers to the riddle of Tariq's death.

The weather could only be described as grey. It was dull and slightly damp after overnight rain and it didn't lift her spirits as she parked in front of the white, single-storey, prefabricated corrugated iron village hall that served Lemington.

Keya drew up beside her and lowered the window. "Jump in," she called.

Dotty locked her car and climbed into the passenger seat of Keya's Ford Focus.

Keya handed Dotty her phone. "When I tell you, click go on the screen." She reversed out of the car park and as soon as she was on the road, she said, "Go," and drove forward.

"Are you timing the drive from Eaton Common?" asked Dotty.

"Yes. I'm doing it twice. On the way here, and then when I go back to interview the Tylers. I called and they're around all morning."

Keya drove out of the village before turning into the drive leading to Lemington Hall.

"So to check David's alibi, we need to see if he could drive to Lemington Hall and back again in half an hour, and have time to kill Tariq."

"Exactly," confirmed Keya. "And we're nearly there."

Keya parked in front of Tariq's office, and Dotty pressed stop on Keya's phone.

"I didn't drive super fast," admitted Keya as she took her phone, "But neither would David have done if he didn't want to draw attention to himself. Let's see, two minutes forty-five seconds from the village hall, added to the eleven minutes twenty-six seconds from the Tylers'. That is …"

"Fourteen minutes, eleven seconds," calculated Dotty. "So a return journey of just under twenty-nine minutes. If he'd driven faster than you, he could have made it to Tariq's office and back."

"But he needed time to kill Tariq and steal the painting. I think I'll let Inspector Evans decide if he thinks it possible and wants to pursue it further."

As they climbed out of her car, Keya said, "You better not come into the office again, in case you drop a hair or something which is later picked up and used as evidence against you. Why not have a look around the outbuildings, but be careful, some of them aren't in great condition."

Disappointed, Dotty watched Keya unlock and enter Tariq's office. She understood why her friend was protecting her. As she wandered away from the office, she noticed a pool of oil on the cobbled yard. She knelt down beside it. It looked fresh. Glancing around, she didn't see any more pools.

She wandered around the buildings. Some parts were still intact with wooden partitions separating the areas where horses once stood, while in other sections, the floor was littered with bird droppings and there were gaps in the roof where tiles had slipped or fallen off.

There was no sign of the buildings being used recently, although Tariq's killer could easily have hidden in one of them.

She wandered back across the cobbled yard as Keya was locking the office. "Anything?" asked Keya.

Dotty smiled regretfully and shook her head.

"I suppose the next thing to do is look for evidence of parked cars, although I'm not sure how."

"You said neither the groundsman nor housekeeper saw anything, which means nobody parked near the hall, so where else could a car have been left?" asked Dotty.

"In one of the tracks leading to the woods, although they couldn't be certain Bob Wicks wouldn't spot it."

"How far is it to walk through the woods to the village?"

"The footpath leads to the far side of the woods and turns towards Eaton Common. From there it's a few minutes' walk back to the village."

"And how long does it take overall?"

"I'm not sure. I've never walked that far," admitted Keya.

"Why don't we try it now? I feel like stretching my legs and I need some fresh air after my time in your police cells." Dotty looked up at the sky. "And we might even get some sunshine." The earlier clouds were thinning, and she spotted a small patch of blue sky.

"I'm not sure I have time," replied Keya.

"Are you worried about helping Ryan?"

Keya nodded.

"Look, he probably has his head buried in Tariq's laptop and I doubt either of us would be much help to him at the moment."

"You're right. And after the week we've both had, a walk would be pleasant. But I'm putting my wellies on. It rained hard last night."

Keya returned to her car as Dotty looked down at her feet, pleased she'd worn a pair of leather boots.

"Ready?" asked Keya. She wore black wellies and a small rucksack.

As Dotty and Keya left the old stable yard and walked up the drive towards the house, Dotty queried, "We're only going for a short walk. Why the rucksack?"

"I don't know how far it is and we might need water. Besides, I thought we could collect your car in Lemington and you can drop me back here. I don't want to leave mud in your car, so I've brought a pair of shoes to change into."

"You didn't need to, but thank you." Dotty smiled at her friend and then looked around her. "The wood is fenced off from the drive, so there's no obvious parking place along here."

Keya reached a gap in the fence. "This is where the path starts. If a driver wanted to, they could have hidden a car between the rhododendron bushes." A tall wooden sign told them it was one and a quarter miles to Lemington and three and a half miles to Eaton Common.

"Only a mile and a quarter to Lemington. That shouldn't take too long," remarked Dotty. She looked down at the wet ground. "I don't see any marks left by a parked car."

"No, but look at this."

Dotty joined Keya at the side of the path, where she'd squatted down beside a thin tyre tread left in the mud between two puddles. She said, "It's a knobbly tread, I guess for off-road and muddy conditions, but I'm not sure if it's from a motorbike or mountain bike."

Keya looked up at her. "And those new style bikes have fat tyres. I've seen people riding them along bridle paths. I'll take some photos and see what I can find out back at the station."

Keya removed her rucksack and took out a tape measure. She pulled out a short length, locked it in place and put it beside, and then across the tyre tread mark while she took her photos.

While she did that, Dotty wandered into the wood, admiring the large pink and purple blooms of the rhododendron bushes which lined the footpath.

"All done," declared Keya, catching up with her. "Oh, can I smell wild garlic?"

As they walked on, the rhododendrons gave way to an open area of woodland, the floor was covered with a carpet of pointed waxy green leaves and balls of spiky white flowers. The smell of the wild garlic was intense.

"I love spring," admitted Dotty. "It's the idea of new life, of nature waking up, of hope."

"I know what you mean," agreed Keya.

They continued to follow the footpath, talking about the Cotswolds in spring, until a floppy-eared, golden-brown cocker spaniel ran towards them.

"It must be great having this wood to walk your dogs. I can see why the villagers would be annoyed if the Kazems stop them using it."

"The Kazems don't mind walkers and dogs, if they keep to the footpath, but people have been treating the woods as their own and wandering wherever they like, and then there are the bikes."

A middle-aged couple came into sight calling, "Bonny. Bonny."

The cocker spaniel bounded back past Keya and Dotty.

When Dotty and Keya reached the couple, the man said, "It's good to see the police taking the issue of the woods seriously. You know Bob Wickes tried to block the entrance to the path again."

Keya replied, "I don't think that's the case. He's happy for you to use the footpath but he put a stile up to stop bikers using it."

"Aye, well, that didn't last long," replied the man, looking down at his feet.

"Have you seen any bikes or motorbikes in here recently?" asked Dotty. "We found some tyre tracks."

The woman shook her head. "They're not from our village. Some of us understand why a stile was erected, but perhaps you can suggest a gap next time to allow dogs through?"

"I'll pass the message on," agreed Keya.

The man said, "We held a village meeting and agreed that only walkers will use the wood for the moment, and we'll keep to the path. Hopefully, once we can prove to the new owners that we are responsible, they'll let the children use the wood during the holidays. It's a safe place for them to run about and they love making dens and playing hide and seek."

Keya looked surprised. Maybe because the inhabitants of Lemington had finally agreed on something sensible. "I'd be happy to arrange a meeting between representatives from both sides to discuss that," suggested Keya.

"So does that mean that none of the kids, and no bikes or motorbikes from the village are using the woods at the moment?" asked Dotty.

"That's right," agreed the woman. She let go of Bonny, who bounded along the path towards Lemington Hall.

"Bonny," called the woman as she stepped past Keya and Dotty.

The man followed but stopped and looked back. He said, "But now you mention it, I'm sure I heard a motorbike on Wednesday afternoon when I was planting bulbs in the garden, or was that Tuesday?" He turned and followed his wife and dog along the path.

Twenty minutes later, Dotty and Keya arrived at the village hall, having walked through the wood and along the footpath back through the village.

"Thank you," declared Keya. "I needed that walk, especially as I'll be spending the afternoon at the station filing reports, following up leads, and helping Ryan." She grinned at Dotty and added, "But I'm enjoying working on a proper case. Where shall I put my boots?"

Keya removed her muddy walking boots and slipped on a pair of shoes as Dotty unlocked the car. "In here," suggested Dotty, opening the back and pulling a plastic bag out of a side compartment. She kept spare ones in the car for shopping. As she flattened it on the floor for Keya's boots, a white glove fell out.

"Is that your glove?" asked Keya.

"No, I don't wear gloves for the antiques I handle. Do you think the perpetrator dropped it when they hid the painting in my car?"

"It's a possibility. I'll take it back to the station." Keya removed an evidence bag from her rucksack as she remarked, "We could have saved ourselves a walk if we'd looked in your car first." But she smiled as she sealed the bag.

Keya carefully placed her boots on the plastic bag and asked, "Would you like to visit the Tylers with me on my way back to the station?"

Dotty nodded. "Yes, please."

CHAPTER THIRTY-ONE

The road to Eaton Common was new to Dotty, and she was surprised when Lemington Hall's wood gave way to rocky heathland, where cows grazed peacefully on tufty grass.

Driving her own car, she followed Keya into the small village and turned left down a winding drive to a small single-storey stone cottage, with a huge double storey extension comprising a wooden frame with glass walls. She also spotted the tennis court and a row of single-storey stone and wooden buildings.

"This is nice and tucked away," commented Keya as they walked towards the front door, which Mrs Tyler opened after they'd rung the bell.

"I'm Sergeant Varma," introduced Keya. "My consultant and I are here to ask you some questions about Wednesday afternoon."

"Of course, you phoned earlier," replied Mrs Tyler. She wore no make-up, and her pink shirt was tucked neatly into blue denim jeans. She was in good shape for someone Dotty judged to be in her early sixties, and she could imagine Mrs Tyler running around the tennis court. "My husband's out in the garage. I was just about to take him a cup of coffee."

"We're happy to speak to you both out there, if that suits," suggested Keya.

Dotty and Keya followed Mrs Tyler through a neat garden where yellow daffodils were still flowering, alongside purple hyacinths and purple, yellow and white crocuses.

"My husband's semi-retired and when he's not working from home, he's outside tinkering with old cars and motorbikes," explained Mrs Tyler. She carried a cafetière and a jug of milk while Dotty and Keya carried mugs.

They arrived at a large garage where two of the three overhead doors had been raised. Inside there was a vintage black car and two other vehicles in various stages of repair. A muddy red motorbike was propped against a side wall.

"Hudson, the police are here to ask us some questions about Wednesday," said Mrs Tyler.

A man wearing blue overalls, his experienced face smeared with oil, appeared from behind another motorbike, holding some sort of hand tool.

"Yes, of course. Is that coffee, Deidre?" asked Mr Tyler.

Mrs Tyler began pouring cups of coffee as Dotty said, "You don't seem surprised to see us."

"That's because Marion called and explained that the police needed to check the alibis of anyone connected with Tariq Kazem," replied Mr Tyler. "Of course, we knew she and David had supper with him the night before he died. Isn't it awful? Not that we were friends."

Mrs Tyler handed her husband a cup of coffee as he placed his tool on the concrete floor with a metallic clang.

Mr Tyler continued, "Of course I know of his father, but the family's new to the area and they aren't part of the social scene yet. But I'm not sure tennis is their thing."

"But Marion and her husband play, and they were here on Wednesday?" queried Keya.

"Yes, Marion has persuaded David to play this year, but he was very rusty to start with. We beat them in the two sets, only conceding a single game, didn't we, Deidre? I thought that was it as David took himself off. We'd just finished our break when he reappeared and suggested a third set. Said he'd given himself a good talking to, and it seemed to work. We only beat them by six games to four in the third set."

"How long was David away for, during the break?" Keya asked the crucial question.

"Twenty or Twenty-five minutes, not as long as half an hour I'd say." Mr Tyler wiped his free hand on the leg of his overalls.

"And how did he seem?" Keya enquired.

"Steely, grim, and determined. Just as I'd expect from someone who's competitive and has been convincingly beaten." Mr Tyler smiled proudly and lifted his chin.

As Keya continued her questioning, Dotty wandered around the garage, stepping over patches of oil. Behind the closed garage door, another car was concealed beneath a grey cover. Along the far wall, metal shelves supported vehicle parts, tools, and cans and containers. Nearest the door there was a tall plastic bin, the muddy leg of a blue overall draped over its side.

Dotty heard Keya say, "Thank you both for your help," and she returned to the garage entrance.

When Dotty and Keya reached their cars, Dotty said, "I might as well follow you to the station. I have to present myself as a condition of my bail, in case Sergeant Unwin has any further questions."

"I'll see you there then," Keya replied.

CHAPTER THIRTY-TWO

Dotty didn't go straight to the police station when she arrived in Cirencester but settled herself in the Copper Kettle outdoor cafe, which she'd visited with Ryan and Keya at the beginning of the week.

It was just after two o'clock when she entered Cirencester police station and was greeted by Sergeant Rowbottom, who stood behind the Perspex screen in reception.

"Afternoon, Mrs Sayers. It's nice to see you at the front of the station, rather than at the back."

"And I could say the same about you." Dotty replied, smiling.

The sergeant smiled back and confided, "They like someone with experience on the front desk on Friday afternoons and over the weekend. I expect I'll have my hands full tomorrow. They're expecting you."

Dotty gulped but relaxed when Sergeant Rowbottom handed her a blue 'Visitor' lanyard. That was a positive sign. He buzzed open the reception door and led her straight to Inspector Evans' team room.

"I'll leave you with Ryan, if that's OK?" said the elderly sergeant.

"Yes, thank you."

Tariq's laptop was open on Ryan's desk, surrounded by files, sheets of paper, and a notepad which Ryan was scribbling on.

He put down his pen and looked up. "Sorry, I had to make a note before I forgot something. I'm glad you're here. Can you help me with some information I've found on Tariq's computer? Keya will join us once she's finished debriefing Inspector Evans."

Dotty looked across at the empty desks in the room and asked, "Where's Sergeant Unwin? I was expecting him to interview me."

"He's in Cheltenham, interviewing friends who Tariq stayed with last weekend." Ryan lowered his voice. "I'm not sure if the inspector is punishing him or just wants him out of the way. Anyway, have a look at these and see if you have any idea what they are." Ryan handed Dotty a sheet of lined paper on which he'd made various notes.

One section had several capital 'C's followed by a dash and different initials including L, NY, D and HK. Below it was S with similar initials, and above it, G with an L and NY. Dotty took the paper and sat down at a spare desk.

She searched for major auction houses on her phone. Christies in London had numerous international offices, including Dubai, New York and Hong Kong, as well as London, and so did Sotheby's. Gainfords had offices in London and New York.

She returned to Ryan, who looked up as she said, "I think this section is the offices of the leading auction houses. And these email addresses might have been used to open accounts."

"And the bottom section could be passwords." Ryan's eye shone. "Pull up a chair and I'll see if you're right. Let's start with one of the London accounts. Which do you suggest?"

"If they're in the same order, then the account details, email address and password for Gainfords' London branch is the third one down on each list."

Ryan found the account section on Gainfords' website and typed in the relevant information. 'Welcome back, Mr Kale' flashed onto the screen.

Ryan looked across at Dotty. "The account details worked, but this isn't Tariq's account."

Dotty glanced at the sheet of paper again. "He's unlikely to open all these accounts in his own name. It would raise too many red flags. Why don't you re-write your list with the relevant auction house, office, email address, and password? Then open the account and add the name that appears on it, and any contact details. Is there a balance on Mr Kale's account?"

Ryan tapped his keyboard. "No, but a painting sold in a recent auction for £12,300."

"Does it tell you where the money was sent?" asked Dotty.

Ryan continued typing as various screens flashed up on the laptop until he stopped at one called account details. "Is it that simple?" asked Ryan, looking at the screen and then some notes he'd made on the pad. He circled a long number. "This is the account number linked to the Gainfords' account."

"Can we work back and find the bank?" asked Dotty.

"I've narrowed it down to one of these. Lloyd's of London, Brooks McMillan's London branch, or ApaBank in Istanbul."

Inspector Evans' office door opened and Keya came out, followed by the inspector, who said, "Good work this morning, Dotty. I've called a colleague at the forensics lab in Gloucester and asked him for a favour.

"He's agreed, so Sergeant Varma is driving over with the glove found in your car and handing it to him in person. He promised to work on it straight away. And why are you grinning, constable?"

"That's it. I've identified the first back account, which is connected to an account at Gainfords in London in the name of Mr Kale. I don't know how much is in it, but by my reckoning there are another eight accounts listed here worldwide."

"Good work, Ryan," praised Inspector Evans.

Dotty's phone rang. "Hi," she answered, knowing from the call recognition it was Aunt Beanie. She stepped away from Ryan's desk.

"Are you at the police station?" asked the older woman.

"Yes."

"And they're not holding you for questioning again, are they?"

"No, in fact, I'm with Ryan, Keya, and Inspector Evans. And Ryan's just discovered some auction house and bank accounts on Tariq's computer."

"Excellent, but can you do me a favour?"

"Sure."

"Go up to my office, or at least what I used to call my office, and see if you can find the file for missing paintings from across the UK for five years ago. I don't seem to have it with me and Ozzie's popping back later so we can complete our check of Tariq's collection."

"OK, but I'm not sure I'll be allowed up there."

"Ask Ryan to escort you. Will you be home soon?"

"Yes, I think so."

Dotty finished her call and relayed Aunt Beanie's request.

"I'll take you up," offered Keya, "before I leave for the forensic lab."

Keya and Dotty climbed the concrete steps to the first floor. They had to turn on the lights when they entered Chief Inspector Ringrose's empty unit area.

"It's funny," admitted Keya, "but I feel so much more at home down with Inspector Evans' team."

Dotty thought the room had a neglected feeling about it. Submitting to a sudden impulse, she strode towards the chief inspector's office and tried the door handle. It turned in her grip and she pulled the door open and stepped inside.

"Dotty," whispered Keya. "You shouldn't be in there."

"Just give me a second."

The chief inspector's office was tidy and free of files and paperwork. She moved across to a pine bookshelf and picked up one of the framed photographs on top of it. It showed the chief inspector with a group of men who all wore cricket whites. The label on the frame read, 'Burford 1st XI Cricket Team'.

Another photograph showed the chief inspector presenting a trophy to a muddy rugby player, while one, which was clearly taken in the summer, was with a group of men and women and the label told her it was taken at Wimbledon. She was surprised to see an immaculately turned-out Marion Rook smiling at the camera from the front row.

"Have you finished?" hissed Keya. "I think I've found the file Aunt Beanie wanted."

"Yes," replied Dotty, as she turned away from the bookcase. She glanced at the chief inspector's desk as she passed, noticing the empty jotter pad beside his telephone and next to it a pen and a black knight chess piece. She didn't know why, but she reached over and picked up the chess piece, hiding it in her pocket before she left the office.

CHAPTER THIRTY-THREE

Before Dotty left Cirencester police station and drove back to Meadowbank Farm, she called Aunt Beanie.

"Have you found the file?" the older woman asked.

"Keya did, and I have it with me. I wondered if it would be OK to invite Edith over for an early supper. I have an urge to go through those papers I brought back from Ethel's house in Gloucester, which are currently gathering dust in your dining room. And I thought Edith might like to help me."

"That's a lovely idea. Will you pick up her?"

"Yes, I'll call the care home and check that's all right. If it is, I'll be back in an hour."

"This is so kind of you," gushed Edith as she clasped Aunt Beanie's hand in the kitchen at Meadowbank Farm.

Dotty had first seen Edith with her counterpart, Ethel, at an Antique Fair. David Rook had explained how the pair, who always wore yellow, persuaded buyers to buy certain antiques and, when they did, the two of them received a cut of the profits.

With their grey hair and aluminium walking sticks, which they sometimes forgot to use, they came across as a harmless pair of old ladies. And for the most part, they were.

But then Ethel had died at another antique fair and Worcestershire Police, within whose jurisdiction the case lay, attributed her death to a heart attack. Because Dotty had found Ethel with her scarf wrapped around her mouth and Keya had identified marks on the old lady's neck, they were convinced there had been foul play. But so far, they hadn't found any evidence to prove it.

Dotty placed the box of magazine cuttings she'd found at Ethels' house, when visiting it for the final time with Edith and Ryan, on the table. She felt she needed to conclude Ethel's case so the old lady could lie in peace.

"Edith, you sit down at the table with Dotty, and I'll make us all a cup of tea," suggested Aunt Beanie.

"Is that the box you were talking about?" asked Edith, staring at the dusty old box with faded images of apples on its sides. Dotty had explained in the car what she wanted to do.

"Yes, and it's the final part of Ethel's life we have. Are you ready to go through it?" Dotty asked.

"I am," replied Edith firmly.

The top articles were dusty but new.

Aunt Beanie glanced at them as she placed cups of tea in front of Dotty and Edith. "Are those the articles Ozzie wrote about Roger Dewhirst's death?"

"Yes," confirmed Dotty, removing the next newspaper clipping. The headline read, "Priceless mask stolen," and there was a picture of an African tribal mask.

Edith read, "A mask was stolen from a house in Cheshire in November and its estimated value was £25,000."

Dotty handed her another clipping, and she read, "At an antique fair in Huddersfield, a first edition Agatha Christie was stolen from a stall and later valued at £80,000." Edith frowned. "Ethel visited Yorkshire in October and she refused to tell me why, or who was paying for the trip. But she did bring me back some lovely soaps and hand cream."

There were other clippings about stolen items and then one which caught Dotty's attention as it mentioned Iraq. A set of six stamp seals had been stolen from an antique fair at Bedford racecourse in June the previous year.

"Aunt Beanie, do these ring any bells?" asked Dotty.

Aunt Beanie pulled a pan off the hotplate on the Aga and, wiping her hands on a towel, approached the kitchen table. She took the magazine clipping Dotty handed her. "No, this is news to me, but it fits the pattern of stolen items. We need to try to find out if these have been returned to the museum in Baghdad."

Edith took the article and, after reading it, said, "Ethel and I visited that fair. I didn't think it was worthwhile for the amount we made."

Aunt Beanie's phone rang, and she strolled across to the kitchen worktop to pick it up. "Hello."

After a pause she said, "Ja, Billy Edwards."

Dotty frowned and looked across at Aunt Beanie, wondering who she was talking to.

"Danka," said Aunt Beanie before finishing her call.

She approached the table and said, "That was the police in Antwerp, in Belgium. Billy Edwards has been spotted, and they want me to pass on their details to the relevant authority over here. Did Keya say Avon and Somerset are looking for him?"

"Yes. Do you want me to call Keya to give her Antwerp police's details?"

"Good idea," agreed the older woman, glancing at her watch. "I'll quickly jot them down as Ozzie will be arriving soon and then we can all have an early supper, before you drop Edith back. I wonder where Norman is? Working late, I guess."

The rest of the clippings were similar to those they'd already seen reporting stolen items, some going back five years.

"I'm not sure if this is helping Ethel," said Edith, "but she clearly had her reasons for saving all these articles."

Dotty reached into the nearly empty box, but instead of touching paper, her fingers brushed against plastic. They closed around a small object and she removed it and gasped. It was a black pawn from a chess set. She removed the black knight she'd found in Chief Inspector Ringrose's office.

"What have you got there?" asked Edith. "Ethel didn't play chess."

CHAPTER THIRTY-FOUR

Dotty allowed herself a lie-in on Saturday morning, although she was aware of Earl Grey yawning, stretching, and jumping off her bed. Clearly, he didn't agree with the concept of sleeping in if it meant missing breakfast.

She went back to sleep.

When she woke up again, the light was bright behind her daisy-print curtains. She yawned and stretched and decided to wander down to the farmhouse kitchen for a cup of tea before she showered and dressed.

Norman entered the kitchen just as she pulled the chrome kettle off the Aga hot plate.

He placed a pile of newspapers on the kitchen table and said, "It's a lovely morning. But make the most of it as rain's due this afternoon. I'm going to feed Agatha and milk Buttercup. Beanie should be down soon. I took her up a cup of tea earlier."

Dotty made herself a cup of tea and had just settled at the pine kitchen table when Aunt Beanie appeared. She looked refreshed and her burnt-orange scarf was tied in her trademark large bow at an angle on top of her head.

Turning the pages of one of the newspapers, a photograph of a painting caught Dotty's eye.

"Is that Ozzie's first article?' asked Aunt Beanie, peering over her shoulder. "She told me last night it should be in one of the national papers today and she has a follow-up piece tomorrow, which is why we needed to confirm all the stolen paintings in Tariq's collection."

"And were there many?" asked Dotty.

"Oh yes, twenty-three, including one of the Lucian Freuds, going back five years. And Jarrod also told me he has his doubts about the authenticity of some of the others. He's trying to persuade the police unit in London which is dealing with the collection to let him be a consultant. He's offered his services for free because he's so interested in it. What have you planned for today?"

"Nothing special." Dotty looked out of the full-height windows at the conservatory end of the kitchen and noticed how the sunshine highlighted streaks and rain splashes on them. "I think I'll start spring cleaning. Yes, that will help me put the last week behind me, so I can look forward more positively."

"Oh, I forgot to give you a letter which dropped through our letterbox yesterday."

Aunt Beanie collected a white envelope from a pile of papers on one of the worktops and placed it on the table beside Dotty.

Dotty stared at the blue University of Oxford logo on the front of the envelope.

"Aren't you going to open it?" queried Aunt Beanie.

"I think it's the results of my Appreciation of Modern Art Course." Dotty continued to hesitate.

"What are you waiting for?" Aunt Beanie said impatiently. "Let's find out how you did."

Cautiously, Dotty peeled back the envelope flap before removing a folded sheet of high-quality cream writing paper. She smoothed it down on the table, preparing to read it, but Aunt Beanie beat her to it.

"A merit. Congratulations. And the presentation ceremony is in two weeks' time. Who will you take with you?"

Dotty looked up at Aunt Beanie's hopeful expression. "I don't know. I hadn't thought about it. Who would want to come?"

"I would, and I'm sure Keya will want to celebrate with you, and I know Gilly wants an excuse to visit her old university. Let's organise a table."

Dotty started the spring clean in her bedroom, stripping the bed and flipping the mattress. How had so many cobwebs developed in the corners and at the edge of the ceiling without her noticing?

But she played the radio loudly and sang along to old, familiar upbeat tunes, and the morning flew by.

It was half-past one when Aunt Beanie called, "Are you joining us for soup and rolls?"

Dotty switched the radio off and called back, "Just coming."

"Very fetching," remarked Norman when she entered the kitchen.

Aunt Beanie removed a string of cobwebs from the scarf Dotty had wrapped round her head and commented, "Very practical, your scarf, although a little dull for my taste."

"I thought the hedgehogs on it were rather fun." Dotty smiled at the older woman as they sat down at the kitchen table.

Three large bowls of minestrone soup were waiting for them, and Norman placed a mound of filled rolls on the table as he joined them.

Dotty had just picked up her soup spoon when the kitchen door opened and Keya called, "Hiya."

"Help yourself to soup," directed Aunt Beanie, "but you'll need to sort out your own sandwich as the ones Norman has made are filled with ham or pâté."

As Keya sat down, she said, "I'm on my way home from the station." She looked across at Aunt Beanie. "Somerset and Avon police were grateful for your tip about Billy and are now liaising directly with the police in Antwerp."

"You see, I can still be useful. I don't need to be consigned to cold cases," retorted Aunt Beanie.

Keya slurped her soup and then said, "Talking of cold cases, or perhaps I should say lukewarm ones, Ryan made an interesting discovery yesterday. He decided to re-look at Ethel's case and realised that a white cotton glove had been found on the floor of the antique stall in the same room where you found Ethel."

Keya turned to Dotty. "I think everyone presumed it was the stallholder's, but as we're already testing a similar glove linked to Tariq's murder, Ryan persuaded Worcestershire Police to deliver the one they have to the lab in Gloucester, so it can also be tested for fingerprints. Inspector Evans' contact said he'll work on them both this morning, but he won't have the results until Monday."

"Did you see Ozzie's article in the paper this morning?" asked Dotty.

"Yes, Ryan showed it to me. I should be happy as it reflects well on my unit, but I don't feel we deserve the credit," complained Keya.

"But you called in Jarrod and his team. If you hadn't, the stolen paintings would never have been found," comforted Dotty.

"I suppose so," accepted Keya.

"Paintings," declared Aunt Beanie. "What's everyone doing in two Saturdays time?"

"I don't think I have any plans," replied Norman.

"Working, I expect," moaned Keya. "Why?"

"Dotty's achieved a merit in her art course, and I thought I'd organise a table and treat us all for lunch."

Keya's eyes brightened. "I like the sound of that," and turning to Dotty added, "well done."

Rain splattered against the conservatory windows.

"I said it was forecast rain," confirmed Norman dully.

Keya glanced out of the window and commented, "At least we had some exercise and fresh air yesterday, didn't we, Dotty?"

"Doing what?" asked Aunt Beanie.

"We walked from Lemington Hall to the village along the footpath through the wood."

"So there is a footpath. I'd heard rumours the Kazems were trying to stop the villagers accessing the wood."

"The groundsman erected a stile to stop bikers, but it annoyed the dog walkers who had to lift their animals over it so, somehow, it was broken. Bob Wicks, the groundsman, was all for blocking the path altogether, but I think I've persuaded him not to."

"Aren't there any other local footpaths they could use?" asked Aunt Beanie.

"I don't know," confessed Keya.

"Let's have a look on the Ordnance Survey map Aunt Beanie brought to me at the police station," Dotty suggested.

She found the map in the plastic bag she'd brought back from the station, along with Jarrod's books.

Norman cleared away the empty soup bowls and side plates providing room for Dotty to open the map out fully on the table.

"That's Lemington," said Keya, stabbing the map with her finger.

"And the hall is on its southern side." Dotty stared at the map, and then corrected herself. "Actually, while the entrance to its drive is south of the village, the house is southwest, separated by the wood."

"And here's the footpath." Keya trailed a dotted line with her finger. "See how it passes out of the wood on the far side before turning to Eaton Common."

Dotty followed the line of the footpath to the neighbouring village. "I think it passes below the Tylers' house," she mused.

"Which is theirs?" asked Keya.

"We turned left off the road and down a drive, so this one, or this." Dotty pointed to the two houses with her finger. "The footpath passes close to both of them. That signpost by the hall said it was three and a half miles to Eaton Common along the footpath, and further by road. But I didn't appreciate how much closer it was as the crow flies."

"What does that mean?" asked Keya.

"The drive by road is much further than the route a bird would take if it flew from the hall to Eaton Common," Dotty clarified.

Aunt Beanie and Dotty stared at the map. There was a polite knock on the kitchen door and Norman, who was washing up, dried his hands on the towel hanging from the rail in front of the Aga before opening it.

"I hope I'm not interrupting," said Jarrod as he walked into the kitchen, "but I wanted to talk to Beanie about the article Miss Winters wrote in the newspaper."

"Come in, Jarrod," called Aunt Beanie. "We're just refreshing our knowledge of the local area."

"Do you think someone on a bike would reach the hall before a person driving a car," Keya asked, still concentrating on the map.

"I'm not sure," replied Dotty. "Did we say fourteen minutes for the drive? If the signpost at the hall is right, and the distance by footpath between the two is three and a half miles, how fast would a cyclist need to go to beat the car?"

"Fifteen miles an hour," concluded Jarrod as he approached the table and looked down at the map. "Ah, I see," he muttered. "The topography of the area is relatively flat, but I imagine the path is twisty in places, particularly through the wood. I'd say a bike would struggle to beat a car even though the route is shorter."

Deflated, Keya sat down muttering, "We haven't found a motive for David Rook, anyway."

"What's this about?" asked Jarrod sharply.

Surprised, Dotty replied, "David and Marion were playing tennis in Eaton Common, but they had a break and David disappeared for between twenty and thirty minutes, depending who you speak to."

"He could have driven to Lemington Hall and back, just, in thirty minutes," explained Keya.

"But he would have needed extra time to steal the painting and kill Tariq if he was the murderer," added Dotty.

"And I'm sure the tennis party would have told you if he'd driven away in his car," pointed out Jarrod.

"Oh. I hadn't thought of that," conceded Keya. "At least that's a line of enquiry we can close."

The kitchen door opened again, and Ryan poked his head around it. "Is it OK to come in?"

"Join the party," Dotty heard Norman mutter.

"Take no notice of him, Ryan, we're delighted to see you, especially if you have an update on the case."

Ryan entered the kitchen and replied, "I do."

CHAPTER THIRTY-FIVE

Dotty folded up the Ordnance Survey map, which had been laid out on the kitchen table at Meadowbank Farm.

"I think I've worked out what's on the laptop, well, some of it," announced Ryan. "I've suggested to Inspector Evans that we send it to a forensic accountant to explain exactly what it all means, but he said it'll depend on the cost and his budget."

"I saw you were busy this morning, and I didn't want to disturb you, so what did you find?" asked Keya.

"Here, let me show you. The inspector said I could continue working on it at home this weekend if I wanted to."

As Ryan unpacked the laptop and his notes, Jarrod wandered across to speak to Aunt Beanie and Norman. "Is it always this social in your house?" he asked.

"More like an extension of the police station," retorted Norman. "Sometimes I think it would be nice to just sit down for an afternoon to watch the TV or play a game."

"What sort of game?" asked Jarrod. "Cards?"

"Yes, the old Duke and I played whist, but it's not ideal with only two players. We sometimes played draughts, but he also taught me a bit of chess. Can't say I'm much good at it, though."

"I've changed the password, so it's easy to access now," said Ryan as he tapped the laptop's keyboard.

"I wouldn't mind a game of chess," remarked Jarrod. "How about it, Norman?"

Norman frowned. "I'm not sure. The entrance hall needs a good clear out and …"

"Norman, stop procrastinating," admonished Aunt Beanie. "You've just said you'd like a quiet afternoon. You can't work outside as it's raining, and the hall can wait. It's been that way for the last four years. I think I know where the old chess set is kept."

"I'm in," reported Ryan, and Dotty and Keya pulled out chairs and sat down on either side of him.

"So we found the accounts held in cover names with the prominent auction houses," Ryan reminded them. "Tariq has been selling items for large sums, but only buying a few low-cost items, like this necklace last week."

Ryan clicked through to the image of a beaded necklace string with delicate gold leaf shapes hanging from it. The ends of some leaves were missing.

Jarrod joined them and examined the image. "That looks old. How much did it sell for?"

"Tariq bought it for £2,700," replied Ryan.

"That doesn't sound right. Which auction house was it?"

"Gainfords. They were auctioning off a private collection last week."

"Here we are," announced Aunt Beanie, returning to the kitchen.

"Come and have a look at this, Beanie," called Jarrod.

She strode across to the kitchen table and peered at the image on the laptop. "Oh, that's old, and very delicate. Is it for sale?"

"It sold last week for less than three thousand pounds and was bought by Tariq, or at least by whoever he's keeping accounts for."

"Why do you say that?" asked Dotty. "Don't you think Tariq was acting alone?"

"No, I don't," replied Jarrod. "He doesn't have the contacts to work something like that."

"Like what?" asked Keya.

"An open auction, where nobody bids and an expensive piece is sold at a bargain price," explained Jarrod.

"Another item heading to a certain museum in the Middle East, I suspect, Jarrod," concluded Aunt Beanie.

"I think you're right. Is that the chess set?" Jarrod asked.

Aunt Beanie and Jarrod moved into the conservatory section of the kitchen and positioned two chairs on either side of a small table.

"This is exquisite," remarked Jarrod, and Dotty looked across and watched them set out the chess pieces. "Carved ivory, and the bishop is an elephant, like the original sets."

"I've also found a document recording sums of money," revealed Ryan. "I think they represent payments, but I can't work out who to, although I did track some to Antwerp and Istanbul."

"Could that be for smuggling items to Baghdad?" asked Dotty.

"I wonder," said Aunt Beanie, as she and Jarrod joined them. "Tea or coffee, everyone?" she asked.

"Ready to play, Norman?" enquired Jarrod.

"Then there were numerous payments to someone, or something, called 'piyada', some to 'wazir' and others to a horse. And finally, a large sum was withdrawn from the account, perhaps by Tariq, I'm not sure, but the reference is 'chariot'."

"That doesn't make any sense," complained Keya.

"Actually, it does," remarked Jarrod as he walked past them. "Come with me."

Jarrod and Norman sat down at the chess set as Dotty, Keya and Ryan joined them. Jarrod was right. The small pieces were delicate and beautifully carved.

Jarrod picked up a white pawn and explained, "Chess is thought to have originated in India and then it spread to Persia, which is modern day Iran, but once covered many other countries including Afghanistan, parts of Iraq, and Turkmenistan. The Persians called the pawn a piyada, which meant foot solider. The knight was known simply as a horse, the rook or castle as a chariot and wazir, which means advisor, or one who bears the burden of office, in Persian chess referred to as the queen."

He moved the white pawn forward two squares.

Norman mirrored his move with a black pawn.

"So," considered Ryan, "those payments may be to people whose real identities are hidden behind the names of ancient chess pieces."

Jarrod moved a second pawn forward, setting it in the square beside the first pawn.

Dotty thought of the chess pieces she'd found in Ethel's box and the chief inspector's office, but she didn't think this was the time to mention them to the others. Two pieces could be a coincidence.

"The most entries were to piyada, but in places piyada was crossed through and next to it the word 'sacrifice' was printed," Ryan explained.

"Sounds a bit morbid," muttered Keya.

Norman moved his black pawn diagonally into the square occupied by Jarrod's pawn, knocking Jarrod's over.

Jarrod picked his piece up and said, "On the chessboard, sometimes a piece has to be sacrificed to gain a tactical advantage."

Norman looked across at Jarrod, scratched his cheek and waited for Jarrod's next move.

Dotty, Keya, and Ryan returned to the kitchen table.

"You've certainly been busy, Ryan, but I'm not sure what it all means," admitted Dotty.

"There is one more thing I think you'll find interesting." Ryan opened another file. "See this," he pointed to the screen, "I think it's the £5,000 that was paid to Bernard Ingram."

"Is that enough evidence for Inspector Evans to re-open the case?" asked Keya.

"I didn't know it was closed," said Dotty.

"Yes, after you were released on Tuesday. The pathologist reported that he died from a heart attack and his death was declared accidental."

Dotty noticed Keya's attention return to the chess set as Jarrod knocked over Norman's queen. "You know it's strange, but I saw a black chess piece on Tariq's desk. One larger than the pawn Jarrod just showed us."

"That makes three different chess pieces," muttered Dotty. "I wonder what it means."

CHAPTER THIRTY-SIX

O n Monday morning, Dotty arrived at Akemans at half past eight in the morning. As she climbed out of her car, Norman drove in and parked in one of the staff spaces next to her. Dotty was surprised to see Aunt Beanie sitting in the passenger seat.

Aunt Beanie climbed out and explained, "Gilly called just after you left, and asked me to come in today to help. As both you and George were away from the office last week, there's a lot of catching up to do. The next auction is in eleven days' time, and the catalogue is far from complete."

The three of them entered the antiques centre and walked across to the interconnecting door with the auction house.

Inside, they found Marion already sitting at the reception desk, a strong smell of cardamom emanating from her cup of coffee. "The team is complete," she declared. "David is already setting estimated prices on items in the main auction room. Perhaps you could help him, Bernadette?"

Aunt Beanie crossed the reception area and entered the main auction room.

"Norman, we're expecting a delivery within the next ten minutes with Didier Vogt's furniture and possessions. Please can you help unload it?" Norman followed Aunt Beanie into the auction room.

Marion picked up the company tablet. "I didn't make as much progress as I wanted last week. Can you continue photographing and writing descriptions of items already in the auction room, and then continue with Didier's delivery?"

"Of course," replied Dotty, taking the tablet. Cleary today was not a day for hanging around the reception area drinking tea. There was work to be done.

A white van reversed up to the open double doors, halfway down the long side of the room. Dotty always wore several layers of clothing when working in the auction room as it was a large, barnlike room which was only heated in the lead up to an auction.

Today she wore tan trousers with comfy ankle boots and a V-neck wool jumper. She wore the same brown scarf with images of hedgehogs on it which she'd worn for spring cleaning and then washed on Sunday. The scarf was fun, and she smiled as she folded it in half and threaded the two loose ends through the folded section.

David was at the far side of the room, and Aunt Beanie was working close to Dotty. Marion strode into the auction room and across to the white van.

"I swear I saw a bureau like this in your hall once when I collected David," Aunt Beanie remarked as Marion passed. "The grain on the wood is exquisite."

Marion ignored the comment and continued striding towards the delivery van.

A few minutes later, a smiling Gilly Wimsey appeared. "I'm so glad to see you're back at work," she gushed when she reached Dotty. "Not least because we have lots of quality items for this month's sale, so I want to market it widely. But of course, just having you here and not locked away in that dingy police station is such a relief. I told George all about it at the weekend and she told me to say welcome back."

Dotty thought George was more likely to be worried about her not being around to prepare for the auction than about her being locked up in a police cell, but she kept her thoughts to herself.

Politely, Dotty asked, "How is George? Has she found her painting?"

"She has a lead," confirmed Gilly, "So she won't be back before the end of the week, and possibly not until Monday or Tuesday next week. And she's heard that Didier might be in Paris later this week, so she'll look out for him."

Dotty turned to the white transit van as its rear doors were slammed shut. "That's Didier's furniture which has just been unloaded."

"So he really has gone. I'll miss him," admitted Gilly. She turned and left the auction room, accompanied by Aunt Beanie and Marion.

"Can you help me move some of this furniture," Norman called over to Dotty. "I need to make room for the new arrivals."

Dotty placed the tablet on an oak sideboard and joined Norman, who said, "We'll start with this blanket chest, and move it into that gap beside David."

The large wooden box was heavier than she had expected and awkward to move. Gasping, she lowered it to the floor, just managing not to trap her fingers.

David tapped the box. "I'll miss this. It's so very useful."

Norman turned and walked away, but Dotty stopped, and with a note of surprise asked, "Is this your furniture?"

David looked around. "Those pieces closest to me, and some of the ones near Norman. We're doing, what do you call it? ... downsizing, Dorothy. Most likely abroad. I'm leaving this evening on a trip and I might combine it with a search for a new house. There's nothing left to keep me here, and Marion likes her golf and tennis. We'll find a place where she can play all year round."

This was news to Dotty, and she was amazed Marion hadn't said anything, but then she was aware of other secrets Marion didn't speak about.

"Come on, Dotty," shouted Norman.

"Excuse me," Dotty muttered, but as she wandered across to Norman, her mind started buzzing.

"Next, I want to move this bookcase with the drawers at the bottom over there." Norman pointed to something, but Dotty didn't look. The pieces of the investigation into Tariq's death, into Ethel's and Bernard Ingram's deaths, into the counterfeit furniture, and Gilmore's scam were all falling into place. But she couldn't quite believe where they were taking her.

"Careful," called Norman, but Dotty didn't heed his advice.

She wasn't concentrating and dropped her end of the bookcase. A bottom drawer fell out scattering playing cards, dice, and pieces of a chess set across the stained carpet.

"Dotty, what are you doing?" cried Norman.

"I'm sorry!" Dotty's mind registered what had happened, and she knelt down to gather up the playing cards.

Norman joined her and as he helped with the cards he asked, "Are you OK?"

"I think so. What does this mean, on the cards?" The backs of the cards were red with a central image of three legs, extending from the centre like spokes of a wheel.

"That's the symbol for the Isle of Man," remarked Norman. "I don't know much about it, except they hold an annual motorbike race."

"The Isle of Man TT," confirmed David, looking down at them. "One of the most dangerous racing events in the world. It's thrilling to watch the competitors push themselves to the edge of their courage. And even more so to take part."

"Norman," called Aunt Beanie from the door leading into the reception area.

"Excuse me," Norman muttered, handing the playing cards to David. "I better see what Aunt Beanie wants."

Dotty returned the cards she'd gathered to the empty drawer and collected up the dice. She could feel David staring at her, but he didn't offer to help.

Next, she gathered up the chess pieces and arranged them in their green baize box. "Oh dear, I think some of the pieces must have rolled under the other furniture." She bent lower and peered under a chest of drawers.

"I thought I'd emptied all the drawers. It's a shame that's the one which fell out," declared David.

"Why?" She looked up at him and realised his large, watchful eyes had lost their sparkle. There was a coldness to them, which made her shiver. Where was Norman?

Dotty looked back at the chess set, realising that it was only black pieces that were missing. Most of the pawns, a bishop, a knight, and the queen. She was drawn to the box and ran her finger over the indentations where the missing pieces should have been.

David bent down and picked up the white queen. As he stood, he guided Dotty to her feet and asked, "Do you know what happens when a pawn makes it across the entire chessboard?"

Dotty slowly shook her head, mesmerised by David's intense gaze. She tried to step back, but he gripped her wrist.

"It is promoted to queen. What a clever pawn. Gathering its supporters around it as it grows braver and more knowledgeable. As its skill increases, its opponent has to be bolder but more careful. He tries to capture the pawn, but somehow it evades him and reaches the far side of the board."

David gave her a disappointed smile. "I congratulate you, Dorothy," he said with icy coldness as he forced the white queen into her clenched fist. "You reached the far side of the board and by doing so you have forced me to run. To relocate. I think we'll call that check."

"But I thought you were the rook," whispered Dotty. "Not the king."

"Then you haven't heard of the move in chess known as castling, where the rook and the king change places. I am both, my dear. Which is all the better for concealing my moves."

"But Gilmore?"

"A bishop, a minor piece which can only see half the game and moves diagonally. You see, in life, as in chess, the best players see how the game will unfold many moves ahead. They are patient and vigilant, and direct play accordingly, altering their strategy to ensure they win. But unlike chess pieces, people are fallible, and greedy."

"Was Tariq greedy?" Dotty thought of all the stolen paintings.

"He was. As my wazir, the queen in my game, he thought he was more important than me, but he took risks. I knew it would only take so long before Inspector Evans intervened and realised you were telling the truth and that you had seen

Tariq at Barnton Manor. Tariq thought himself cleverer than me, so he had to go. But he ruined everything."

"Ow," Dotty cried out in pain and winced as David's grip on her wrist tightened.

She could hear voices in the reception area, but the door between it and the auction room remained closed.

Maybe David heard them too as suddenly he grabbed her scarf with his free hand and pulled the two ends. It tightened like a noose around her neck.

Gasping, she reached for David's steely, emotionless eyes, but only succeeded in scratching his cheek. He sidestepped around her, clinging to the ends of the scarf which continued to tighten and now as he pulled from behind, she felt her throat contract. She grabbed at the scarf, but it was useless.

Her knees began to buckle as her vision blurred and spots formed in front of her eyes.

"No!" cried a deep, primeval voice which was followed by a thwack and, as the scarf loosened slightly, a crashing sound and a horrible thud.

Dotty fell forwards onto the dirty nylon carpet, grabbing at her scarf until it loosened enough for her to gasp in some air.

She was aware of pounding feet and raised voices and then Keya was pulling at the scarf calling, "Dotty, can you hear me?"

Dotty tried to respond, but her throat felt rough and sore and she could only croak.

"Ambulance, please," she heard someone else say. Ryan?

Then she felt a pair of strong arms lift her up as she closed her eyes, and with her head pounding, she murmured, "Checkmate."

CHAPTER THIRTY-SEVEN

"Lie her on the sofa," the unmistakable voice of Gilly Wimsey instructed. "I've called Peter, and he's on his way."

Dotty opened her eyes as Ryan gently placed her on the sofa, although it was too short and he had to lift her legs over one arm. With her legs raised, it would at least save Gilly's husband, Dr Peter, insisting she was put in the position for shock. She felt the blood rush to her head.

Amazingly, apart from a sore neck and her throat feeling like sandpaper, she was unscathed. But how did she not realise David Rook was the mastermind behind everything? It seemed so obvious now. His intelligent, watchful eyes. His unknown family history. His understanding of the antiques industry and his prominent position within it.

Had he been grooming her to join him from the beginning?

She remembered recent discussions about institutions like the British Museum and wealthy individuals who collected and displayed antiquities from foreign nations rather than returning them to their country of origin.

And it had been happening from the very beginning, from the first case she helped the police with, the one involving her late husband's regiment. This had been about the treasures plundered during the war in Iraq in 2003. The commanding officer's dagger.

David must have taken it and shipped it back to Iraq. Was he wrong to do so? Part of her understood his reasoning and could respect his point of view. But to kill people in the pursuit of his cause was an entirely different matter.

"Is she conscious?" asked the unusually serious voice of Dr Peter Wimsey, Gilly's husband.

Dotty opened her eyes and stared up at him. Too much blood in her head. She unfolded her legs and lifted them off the arm of the sofa as she manoeuvred herself into a sitting position. Gilly rushed to help her while Dr Peter watched her critically.

"Can you speak?" Dr Peter asked.

"Yes," she rasped.

"Sweet tea with honey is what she needs. We might have some at the back of the cupboard for colds," babbled Gilly.

While Gilly bustled away, Dr Peter sat down next to Dotty and examined her throat. "You have a nasty welt, but it will heal, and I don't think there's any long-term damage to your voice box. Norman acted quickly and without hesitation, or so I hear."

"Did he hit David?" Dotty whispered painfully.

Peter smiled. "Aunt Beanie said they opened the door to the auction room and before she realised what was happening, Norman charged like a bull across the room, sending furniture flying and grabbing a vintage fire extinguisher lamp. That's what he hit David with. I'm not sure if it was the blow to the head or landing on the concrete floor which knocked him unconscious. But at least it made Keya's life easier, as she didn't have to restrain him while Ryan carried you through here."

Dotty was about to speak again but Peter continued, "An ambulance arrived five minutes ago and David's on his way to Cheltenham Hospital, with Marion accompanying him."

Gilly placed a mug of tea on the reclaimed-elm coffee table. "I hope this helps." Her voice was still full of concern.

The door to the auction room opened and Keya and Ryan walked into reception.

Keya's eyes were bulging, and she looked like the one suffering from shock. Gilly must have thought the same as she said, "The kettle just boiled," and she rushed back to the office kitchenette.

Keya sat opposite Dotty and in a disbelieving voice said, "David tried to kill you. Did he murder Tariq?"

Dr Peter stood up. "This is police business. I'll examine you again when they've finished, Dotty." He followed his wife into the office area.

"Did he?" repeated Keya uncertainly.

Dotty nodded as she leaned forward and picked up her cup of tea. Gilly must have found the honey, as the liquid was hot, sweet, and thick, and it soothed her aching throat.

Ryan, who was still standing, looked down at Dotty with a serious expression. When she met his eyes, he asked quietly, "Was it David all along?"

Again, Dotty nodded.

"Was he the chariot referred to in the files?"

"Yes," she whispered, less hoarsely.

Keya looked from Dotty to Ryan and asked, "What do you mean?"

Ryan glanced across at Dotty, but she pointed to her throat and slowly shook her head. She continued to sip her tea.

"Jarrod told us about the Persian names of chess pieces which were the same names used in the files I found on Tariq's laptop." Ryan paused and addressed Dotty. "Do you think Jarrod guessed David was behind it all?"

"I think so," and as her throat didn't feel too sore, Dotty continued, "although, like me, he might have thought David was only the rook and was taking orders from someone else, the king on the chessboard." Dotty sipped her tea before continuing, "But David admitted to being both. He said something about a chess move called castling, where the rook and king swap places."

Gilly returned, handing both Keya and Ryan cups of tea.

As Keya gratefully sipped hers, she visibly calmed down, and said, "I presume the names on the files which were crossed off, or 'sacrificed', represent the people who have died. The people David killed."

"I don't think we'll ever know that for certain, unless David confesses," Dotty responded with regret.

"We might," exclaimed Keya, suddenly sitting up excitedly. "That's why Ryan and I drove over this morning, to tell you about the results from the glove examinations. Guess what? The same fingerprints were found on the inside of the glove found at Ethel's crime scene as the one found in the back of your car?"

"Whose?" asked Dotty.

Keya's smile faded. "That's the trouble. We don't know, but," her smile reappeared, "I photographed the pads of David's fingers while I waited for the ambulance. I used Ryan's phone, as his camera is better than mine."

She paused and composed herself. "I've sent them to the lab to see if they're good enough for an initial match. It may be a while before we can arrest him and formally take his prints, as I understand Norman didn't hold back. David's likely to have internal bleeding, as well as a damaged skull."

Dotty thought back to the very first case she'd been caught up in, when she'd also ended up at Cheltenham Hospital with a fractured skull. For all his faults, she hoped David didn't have permanent brain damage. His mind was full of knowledge which could still benefit the world.

The door to the auction room opened again, and a wild-looking Norman was escorted by Aunt Beanie.

"I'm so sorry I left you alone, Dotty," cried Norman, stepping forward.

"Now, now, we've just been through this," cautioned Aunt Beanie in a firm tone as she tried to restrain Norman. "It wasn't your fault. Dotty and David have spent a lot of time together in the past and he hasn't tried to strangle her."

Dotty winced and her hand involuntarily touched her neck. "Ow." It was sore. Her brown hedgehog scarf was hanging across her shoulders, so she wrapped it loosely around her neck, hoping to cover any red marks. Although it had been used as a weapon against her, it felt comforting.

Keya's radio crackled. She jumped up and walked away from the rest of the group. When she returned, she said, "Sergeant Unwin has been sent to Cheltenham Hospital. Inspector Evans wants to speak to all of us."

Keya looked around the group with a serious expression on her face. "He's asked if we can meet him at Meadowbank Farm in half an hour."

"Good idea," agreed Aunt Beanie. "Norman, I'll drive." She escorted a bewildered-looking Norman out of the reception area.

Keya watched them go and then said, "I'll drive your car, Dotty."

CHAPTER THIRTY-EIGHT

When Dotty, Ryan, and Keya walked into the kitchen at Meadowbank Farm, it was empty. Aunt Beanie appeared carrying a large pan and said, "I'll heat this soup up for lunch. I've told Norman to have a shower."

Ryan sat down at the kitchen table, concentrating on his phone. As Dotty and Keya joined him, he looked up and reported, "Birmingham University has successfully lifted a palm print from the scan of the hilt of the dagger I sent them.

Now all they need is one to match it with. I'll sort that out when we process David. I'm dying to hear how you think David killed Tariq, but we better wait for the chief inspector."

There was a knock at the kitchen door. "Is that him already?" asked Keya.

But Ozzie Winters stepped through. Dotty glanced across at Ryan, but he raised his hands defensively. "I didn't call her."

Ozzie exchanged flamboyant air kisses with Aunt Beanie.

"Great articles, last week. Well done," congratulated Aunt Beanie.

Ozzie was actually blushing as she approached the kitchen table and asked, "Is everyone OK? I heard reports that an ambulance picked someone up from Akemans who'd been attacked and was suffering head injuries?"

"David Rook," said Ryan.

"And Norman only hit him to stop him hurting Dotty, although he may have used slightly more force than was necessary," admitted Aunt Beanie.

"Tell me all the gory details," insisted Ozzie, sitting down.

"We can't," replied Ryan. "Not yet anyway, as we haven't discussed the case with our boss."

"Chief Inspector Ringrose?" asked Ozzie, her eyes narrowing.

"No, Inspector Evans," replied Ryan.

"Why did you mention the chief inspector?" Dotty enquired.

"He was away last weekend at an international rugby match, and people have started asking about his links to certain Arab gentlemen and if his trip, and attendances at other sporting events, are self-funded. If they're hospitality trips, the question is, what is he providing in return?"

Keya and Ryan looked at each other.

Ozzie stood but asked, "Is there anything you can tell me on the record about the incident at Akemans earlier? It's better coming from me than letting rumours start."

Ryan sighed. "Honestly, I don't think we can. I don't understand it all at the moment. But I'll ask the inspector what we can release to the press and call you."

"Fair enough. Catch you later," and Ozzie strode purposefully out of the kitchen.

"What was that young reporter doing here? Have you lot been blabbing?" asked the baritone voice of Inspector Evans as he entered the kitchen.

"Morning, Inspector, or is it afternoon? I have no idea what time it is," admitted Aunt Beanie.

"It's half-past twelve and my stomach tells me it's nearly lunchtime, and the delicious smell coming from that pan isn't helping."

"Carrot and coriander soup, and I'll make cheese on toast to go with it," Aunt Beanie suggested.

A fresh-faced Norman appeared.

"And Norman can help me, unless you need to interview him."

"All in good time," confirmed Inspector Evans, "And thank you, Bernadette, I'd be very grateful for lunch. It could be a long afternoon."

Dotty, Keya and Ryan watched the inspector as he walked deliberately across the kitchen and sat down in Norman's usual place at the end of the table. Placing both hands on the table, he regarded Dotty. "I'm glad to see no permanent damage has been done. I presume David Rook's attempt on your life was because you accused him of murdering Tariq Kazem?"

"Not exactly," Dotty replied. "He didn't actually say he'd killed Tariq, or anyone else. Typically, he talked in intellectual riddles, mainly involving chess moves and pieces."

"But do you believe he killed Tariq? Why else would he attack you?"

Dotty sat back, considering how best to answer the question. "Tariq's death was the final move. David said you would believe me, in the end, about seeing Tariq at Sir Reginald's and look to him for stealing the painting. Ironically, Tariq's death meant that we, Keya, did investigate Tariq and his art collection and found the painting, and many others he either stole or acquired illegally."

"You said final move," raised the inspector. "What do you mean by that?"

"I think David has been conducting illicit activities for several years, maybe more, in his fundamental belief that the treasures plundered from Iraq during the 2003 war should be returned. That was the basis for everything he did. He stole some items, like the dagger from Colonel Sutherland, or had others steal for him, like Ethel taking the copper jug at the Cotswold Antique Fair or, more recently, Billy Edwards stealing the headless limestone statue from a house in Bristol."

"Colonel Sutherland's dagger? But that was ages ago," blurted Keya.

"It was. You were still a constable, and I'd just started working at Akemans."

"I'm not going to ask, for the moment, why you think those people and events are connected," said Inspector Evans, "as I'd rather move forward, and while theft is important, I'm more concerned about unsolved murder cases. To start with, Dotty, are there others, apart from Tariq's, which you believe are linked to David?"

"I think the fingerprints found on the inside of a glove from the crime scene will prove he killed Ethel. I'm certain he instigated Bernard Ingram's death, but I doubt we can prove it was murder, never mind who committed it."

"So, for now, we'll concentrate on the deaths of Ethel Lee and Tariq Kazem. You mentioned fingerprints? Has the forensic lab come back with results?" The inspector turned to Keya.

"Ryan, PC Jenkins is liaising with them," Keya replied.

"That's right, Inspector. The lab has found prints, but we haven't matched them to David Rook yet. We're working on it."

Inspector Evans wrinkled his brow as he regarded Ryan.

"That'll be critical evidence for a conviction as much of what Dotty is about to tell me will be conjecture, although I doubt I'll disagree with her." The inspector turned back to Dotty.

"Here we are, everyone. Soup, and cheese on toast." Aunt Beanie and Norman placed lunch on the table and, when they'd finished, sat down to join the others.

Inspector Evans explained, "Dotty was about to tell us how she thinks David killed Tariq."

"Good," said Aunt Beanie as she cut her cheese on toast in half. "Because I think he had to be the one who did, but I've no idea how."

"I'd been trying to work it out since Saturday," said Dotty, "when we examined the map of Lemington, the hall, and Eaton Common, and the road route between them versus the shorter footpath. It appeared possible, but unlikely, that David could have driven between the two and committed murder, and done so without his wife or friends seeing him. And Jarrod calculated that a bike wouldn't be any quicker than a car."

"I agree. I considered both those options," agreed the inspector.

"But Mr Tyler had motorbikes in his garage," revealed Dotty.

"Of course," interjected Keya. "People kept mentioning they heard a motorbike in the woods. I just thought it was local youths, but what if they heard David using the footpath to get to Lemington Hall? And the tyre track. Have you had time to look at it, Ryan?"

"Sorry, it slipped my mind, but I will when we get back to the station. Any idea what sort of motorbike?" asked Ryan.

"A red one," said Dotty, remembering the mud splattered motorbike propped against the wall in the Tylers' garage. "And the one at the Tylers' wasn't like a bike used on roads. It was more wheels and less body, if that makes any sense?"

"It does, and I'll check the tyre against Honda off-road bikes first, as they are usually red."

Keya sighed. "That all sounds possible, but David was wearing tennis kit. I think grey rather than white, but even so, the path through the wood was muddy, and he'd have been filthy. And it's likely he would have been sprayed with some blood from stabbing Tariq."

"Did you notice the plastic bin in the Tylers' garage?" asked Dotty.

"No," replied Keya hesitantly.

"It was full of dirty overalls, like the ones Mr Tyler was wearing when we spoke to him. I bet David covered his sports kit with a set of those and threw them back in the washing basket when he finished."

"I'll drive back via the Tylers," Keya said. "Fingers crossed they haven't done any washing since we visited."

"But what about the painting which was found in Dotty's car?" Ryan asked.

"That always puzzled me," replied Dotty. "Whoever put it there must have done so during the short time I went to look for Tariq in his office. Or so I thought, and that the person then disappeared."

"That's why we were looking for a car parked nearby," confirmed Keya.

"But David actually transferred it from his car to mine after he and Marion arrived."

"You mean when I was there?" asked Keya incredulously.

"Yes, and he would have needed gloves, or one glove, so that he didn't leave fingerprints. Either accidentally, or deliberately, he left one in my car. Part of me thinks he did it on purpose and so any subsequent search would have found it and further incriminated me."

"I thought David liked you, but he hasn't treated you very well," Keya commiserated.

Dotty looked down at the table and drew a figure of eight with her finger.

"I don't think David would see it like that. In fact, quite the opposite." She reached into her pocket and pulled out the white queen chess piece.

"He gave me this and said I was a pawn who had gained knowledge and strength, and with the help of my friends, evaded trouble. As he viewed it, I had reached the end of the current phase of my life and, as in chess, when a pawn reaches the far side of the board, transformed into a higher-level player."

She fingered the plastic chess figure.

"That's all very well," exclaimed Aunt Beanie. "But he still tried to kill you and if Norman hadn't acted so bravely, and slightly recklessly, he'd have succeeded."

"I know, and I am very grateful, Norman." Dotty smiled at him. "Perhaps I should have seen David for who he was earlier. I don't know.

But I don't hate him, or really even blame him for what he did.

"It came naturally to him and the fact that he saw me, who less than two years ago was a timid military wife whose only role in life was to make her husband's life comfortable, as an equal, or as close as, makes me feel honoured. I know that sounds strange."

Inspector Evans shook his head. "It does, lass, but there's always been something about you I couldn't put my finger on."

CHAPTER THIRTY-NINE

"Turning to the death of Ethel Lee," said Inspector Evans. "Nobody mentioned seeing David Rook at that antique fair and you, and Sergeants Unwin and Varma were there."

Dotty nodded. "But I did spot David's car when we first arrived and I thought I saw him enter one of the rooms, the one where we later found Ethel. I followed him inside but couldn't find him at the stall. I didn't realise there was a gap allowing access to the room beyond. I think that's where David went and he was meeting Ethel, although I doubt we can prove it."

"We could if the fingerprints inside the glove are David's," argued Keya.

"But why kill Ethel?" asked Aunt Beanie, who had been quiet up to this point.

Dotty gave her a thin smile. "I think she was one of his pawns, but she wanted more money, although, once again, this is just my theory. Ethel had her terraced house and her cats, and she ran a car. Her outgoings were modest, but I'm not sure if she had any other source of income besides that which she and Edith made at fairs.

She may have needed the money she earned working for David to survive. But I doubt you'll find evidence of money transfers, as she's likely to have insisted on cash."

"So what did she do?" asked Keya, leaning forward.

"Stole to order. I believe she took the copper jug and brass plate at the Cotswold fair."

"When?" pressed Keya.

"Edith mentioned that when Roger Dewhirst's body was found, everyone crowded around his stall, everyone except Ethel. I think she took the opportunity to rob Ernie's stall."

"But she didn't steal the chapman robe, did she?" asked Keya.

"I don't know. She may have done and before she handed it over demanded more money, or she may have refused to steal it unless she was paid more. Or David could have instructed Billy to take it, while we were concentrating on Ethel's body. I don't think we'll ever know the answer to that."

"What I don't understand," began Aunt Beanie, "is why Sergeant Unwin was so convinced you were the culprit? And why he and Chief Inspector Ringrose were trying to link you to all the crimes?"

Inspector Evans cleared his throat. "I think I can answer that. I've been tasked with looking into the chief inspector. It's been noticed that he's been living beyond his means and questions have been asked higher up the police hierarchy. I also became concerned about his running of Operation Bumblebee."

"Of course," cried Dotty. "What was that all about? Every time I mentioned it, you all clammed up."

"It was a sting operation, hence the name," replied Inspector Evans dryly, "To catch those involved in fake or stolen antiques. The chief inspector was in charge, but I became concerned about his team when he procured my sergeant but kept his own out of the office and engaged with minor policing tasks.

And you, Bernadette," he looked up at Aunt Beanie, "had his ear in the past and you worked successfully together. I noticed he was excluding you from the operation and other current investigations, and limiting your involvement to cold cases. Although he may find that was a mistake if Ms Winter's articles are to be believed. I presume one of her sources on stolen paintings was you."

"It was," agreed Aunt Beanie proudly. "I'm delighted that we've found so many of them."

Dotty remembered, "There are photographs in the chief inspector's office of him at various sporting events, including one at Wimbledon with Marion Rook."

"I won't ask how you know that," remarked Inspector Evans.

Dotty looked down at the table before admitting, "I also took something from his office."

"You have the chess piece?" the inspector sounded relieved.

"Sorry, I'm not sure why I grabbed it, but it seemed important at the time."

"What piece did he have?" asked Ryan.

"The knight," replied Dotty.

"Referred to as the horse in Tariq's files. We should be able to identify the payments made to the chief inspector." Ryan enthused and then looked serious. Maybe he realised he was discussing a senior police officer.

"That would be useful," agreed Inspector Evans, "Although the chief inspector has already requested a plea deal. Now we have David Rook in custody, I'm not sure how useful his evidence will be, but that is a matter above my pay grade."

"Do you know why he did it?" asked Aunt Beanie.

"I only interviewed him for the first time this morning, as he's just returned from a weekend away at an international rugby match. And I didn't know then about David and how his operation worked. But what the chief inspector did admit, is that he believed he was part of a cause, and what he was doing was right."

"If he was such a believer, why not do it for nothing? Why the big payouts?" asked Keya.

"Corporate hospitality is big business and doesn't need to be declared as income," replied Ryan. "Maybe the chief inspector felt that morally he could accept it, or that he deserved it, or he just enjoyed being around powerful and important people. And he does love his sport."

Keya bit her lip, looking troubled.

"What's wrong?" asked Dotty.

"What's going to happen to the chief inspector's team? To me and Aunt Beanie?"

"I'm afraid I can't say," replied the inspector. "It will need to be discussed, but there's always a place for you on my team."

"Two sergeants?" Keya asked despondently.

"Let's not worry about that now." Inspector Evans gave her a sympathetic look.

Norman cleared his throat, and everyone stared at him.

Self-consciously, he asked, "What about Marion? Do you think she knew what was going on?"

"She certainly knew David's politics and views on the repatriation of antiquities," remarked Aunt Beanie. "And I presume she knew where he went on his trips and had some idea what he was doing."

Keya said slowly, "I had a chat with Marion after the inspector and I interviewed her. She said something about never being free from the choices we make, and that the consequences follow us. I thought she was talking about her previous life, when she was much younger, but what if she was referring to David? Because she also talked about turning a blind eye and not asking questions she didn't want to know the answers to."

"I think that's a good summary of her position," agreed Aunt Beanie. "She's loyal to David but, if she buries her head and pretends nothing is wrong, she can continue with her life. And she has done so for the past few years."

Dotty wondered, "Why didn't she tell me it was her and David's furniture being auctioned, and that she and David were planning to leave the country?"

"Were they?" queried Aunt Beanie.

"That's what David told me. In fact, he was due to travel tonight, and I don't think he intended to return."

"Like Didier," noted Keya.

"Like Didier," repeated Dotty.

"Why?" asked Ryan.

"I think Didier was another pawn who David used in the counterfeit furniture scam which Keya broke up when she arrested the furniture maker," explained Dotty.

"But with all that's happened, Didier's priority will be his girls and his flight to France was his way of getting out. He might have been scared, as others were dying, or just felt that the distance would be sufficient. He was very secretive about where he was going, although

I'm sure David had the contacts to find him if he'd wanted to."

Dotty paused before adding, "And in his own way, Gilmore did the same. Perhaps the blame for copying paintings, selling the originals, and returning the fakes wasn't all his, but he took the fall to protect himself."

"So you don't think Gilmore was the only one involved in that scam," concluded Aunt Beanie. "What about Tariq? Could he have been involved to make money for himself?"

"He could, for himself or to fund David's operation," concluded Dotty. "If I'm right, David must have been furious with Gilmore for exposing the hoax and cutting off a major source of income. I think it'll be worth speaking to Jarrod about it, Keya, as he's probably had his suspicions for a while and I bet he's been working on it privately."

"I will," agreed Keya.

CHAPTER FORTY

Dotty didn't have much time to recover after being attacked by David. Marion refused to return to Akemans, so Gilly begged Dotty and Aunt Beanie to help her prepare for the upcoming auction.

Even Keya had been drafted in to work on reception for the two days leading up to the auction, and the auction day itself.

Her department had been closed down and she, Aunt Beanie and the chief inspector were all under investigation, so she wasn't allowed back to Cirencester police station until her case had been concluded.

The following Wednesday, the day before the auction, was a viewing day which meant members of the public could look round the auction rooms and ask questions about the items being sold, their expected prices, and their condition.

"People filled these forms in last night during the viewing. What do I do with them?" asked Keya.

She was sitting at the reception desk and Dotty was standing beside her.

"Those are bidding sheets. People who can't attend the auction leave a bid, which is the highest price they are prepared to pay for an item. You need to enter them into the system and, tomorrow, before the auction starts, we'll print them off.

"When the bidding for an item starts, George will refer to them as well as taking bids from the room and those that appear automatically on the internet. One change Marion persuaded George to make was to only use one internet auction site, which will make my job up on the rostrum, helping George, much easier."

Keya nodded. "I think I've got that. And tomorrow I'll be issuing bidder numbers to people who fill out the form, and during the auction enter the details of who bought which Lot and the price they bid. But what if I get in a muddle?"

"Ask Aunt Beanie or, if she's dealing with one of the many telephone bids, ask Gilly. I know she's hoping one of the girls from the village will help her in the cafe."

"She's agreed to come," confirmed Gilly, as she joined them. "A sweet girl called Ashley. Quiet, and not particularly dynamic, but hopefully she'll get the hang of things once I've shown her a few times. And are you both bringing cakes?"

"I am, and so is Ryan," confirmed Keya. "And we'll have a full police presence since the money raised from David's furniture and possessions will go to the government if he's found guilty."

"I'm pleased about the cakes, but not the police," remarked Gilly, wrinkling her brow. "Still, at least everyone will behave themselves. After all the publicity, especially from the articles Ozzie Winters has written, I'm expecting a large crowd."

"Gilly," called Aunt Beanie.

"Excuse me, my work is never finished," and Gilly left them.

Dotty and Keya were about to return to the forms when Keya's phone rang.

"It's Ryan," Keya disclosed. "Hiya."

She listened for several minutes. "That's good news, isn't it?"

She listened again before saying, "I'll let Dotty know. See you tomorrow."

"Let me know what?" asked Dotty when Keya finished the call.

"The lab finally confirmed that David's prints were on both gloves and, yesterday, Birmingham University said it was 75% certain that the palm print on the dagger matched David's.

"That, together with the dirty and bloody overalls from the Tylers', with David's DNA on them, should be enough to convict him for Tariq's murder, and hopefully Ethel's. Inspector Evans had to drop Bernard Ingram's case through lack of evidence."

"Which is what we expected," conceded Dotty, "but I'll be most pleased if we get justice for Ethel, and I think Edith would like that. She's been great with Uncle Cliff in the care home, and Aunt Beanie is so grateful she's paying to upgrade Edith's room, so she's next to Uncle Cliff. In the summer, they'll be able to sit out on their patio together."

"That's thoughtful," agreed Keya.

"And she's managed to get an increase in rent from the people who farm the land at Meadowbank Farm to pay for it, which is a relief, although I think Norman was quite looking forward to decluttering the farmhouse and selling some of the furniture and unwanted items."

"Everything under control?" asked George Carey-Boyd, in a less haughty voice than Keya and Dotty were used to.

"I think so," replied Keya.

"We are most grateful for your help. It's been a trying time." George looked genuinely appreciative.

Keya bit her lip before asking, "Did you really find your painting?"

"A print," conceded George. "We found out that the original is hanging in a gallery in Marseille. My next trip will be to see it."

"Did you buy the print?"

"I did, and one day I may even let you see it." George grinned mischievously and as she sauntered away, Dotty and Keya exchanged glances and laughed.

"I like the new George. Let's hope she stays like this," Keya remarked.

Dotty, Aunt Beanie and Norman arrived at Akemans at a quarter to eight on Thursday morning. They found the front door of the auction house locked, which was unusual during the week of an auction when it was always open.

"Do you think we're the first to arrive?" Aunt Beanie sounded surprised.

"Beanie, there are other cars here," replied Norman, knocking on the door.

Gilly peered at them through the glass panes before opening the door. "Good, it's you. Customers are already wanting to come in and I need someone to man reception until Keya gets here."

"I'll do that," volunteered Dotty, "if you take these for me." She handed Gilly her wicker basket containing tins of biscuits and traybakes, and a large cake tin. "That's a Victoria sponge."

"Wonderful," exclaimed Gilly.

Dotty settled herself at the reception desk and when she had the forms she needed ready, and the computer program open, she unlocked the front door.

Most people filed past her or asked for brochures, which were piled up on a plastic table between the reception desk and the entrance door to the auction room.

"Morning," greeted Ryan. "Where shall I take these?" He carried two tins stacked on top of each other.

"Through to Gilly in the auction room. She's set up the cafe in the corner on the right."

A few people asked for a bidder's form and then Dotty busied herself entering the proxy bids which had been emailed during the night.

"Good morning, Dotty," said a familiar male voice, with a note of trepidation.

She looked up into the uncertain face of Sergeant Unwin.

"I brought you these." He handed her a fragrant bunch of pink lilies.

They were lovely but …

"I know it doesn't atone for my behaviour and I really am sorry. Perhaps I could make it up to you by taking you out for supper, or you could come over to my place like we once discussed?"

Dotty looked up at the attractive face of Sergeant Unwin - Nick. A face that had looked at her with disappointment and even contempt. How could she ever trust him?

"I'm sorry, but I don't think that will work."

Ryan appeared, carrying a cup of tea. "Gilly thought you might appreciate this. Hi, Nick. Looking forward to the auction?"

"I was."

"I'm going to look round. See you later," and Ryan left Nick and Dotty alone.

Dotty sat up taller and said, "You see, for me, friends are those who stand together through thick and thin. Who don't judge, and don't doubt each other."

Nick swallowed hard. "But …"

Dotty held up her hand. "Please. Don't. I'm thinking of going away for a while. I need a break from all this. From the men in my life."

"And when you come back?"

"Who knows?"

The door opened and Keya stepped inside reception calling, "Hiya. Sorry if I'm late."

"You're not. It's just customers who are early."

Nick gave Dotty a final pleading look before picking up a brochure and entering the auction room.

"Is everything all right?" asked Keya. "Oh, what lovely flowers."

"I'll put them in water while you get settled. Then, can you finish entering the proxy bids and print the sheet off for me." Dotty stood up, putting Nick out of her mind. Today was auction day. She didn't have time to ruminate over matters of the heart.

"Any advance on £6,200?" announced George into her microphone. "I'm selling once, selling twice, sold to …"

Dotty stared at the number the winning bidder held up. "72." She noted it and the price on the green sheet in front of her.

"Thank you, ladies and gentlemen. We'll now take a ten-minute break." George switched off the microphone and remarked, "Didier should be pleased with what his Lots made." She lowered her voice and continued, "I met him for coffee in Paris and he told me everything. Such a shame he got involved with David. And we were so lucky not to, although I have heard rumours a special unit from London will be going through our records checking we haven't sold counterfeit or stolen pieces."

Dotty gasped.

"Don't worry, we haven't. Do you remember that Queen Anne table you inadvertently bought?"

Dotty nodded in shame. She thought she'd bagged a bargain, but it turned out to be a piece of the counterfeit furniture.

"David arranged for it to be sold in London, not here. I believe we are clean. Anyway, returning to Didier. Here's his number. He asked if you could call him to let him know how the auction went. Why don't you do it now?"

Dotty climbed down from the rostrum but instead of returning to reception, she found a quiet corner of the auction room and called the number George had given her.

"Hello," Didier answered.

"It's Dotty. George asked me to call and tell you your items did very well in the auction."

"That's great. Thank you. I caught some of it online but our internet's hit and miss. What did the last lot make?"

"£6,200."

"That's excellent. I'll be able to buy my parents a new car. Look, the reason I asked George if you could call me is that I have a proposition for you. The girls are struggling and they're too much for my mum. But I can't spend all my time with them, as I have things to organise and I'm helping my father on the farm and in the vineyard.

"Would you be interested in working for me for a few months and looking after the girls until they're settled? There are some interesting galleries here, and we can visit towns in the region and I can teach you about French antiques."

"Wow, I'm not sure what to say."

"Why don't you think about it? I just thought you might need a break after all that's happened, and George agreed."

"Ladies and gentlemen, we'll start again in two minutes," announced George's amplified voice.

"I have to go," said Dotty.

"Give me a call with your answer. You have my phone number."

"I will, thank you."

After the auction, Dotty joined Keya, Aunt Beanie, and Gilly in the small cafe.

"Wow, that was hard work," confessed Keya. "I think I only overcharged one man, but he soon corrected my mistake and, luckily, he was charming about it. I think he realised how busy I was. How did you get on in the cafe, Gilly?"

"Like you, rushed off our feet. I had to send Ashley home just before the end as she was exhausted, but I think she'll help again, if we need her."

Keya bit her lip before asking, "And are you progressing with the permanent cafe?"

"What permanent cafe?" asked Aunt Beanie and Dotty in unison.

"A local architect is drawing up plans to open up the rear area of the antiques centre and restore the old waterwheel as a feature. We're also adding a small extension and some covered outdoor seating."

"So you're adding running a cafe to your already busy schedule," remarked Aunt Beanie.

"Gosh, no. I'm not running it. I might look for a manager, but I'd prefer to rent the space out, then it's not my responsibility."

"But you'll lose any say over how it's run," Aunt Beanie pointed out.

"I know, that's why I haven't made up my mind what I'm going to do."

CHAPTER FORTY-ONE

"Gilly looks smart wearing her Oxford gown and mortarboard, but I'm pleased I opted for a dress," Dotty admitted to Keya.

They were sitting at a round table in Oxford's Sheldonian Theatre with Aunt Beanie, Norman, Ryan, Dr Peter and Gilly Wimsey, Inspector Evans, and Jay Newton.

Aunt Beanie had booked it although Dotty suspected Jay was paying for the meal, which was to celebrate Dotty passing, with merit, her Appreciation of Modern Art Course.

So much had happened since she started the course in November and she remembered, with regret, the lectures in the dome-roofed Sheldonian Theatre and her drinks and supper afterwards with Gilmore Chapman. She had really felt she was making progress with life and moving forward.

"A toast to Dotty," declared Jay. "Congratulations on your graduation and clearing your name." He glanced across at Inspector Evans.

"Congratulations," chorused the others, lifting their glasses of champagne.

Dotty sipped hers, but she still didn't really feel like celebrating.

Keya turned to Norman and asked, "Are you still searching for the meaning of life?"

"No," he replied, placing his champagne glass on the table and picking up a pint of Wiltshire Gold beer. "My purpose is to help others, like the old Duke, and Beanie and Cliff, and Dotty, when she finds herself in trouble. I'm proud I protected her from a nasty incident, and she can live a full and meaningful life."

Dotty wasn't sure she felt able to do either at the moment.

"That's very generous of you, Norman. You should become a police officer," suggested Inspector Evans.

"I suppose you have a vacancy now Chief Inspector Ringrose has retired," remarked Jay.

"Not really. The Rural, Heritage and Wildlife Unit is being closed down. Cost cutting, they say," replied Inspector Evans.

"Which means I'm out of a job," muttered Aunt Beanie.

"I thought you were joining Jarrod and Lady Violet," claimed Inspector Evans.

"How did you know about that?" Aunt Beanie gasped, her eyes flashing.

"I am a policeman." Inspector Evans also exchanged his champagne for a pint of beer.

"And what does that mean for you, Keya?" asked Jay.

Inspector Evans returned his pint of beer to the table and wiped froth from his top lip before replying, "She's rejoining my team. It's scandalous, but we've been given a budget for one constable to oversee the whole of the rural area of the Cotswolds. But after some creative accounting from young Ryan, we've changed this to a slightly more than part time Sergeant's role. So Keya will continue to sit in on Parish Council meetings, appease argumentative villagers, and hand out prizes at school sports days."

"And are you happy with that?" Jay asked uncertainly.

"I am because …" Keya glanced at Gilly, who nodded, "I'm taking over the licence of the Waterwheel Cafe at Akemans. I've always dreamed of running a cafe and deli selling local products."

"Brilliant," agreed Aunt Beanie.

"We should drink to that," proclaimed Jay and he lifted his champagne glass again. "To Keya's Waterwheel Cafe!"

They all toasted her. Norman and Inspector Evans with their beers.

After the formal graduation ceremony, they swapped seats and Dotty found herself next to Jay Newton.

"You don't look particularly excited about your award," Jay said. "In fact, you look exhausted. Have you considered a holiday?"

Dotty looked up at him and admitted, "I am going away, but it'll be more than a holiday. Didier Vogt has asked me to help look after his girls in France for a few months, and I've agreed to go. I need the break, and to consider my future. After all that's happened, I'm not sure I can continue at Akemans."

"That sounds like an excellent idea, but what's worrying you?"

"I haven't told Aunt Beanie yet, and I don't want to let her and Norman down. And I'm planning to take Earl Grey with me. I hope they won't mind."

"Of course they won't, and I'm sure they'll understand. It's your life, and I think you're ready to go out into the world and embrace your next adventure."

Dotty smiled at Jay and raised her glass of champagne. Finally, she felt she had something to celebrate, and she toasted, "To the next adventure."

After her holiday in the south of France, Dotty decides it's time to face her parents and either reconcile her differences with them, or move on with her life.

But even in Edinburgh, during the world famous Fringe Festival, intrigue and mystery threaten their reunion.

A murder on stage. Her father a prime suspect. Can an amateur sleuth step into the limelight and find the killer before the final curtain falls?

Claim Your Copy of Deadly Performance at www.books2read.com/DeadlyPerformance

Earl Grey and Shallow Graves

With Dotty away in France, who will solve new murder cases in the Cotswolds? Will Keya continue to work at Cirencester Police Station?

A 30-year-old skeleton. A missing girl. Can a community police officer read the tea leaves or will a deadly secret remain buried for ever?

Claim Your Copy of Earl Grey and Shallow Graves at www.Books2Read.com/EarlGrey

Would you like to read about Dotty's first case, and discover why she joined Akemans?

Find out in the prequel, *Hour is Come,* when you sign up to my newsletter for updates at VictoriaTait.com

If you enjoyed this book, please tell someone you know. And for those people you don't know, leave a review to help them decide whether or not to read it.

Leave a review on Amazon

For more information visit VictoriaTait.com

Printed in Great Britain
by Amazon

29854554R00245